UNBOUND

THE BLOOD PIRATE: BOOK 2

STEPHANIE EDING

Unbound

by Stephanie Eding

Copyright © 2020 Stephanie Eding

Published by Stephanie Eding

Convoy, OH, USA

Cover art by German Creative

Book Design by Chace Verity

ONE

Nothing on earth compared to the stench of a pirate.

The heavy smoke made my eyelids stick every time I blinked. By now, all the breathable air had turned black by the cigar-toting patrons. Spilt alcohol covered every pub surface and pasted my arms in place on the tabletop, nearly ripping the skin from my bones every time I moved. And all of it stank.

All of it.

Still, none of that competed with the monstrous odor wafting from the blackguard sitting beside me.

"Did you want to sign him up, or shall I?" Long stretched his skeletal fingers across the table and crumpled the page in front of me.

I scowled at the joke he'd already told three times that hour. Once my lessons with Nikolaus picked up again, I'd write and read just like any educated person. The islands hadn't provided us with much learning time, but I could at least write my name now.

Ezra Long, our acting first mate, had been a burden since the day we brought him on board. Old compared to the other pirates I'd met, he could be someone's grandfather. Well, if anyone brave enough to reproduce with him even existed on this earth.

He hated me, and I returned the sentiment.

"Just sign your name here." I pushed the parchment forward, and the man wrote his name in illegible scratches. He shook Long's hand, ignoring me, and headed for the bar to celebrate his new commission.

For mid-afternoon, the place hummed with activity. Although a line at our table hadn't actually formed, we kept a steady flow of men wanting to sign up for the crew. Finn had told me it'd be like this. In late summer, people wanted off the islands to avoid the hurricanes. I'd never experienced such a storm, but if it made men abandon their homes for a life of servitude and impending doom, it couldn't be good.

Now, if only Finn had shown up to help establish his crew rather than leaving me at the mercy of Long, who took immense pride in using me as his personal servant. With no legitimate rank on the *Hellbound*, I had no choice but to oblige.

Our dear captain had disappeared two days ago, with no warning given to me at all. Nikolaus, our ever-informed cabin boy, let me know that Finn had left on his own will and hadn't been kidnapped or killed. Of course, Nik waited until I'd searched everywhere and had nearly driven myself mad with worry before he fed me this information. Typical of him.

Apparently, Finn had dealings to attend to elsewhere on the island and would return presently. I had many questions that went unanswered in his absence, which provided Nik with endless entertainment and me with agonizing frustration. Still, I missed Finn. His presence brought me peace in the chaos of our lives. Without him, nothing felt right.

A burst of light in the rear corner of the pub broke through the smoke, signaling someone's entrance. The skinny stature and juvenile saunter told me exactly who had entered, and I excused myself from Long's *delightful* company to catch Nikolaus before he made his way too far into the haze.

"Please tell me you've been sent on captain's orders to bring us back to the ship so we can be done with this madness," I said.

Nik smiled but didn't slow his progression toward the counter. I followed behind him, trying to keep close enough that I could hear his response against the bellowing crowd.

"Sorry, Cecily. No captain means no commands," he finally said.

I grabbed his arm to demand he face me. "No captain? He's still not returned? It's been three days. This island is not *that* big."

Nik shrugged. "He didn't give me an expected time, but he wasn't back when I left to come here either."

"And where *is* he?" I leaned in closer to avoid being overheard. We had no way of knowing Finn's well-being when he vanished this way. Anything could have happened to him.

"I told you before: I don't know." Nik turned from me and continued toward the bar.

I followed.

"If you're going to keep asking me about it, I suggest you give up. Asking won't help me remember information I don't know." Nikolaus then yelled above the roar of patrons sitting at the counter, "I'm ordering supplies for the journey. Have your new crew bring them back to the ship when they come, will you?"

He couldn't distract me that easily. "But I know you know where he went, Nikolaus. You're a terrible liar. And are you not even the least bit concerned for him after three days?"

"Why? He's done this before," Nik said.

"Not for this long."

Finn could have at least given me a location, rather than let my mind wander. When he did this, I wavered between worry and anger. If he walked through that door right now, I wouldn't know whether to throw my arms around him and thank the stars he lived or punch him in the throat.

The barkeep slapped two mugs in front of Nik and me, the foamy drink spilling over the rim.

I pushed it away and continued, "Finn means to sail tonight, and our new recruits are barely twenty men strong. He requested forty, at least."

Nikolaus swirled the drink around in front of him and frowned. "His mind has failed him if he thinks he'll get forty men from a place like this. He sent you on an impossible mission, Cecily. You'll have to carry two sacks of supplies each to make up the difference. I wish you the best of luck."

I leaned far over on my chair to kick his stool out from under him but lost my balance, catching myself on the sticky countertop.

The barkeep took notice that neither Nikolaus nor I had tasted our drink, so he made his way down to our end of the counter to find offense, like he did every time we came here. Nik stood taller as he slid the written order across the surface, followed by a bag of coins to pay the bill. The barkeep nodded without a single word and signaled for another to watch the patrons in his absence.

"You could have gone with him, you know." Nik lifted the mug and sniffed the foam. His lip curled, and he set it back down.

"The barkeep?" I asked.

"No, idiot. With Finn. Then you'd know where he went."

"He never once asked me to join him or gave me warning he planned to leave at all. I assume it must have something to do with our return to England. At least, that's all I can fathom." My scratchy throat begged me to drink my ale, but my stomach roiled in protest.

After an entire year at his side, secret trysts away from the crew, and sharing in the hardships and danger attached to this lifestyle, Finn still didn't trust me. He kept me in the dark, leaving me to find out many of his plans at the same time he informed the rest of the crew.

Nik scoffed. "If you'd put in for first mate or quarter—"

"Rubbish. He won't let me." And I'd asked him multiple times.

4

If I held more power on the ship, our meetings wouldn't need to be in secret, and the other men might show me an inkling of respect, rather than treating me as a barnacle to scrape from the boat. "Besides, Long didn't go with him, so Finn wouldn't have taken me either if I had a higher standing on board."

"Long's an incompetent rat," Nik said.

Nik and I glanced across the room at our commanding officer. By now, he'd had enough ale that dried bubbles gathered in his patchy gray beard. His hand rested atop the page of recruits, probably smudging the writing, and he laughed loudly with Frans and Eggert, two more horrific pirates we'd picked up in Nassau. If only we could trade all three mongrels for new men. Or *women*. A friend amongst these beasts would be a welcome balm for my soul.

"As long as Finn is content to have men like that in command on his ship, you and I don't stand a chance. He won't let me be anything but his..." The word I needed escaped me.

"His what, Cecily?" Nik showed all his teeth as he bent closer.

"His rigger. I'm his rigger." I pushed Nik's elbow out from under him, sending him toppling into the bar.

He composed himself and moved to shove me back, but stopped just short of touching me. We both straightened in the same moment. The last time we'd gotten into a shoving match, we'd accidentally caused a bar fight in St. Mary's that got our entire crew thrown into the street.

"Bags are out back." The barkeep startled me from my memory. Nikolaus extended his hand across the counter to seal the deal and hopped off his stool.

He'd grown so much since last spring, both in height and maturity. Nearly losing our lives to the Royal Navy a year ago had thrown us all into an older age.

"Our crew will gather the supplies within the hour." Nik nodded to me and bid the man a good day.

With a groan, I returned to my seat beside Long and the native barmaid in his lap—perhaps the only woman in the world foolish enough to flirt with the feral brute. I pulled the parchment out from under his wrist and surveyed the names, a few of which I could read. As predicted, several had smeared with the combination of Long's sweat and spilt ale.

Nineteen new men that week.

That made for about thirty-eight on a ship that required fifty men for full operation. Finn still planned to set sail for England shortly after nightfall, whether we had the desired crew or not. At least, that had been the plan before he disappeared.

I wouldn't have minded staying around the island longer. Of all the Caribbean islands, Barbados held my heart. It was the first place we'd stayed, spent some time alone, and not worried about keeping up appearances for the crew. At least, not when we snuck away from them.

Then Finn had to collect a bunch of scallywags to join us. Nothing had been the same since, and now we meant to trap ourselves on a boat with them for the next few months as we returned to England. Would any of these blokes support our mission to save poor souls in need? Or did Finn mean to use them for another purpose? Surely not pillaging merchant ships or waging war on unsuspecting ports. That proved entirely too *pirate* for my miscreant captain.

"Forgive me, but are you still obtaining men for your crew?"

A well-groomed man, perhaps a decade my senior, his skin dark like the other island natives stood before me. His cleanliness and charming manners put him quite out of place amongst the others.

"What's it to you?" Long growled.

The man swallowed hard and continued, "Sir, I'd like to sail with you. I have many years at sea behind me and possess skills as a cooper. I—"

"We have no need for a cooper." Long spat into his mug.

How had Finn determined this man had the competency to stand on his own two feet, let alone lead a crew in a captain's stead?

If he stopped moving for even a moment, he drank himself into oblivion.

"In fact, we *do* require a cooper, Mr. Long." I pushed the parchment ahead of me toward the man. "Your name?"

"Matthew Stevens, miss. Thank you." He took the quill and signed the page. "Is the captain present?"

That he assumed Long *wasn't* the captain brought me a joy like none other.

Long snatched the parchment and wadded it up in his hand. "No. Be gone with you."

"We need men, and *you* need to stop drinking." I pushed Long's mug over until the remaining contents trickled into his lap. He flew to his feet, pushing the table forward and knocking Stevens farther away.

Long took a giant step toward me, ready for a fight, but the barkeep's shrill whistle stilled his act.

"Get out of my pub," the man yelled over the chatter around the room.

A few of our men headed for the door, some with beverages still in hand.

"Wait. We have supplies to take back to the ship," I called out. If all the men left, we'd sail to England with nothing but some rotting fruit and fish to survive. A deserving first mate would have remembered that aspect of our presence in this pub.

Long nodded at the men nearing the door. They rounded the corner to the rear of the building when they exited, hopefully on their way to grab some bags or barrels—or whatever Nik had ordered. Though, I hadn't expected Long to comply with my direction so easily...

"Eggert, Frans, you heard Miss Hastings. She needs your assistance collecting the captain's supplies. Why don't you help her and her friend out back, would you?" Long reached forward to collect the list of sailors' names. His one wooden tooth showed with the size of his proud grin.

Ah. Not so easily after all.

"Would be my pleasure." Frans bowed low with one hand flourishing in the air above him. He belched loudly as he straightened.

Disgusting ogre.

I nodded for Stevens to follow me toward the door and slid my hand down to my waistband to assure I had my knives at the ready. Nothing would bring Long more joy than his man incapacitating me to ensure I didn't return to the ship.

"Do they mean to fight us?" Stevens whispered as we navigated our way through the lingering smoke.

"Almost certainly," I said.

Stevens surveyed his surroundings and patted down his shirt. "I am not a fighter, Miss Hastings."

"Nor I. In fact, I have a reputation for being quite bad at it." I, too, inspected the rear of the pub. The men had done fairly well collecting items to bring back to the *Hellbound*, leaving only a few bags of flour for those of us left. No doubt Long wouldn't partici-pate in any manual labor if he could avoid it. He meant for these mongrels to dispose of us and carry the remaining goods themselves.

We had little hope of taking the two men on in combat, as our sizes together barely made up for one of them. Stevens couldn't have been much taller than Nik. But if needed, we could outrun them. They'd drunk themselves silly, while Stevens and I had clear heads and were rather determined not to die.

Running sounded better and better as I took stock of our surrounding resources. A latrine sat close to the building, a pen of pigs rivaled the stench a few paces away, and then there was the barkeep's rickety shed propped against a tree, a rusty lock the only thing keeping curious patrons from exploring its contents.

Eggert rounded the corner first.

"There's the flour." I pointed to the pile and took another step back, my other hand hovering above my first knife. Finn always came for me in these moments of peril. He kept me from harm whenever the men grew restless or felt the need to prove themselves superior to my female sex. But he wasn't here this time.

"Why don't you come over here and help me with it," Eggert snarled.

Stevens moved closer to me, placing his body slightly in front of mine—perhaps the most gentlemanly gesture I'd ever seen from a pirate.

The pigs grunted and snuffled when Frans joined us and took a few steps toward their pen like he meant to come at us from a different angle. In my former life, the Collins's pigs had done the same on the farm, growing frantic in the company of bad men. They hated Mr. Collins. He hardly ever attended them without getting knocked off his feet in their chaotic attempt to escape him.

Huh.

"Of course," I said a bit too cheerfully for the situation.

Stevens peeked over his shoulder to evaluate my mental state. I nodded toward the pigpen and made my way nearer to our enemy by way of my smelliest ally.

Frans clapped his hands together and yelled some incoherent battle cry. That did it for the pigs. They screeched and ran around their pen, crashing into the fence and trampling one another for safety. Now was my chance.

I ran at the pen, flipping the latch that kept the animals captive, and climbed atop the gate before they could take me down with them. The pigs charged forward, right at my intended target. Frans shrieked in a way I'd only ever heard from a newborn babe, and he ran off into the trees, a trail of swine at his heels.

Eggert took a special route, clambering atop the latrine to avoid the stampede. I leapt from the fence and grabbed Stevens' sleeve, dragging him behind me toward the next phase of my plan—the one I made up entirely on the spot.

In the shadows, we wedged ourselves behind the latrine. Stevens followed suit when I propped my legs against the wooden back. Together, we rocked the heavy structure until Eggert lost his footing and fell to the ground, shrieking the entire way. With one last heave, we forced the latrine to topple forward, pinning Eggert inside.

The remaining pigs scattered at the crash. Any moment, the barkeep would appear to assess the commotion. We had to get out of there. If caught, no one could save us from an angry barkeep.

"Grab what you can. We need to move." I stumbled in the dark, tripping over piles of dirt until I found the supplies.

Stevens picked up a sack and hoisted it up onto his shoulder. "I cannot believe what just happened. This is absolute madness."

"I have seen much stranger things, Mr. Stevens. If you continue on to the *Hellbound* with me, you will too." I flashed a smile and wrestled a bag into my arms.

Together, we ran off toward the shore, my feet swift when I focused on the joy of thwarting Long's plan and simultaneously ridding myself of Frans and Eggert's company.

I'd found a way when no way seemed to exist, even without Finn to rescue me. I'd discovered a man worthy to sail on the *Hellbound* for a change. I'd even summoned the strength to perform something similar to a run with forty pounds of flour on my shoulders.

Now, if only I could find my captain.

TWO

THE MOONLIGHT GLISTENED OVER THE WATER, REVEALING THE haunting outline of a carrack swaying on the horizon. With the changing tide, the *Hellbound* appeared farther out to sea than it had earlier. Unfortunately, no one had left a longboat for our return, a detail I blamed on Long.

I growled and dropped the flour sack to the sand. "I hope you can swim. You'll find our crew isn't made up of the most considerate men."

Stevens stepped into the warm waters. "I doubt they can be as harsh as the last crew I sailed with. The captain alone was one of the most vile, evil men I've ever encountered. God forgive me for abandoning my mission."

"Your mission?" My boots drank in water, anchoring me to the ocean floor. It'd be hard enough to swim in my full attire, let alone bear a forty-pound bag of flour over my shoulder, too. I would assure Finn knew Long held all responsibility for us leaving the goods on the beach.

"I'm a clergyman," Stevens replied as if stating a very common fact.

"A clergyman? On a pirate ship?" The question shot out of my mouth without my will.

Stevens laughed. "No offense, Miss Hastings, but wouldn't you say that's where I'm needed most? And I must admit, I also find myself wondering how a young woman such as yourself ended up with the same lot."

We waded into the water up to our chests, and I smiled at my companion. "I suppose we're both a bit out of place. And you can call me Cecily. If we die by sharks tonight, I'd rather die beside a friend than a stranger."

"Agreed. Though, a true friend would not mention sharks." He laughed.

I caught the glow in his teeth when he looked back at me and pushed off into the water.

"Then you will not find camaraderie with our cabin boy," I called out and dove in after him.

The journey to the ship didn't take long in the calm evening waters, even though my swimming skills remained frenzied at best with the little practice I'd had. At least the sea creatures left our limbs intact. Above us on deck, voices called out to one another, the crew preparing the ship for sail.

The pair of us climbed our way up the ropes in silence. Perhaps we could slip past the men without their notice—or, at least, past Long's notice. I had no desire to banter with that wretch at such an hour. I only needed proof of Finn's return, Stevens secured in his cooper work, and to assume my place at the rigs before anyone took my job.

But what if Finn hadn't returned at all? Long could have orchestrated a mutiny in his absence. If I jumped ship now before he found me, it wouldn't be the worst thing to live as a permanent resident of Barbados, hurricanes or not. Unless I still couldn't find Finn. Or Nik. Had *he* made it back to the ship on time, or had Long intercepted him as well?

Ringing water from my shirt, I nodded for Stevens to continue on toward the lower decks. "See if you can find the cabin boy, Niko-laus. He'll show you where you'll work and sleep. I'm going to—"

"Hastings!" Long shouted and stomped across the deck, his accusing finger pointed at my head.

I held my hands up in surrender. "Sir, I—"

Long's hand shot forward and coiled around my neck. He shoved me until my rear end met the railing. His grip tightened, and he pressed harder. I gasped for air, clawing at his hands. My balance teetered, his arm the only thing keeping me from tumbling overboard.

Stevens lunged for me, but the other crewmembers cut in between us. When pirates craved a show, nothing kept them from it.

"Where's the goods, Hastings?" he growled.

I couldn't respond. His image grew blurry before me when I battled for air. I kicked to force him away, but he pinned my leg to the edge of the ship with his sharp knee. While I'd likely survive a fall from this height, my chances of survival diminished if I lost consciousness.

Where was Finn?

"You're late, and you have no supplies. What reason do I have to keep you on this ship?" His other hand grabbed my upper arm so I couldn't take hold of the railing for support. "You have no place here."

As he pushed again, a hand clapped against his shoulder and yanked him backward. I tumbled forward and sucked in a breath, trying desperately to keep on my feet and not give them the satis-faction of crumpling to the floor.

When I straightened, my rescuer came into focus. Finn stood between Long and me, his hand resting on the pistol in his belt. The spectators hushed at once. My heart beat faster in my chest, my fists balling to hold back the shock of his appearance.

"Mr. Long, have we not discussed only recently that you're discouraged from throwing crewmembers overboard without my permission?" Finn's head tilted, though I couldn't read his expression at such an angle.

"Aye," Long grumbled under his breath.

Finn turned so I could make out his profile, shaded under his tricorn hat. He appeared unharmed in any way, every inch the powerful captain I knew him to be. "And what, pray, has Hastings done this time?"

"She's late. Left the supplies. Leeson's been up in the rigs to make up for her slack." Long spit on the deck beside him.

Finn sighed as he glanced up at the rigging. "Mr. Long, we haven't even set sail yet, and you've already exhausted me."

Just the sound of his voice brought me home again, steadied me on the swaying ship. I stepped forward and cleared my scratchy throat that still ached from Long's tight grasp. "Captain, I've brought a new man, able-bodied and with experience in woodworking."

Finn turned slowly in my direction, but not because he, too, had longed to hear my voice again.

Gadsbobs.

I'd spoken out of turn again. He'd warned me about that many times. The crew shouldn't address him so casually. And if we meant to keep our relationship a mystery to the men, I needed to act as the rest of them. No matter how long it'd been since we saw each other last.

He rubbed the bridge of his nose and released a lengthy breath. "Men, ready the ship. Long, see that our new 'able-bodied' seaman has a place among us. Hastings, you will follow me to explain yourself and what exactly it was you left behind."

Long smirked. I lowered my head to avoid his ugly gaze. He then began shouting orders at his men to continue on, throwing out in his favorite insults to motivate them. I searched the crowd for Stevens and found him standing wide-eyed in the presence of Long. The two men vanished into the chaos, while the remaining bunch cast jeers in my direction. They all knew what a private audience with an angry captain entailed and beamed when the fate fell on me rather than them.

The short distance from the ship's poop deck to the captain's quarters had never seemed longer, but I followed the captain silently with my head bowed in submission to his orders—and also to hide the stupid smile on my face.

Finn opened the door and ushered me inside. The scent of oak filled the room from the extinguished fireplace and mixed with a lingering sweetness of the hot tea sitting on the table. Light beamed through the windows in lines that shimmered from the reflecting water, creating constant motion across the hardwood floor. Nothing ever changed here. Not even the unmade bed in the corner, the desk full of musty maps, or the unwavering warmth that always wrapped around me when I entered.

Behind me, Finn flipped the latch on the door, locking it with a loud click. Above him, a thick board covered the hole left when the Royal Navy shattered the thick stained glass. It made for a haunting reminder of what we'd been through together when we nearly lost our lives to the enemy.

I took hold of the oversized chair at the center table, the steady sway of the anchored ship mixing with the memories that flooded my mind inside this room. Finn lingered at the door, then shifted slowly in my direction.

His sapphire gaze worked its way across to me, wandering up my body until it came to rest on my face. My fingers trembled against the chair, and I ached for him to say something, *do* something. But he didn't.

So I did.

My chest pounded as I ran to him and shoved him against the door. He clutched each of my elbows in his hands, steadying us both, and pulling me with the same force I used on him. Our lips collided with all the pent up desire of our time apart.

His fingers walked their way up my arms until they reached my back, taking me fully into his embrace. If his grip were any tighter, I wouldn't have been able to breathe, though I hardly cared now. I pulled his hat from his head, letting my anxious fingers coil into the blond strands of his hair, and I tugged him closer still.

His mouth curled into a smile that broke our kiss, and he bent his head to rest his brow on mine.

"Hello, love," he whispered.

I buried my head into the crook of his neck, hugging him in close. His familiar scent of the salty sea air filled me with a calm I hadn't felt in days.

"Where the hell were you?" I asked into his collarbone. "I almost died today."

Finn groaned but didn't release his grip on my waist. "You didn't though."

"A bit close, wouldn't you say? If you'd been here to control your crew, I wouldn't have to hang over the edge of a ship at all." My fingers twirled through the hair at the base of his neck. If he never let go, it wouldn't be the worst thing in the world. I could scold him all day just like this.

"Cess, can we just enjoy this moment?" He sighed into my hair, and his hands gripped harder on my hips when he drew me back to look me in the eye.

My arms fell limp at my sides. It took all I had not to smile at his raised eyebrow. "I am very much enjoying this moment, while also keeping you informed on what happened after you abandoned us this week."

He laughed then, wrapped his hands around my middle, and lifted me from the ground. I covered my mouth to silence my squeal. After all, he'd brought me in here to issue a punishment and discuss my unruliness, not generally a task that involved flirtatious giggling, especially on a pirate ship.

Finn sauntered forward and plopped me down on the edge of his desk as he'd done so many times before. I spun on its surface to follow him around until he sat in his chair.

"You're right. I should be here at all times to control my *crew*."

He leaned toward me and steepled his fingers against his lips, his elbows propped on the desktop beside my legs. "I suppose I have to figure out your punishment now, eh, Hastings?"

So much for our beautiful reunion. It never lasted long. "If you must."

"What did you forget, anyway?" He slid back in his chair and kicked his feet up on the desktop.

"Flour. Long tried to detain me at the pub and sent all the men back in the boats before I returned. If you want the bags, they're sitting on the shore." *Detain* summed it up nicely without giving away the absurdity of what actually happened.

"At least until the tide comes in." The tip of his boot nudged me. "And you realize you spoke out of turn again, don't you?"

I hopped off the desk and walked quietly to the table to pour myself a cup of tea.

He sighed as he watched me, knowing full well he wouldn't get an answer on that one.

"And this new able-bodied fellow? What of him?" he asked.

I took a long sip. Maybe the change of subject could keep me from listening to another lecture on pirate etiquette. "Matthew Stevens. He's a minister of some sort. Says he's sailed before."

"A minister? Did you neglect to tell him we aren't an angler ship?" Finn's chair grated on the wooden floor when he stood and joined me at the table.

"He knows what he's gettin' himself into. Might be mad. Or valiant. I can't decide." I poured another cup for Finn and refilled mine to the brim. "May I suggest he replaces Long? The old man is better suited for scraping seagull dung off the figurehead than running this ship as first mate."

Finn looked at me over the rim of his cup. "*Acting* first mate. He's working on a trial basis."

"I'd like to end the trial, please. He is horrible," I said.

"Doesn't work like that."

"Well, I'd love to apply for the position in his stead." I slunk closer and winked up at him when my shoulder brushed his. "Quartermaster, perhaps?"

Finn's half smirk won over his expression as he shook his head. "Not a chance. As if making you second-in-command wouldn't already spread suspicion, you are, by far, my most insubordinate crewmember."

"Excuse me?" I set my cup down with a thud that sent tea spilling onto the table. While I lacked many of the qualifications he sought in his men, I knew I'd do a better job than Long and almost any of the others out there.

He grabbed my hand and pulled it to his chest. "I'm still a captain in spite of everything else. I have to do what's best for my ship. And you, obviously."

My eyes narrowed. His excuses about keeping us "safe" had grown wearisome. We were on a pirate ship for star's sake! The men didn't esteem me. None of them deemed me worthy of any space on the *Hellbound*. If Finn gave me power, they'd see me for what I could do and not just as a woman hanging around where she didn't belong.

"That response has run its course, Finnigan," I said.

He released my hand and ruffled his hair. "It's still my highest priority, regardless. And you've killed the moment, by the way. This could have been terribly romantic and all that."

"*I've* killed the moment? What about *you*? You disappear for days at a time without telling me where you're going? Give first mate to a lunatic? Call me insubordinate? I am not the one lacking in romantic gestures. And you still have yet to tell me where you've been all this time. I tried to get it out of Nikolaus, but he gave me nothing. I know you told him where—"

"A meeting." He walked to his desk and shuffled through the maps in a seemingly pointless manner. "A pirate meeting."

"Of course. How silly of me to forget that pirates often have meetings to discuss important pirate matters." I crossed my arms and sat back on the table.

He grinned at me over his shoulder. "You'd be surprised."

"Would I?"

Finn shook his head but never lost that smirk. Though the answer didn't explain as much as I wanted, it gave me more than the nothing I had to go on earlier.

When Finn found his compass amongst the maps, he dropped it into his coat pocket and returned to me. Clutching hold of my wrists, he pulled me from the table's edge and back into his arms. His chin rested on top of my head as he spoke.

"If Long asks, I've cut your rations for the next month. Nik will feed you, but don't let the lot of 'em see," he said.

"Aye," I mumbled into his neck.

He cupped my chin and lifted my face so he could kiss my nose, then my cheek. His lips hovered over mine for a moment, his warm breath urging me to close the gap between us.

"Cecily?" he cooed.

My insides turned to liquid, as they often did when he spoke to me in such a gentle tone. He held an amazing power over me to make me forget everything, even when we fought. I hated it. And loved it. I could barely make a real sound to answer him. "Yes?"

"What happened to Eggert and Frans?"

The haze fell away when I started, and my hands froze against his chest.

"Why do you think I had anything to do with them not showing up?" I took a few steps backward to put some space between us.

"I didn't tell you they didn't show up. I just asked what happened to them." His smile grew as he walked to keep up with my reverse motion.

My back pressed to the door. I had nowhere else to go.

I bit my lip and tried hard to bat my lashes flirtatiously. "You were so right about enjoying this romantic moment. It's been such a long time—"

"Cecily Hastings, I command that you tell me what you've done with my men."

"Now who's killing the moment?" I whined.

Finn's hands flattened on the door on either side of me. His voice lowered with our closer proximity to the rest of the crew. "What did you do, Cess?"

I brushed past him and threw my hands in the air. "I fell in love with a pirate. That's what I did. *That* is my crime. If I'd been able to escape my life at the Collins's on my own accord, I might have stood a chance at becoming a respectable lady, but no. You corrupted me. Anything that happened because of your interference is no one's fault but your own."

"Is that so?" His smile widened. "So, whatever happened today —whatever mysterious event you're trying to hide—is really *my* fault?"

"Yes, it is." I marched to the doorway and unhinged the lock, opening it only partway before looking over my shoulder at him. "I unleashed a pen of pigs on Frans and trapped Eggert beneath a latrine. I missed you. Terribly."

With that, I shut the door between us, Finn's stunned silence following me out.

THREE

From my point high above the decks, I relished the warm sun peeking over the horizon. Beginning my work mid-night wasn't ideal, but the fiery sunrise that followed made it worth it. Wherever my task took me, I always climbed to the ship's highest point to take it in, to see it first. Never in my life had I felt as free as in those moments with the wind in my hair and the sun guiding the ship onward.

As badly as I'd wanted to become first mate, the job meant giving up my position as rigger. Somehow, Finn's excuse to keep me safe juxtaposed allowing me to work in the ship's most dangerous occupation of flying high with the sails. Long, however, couldn't have been happier to send me upward, probably hoping I'd meet my doom and be out of his greasy hair forever.

At least I'd gotten farther in the ranks than Nikolaus. Finn wouldn't even hear of him working as anything other than the cabin boy and cook. Nik had voiced his discontent more often than usual, perhaps growing weary of his duties that continued even on shore. His loyalty knew no end, though. Nik served his captain with all of his energy, regardless of the complaints he mumbled under his breath as he worked.

I climbed down the ropes to join the rest of the men, groggily going about their morning duties. A good many of them still had much to learn with sailing a ship of this size. Several months at sea with Finn and Nikolaus had forced me to learn everything quickly after we exploded the Royal Navy's ship and made our way to the Caribbean.

"You aren't tying that properly." I took hold of the rope beside Long and twisted it against the hook.

Long froze, the rest of the rope falling limp in his hand as he cursed me under his breath.

"If you don't pull the bottom rope through that second loop, it will not hold. You'll have to retie it all again in an hour," I said.

He slammed the ropes against the deck and turned to me with fire in his eyes. "You want to tell me how to do my job, girl?"

I held his gaze, unwavering. "You know my name."

"Yes. Unfortunately, I do."

He bullied past me, his shoulder ramming into mine, and I caught the stench of his bodily odors mixed with a hint of tobacco. I followed him, clenching my teeth with determination to fulfill my duty on the ship. And that duty, as always, involved keeping up appearances. I was a pirate, and we had to do our part to keep the ship afloat. In this case, it meant confronting the first mate on a piss-poor effort.

"Do you want me to redo this?" I called over to him.

Long looked about the ship, a loud, breathy sigh rattling his ribs when he exhaled. Just then, the door to the lower decks opened, and Nikolaus stepped out, a mop in one hand and a bucket in the other. Long's sneer grew into a smile that showed all his rotting teeth.

"I've a wonderful idea for you, Hastings. We've got fresh blood on board now, strong backs and willing workers. Why don't you go down below to the galley? It's woman's work, anyway."

Nikolaus froze, looking both alarmed at my presence and offended by Long's remarks—nearly as offended as myself. Woman's work? I could do every job aboard this vessel and with more spirit and accuracy than most of them. Finn and Nik proved excellent instructors when the three of us sailed the massive ship alone.

"I already have a position on the *Hellbound*, Mr. Long. Or have you forgotten it?" I stiffened as his glare bore into me, though I could hear Finn's voice in the back of my mind, warning me to obey the ship's command.

He leaned in closer. "Oh, I haven't forgotten. But as the first mate, I'm charged with assigning tasks to the most suited men. And I know exactly where I want you. Now sod off. Nikolaus, you've no business on deck today. Get on with ya."

Nik squeaked beside me, biting hard into his lip. He puffed his chest and turned on his heel. He often took verbal beatings from the crew, forced to deal with it for appearance's sake. If we didn't have our own alliances, I didn't know how we would have survived any of it.

"Go on. You've got a crew to feed." Long said over his shoulder as he headed back to the ropes.

Just like that, the beast put an end to the job I loved. I doubted I could contest the idea with Finn. He'd probably prefer me tucked away with Nikolaus in the safest part of the ship.

I'd show them, though. I was a terrible cook. Mr. Collins had said as much every day I lived with him on the farm. Still, Long might want to mind his comments if he wanted his food prepared pleasantly. We were pirates, after all. Our moral codes were a bit shaky.

Nikolaus looked to me, his brow furrowed. He'd grown over the past few months, losing more of his boyish appearance every day. He wore his blond hair tied back, a red kerchief covering most of his forehead. He nodded at me, and I followed him until we reached the door to the lower decks.

We descended the stairs, led by the dim light squeezing its way through the portholes along the side of the ship. I looked toward the closed-off room in the corner as I so often did—the room where I once cared for the slaves Finn had freed in Ireland. What had their lives become?

"Can't believe I'm stuck with you now." Nikolaus kicked the door open and sank down onto a stool against the wall. His arms folded with a thump over his chest.

"I expected more delight from you, Nik. We get to spend all our time together. Just the two of us." I probably shouldn't have poked at him, but I'd lived with Finn for so long, it was impossible to resist.

He stared at me, expressionless. I shook my head and sat on the floor beside his stool, folding my arms similarly to his.

"I asked Finn if we could leave you in Barbados like we originally planned. He said no." Nik's boot buckle clicked when he kicked at the side of his stool.

I smiled and tried to see past his pout. Not all of his boyishness had vanished forever. At least, not just yet. "Well, you should know I'm not thrilled with this arrangement either. I liked being a rigger."

"I'd be happier with any other work, too. That is, if Finn would stop being such a scab. I'll be fourteen soon, and I can do any job on this ship, including his."

"I cannot argue that. But you know he's got his reasons, no matter how much we dislike them and question their validity." The dank kitchen made me miss the warm sunshine already. How had Nik survived down here all this time? The galley might as well have been a prison.

Nikolaus tugged at his shirt collar. "His reasons are garbage. Simple as that."

We sat still for another quiet moment. The faintly lit room held its share of dust and mold, but otherwise the small fire in the stove made it cozy enough for a nap. On deck, the daily chores would last all day. We'd attempted to participate, but Long sent us away.

What could we possibly do with free time when we couldn't even move about the ship?

Nikolaus lived in this room, his hammock overflowing with blankets in the corner. He didn't have to sleep with the rest of the crew, which gave him extra safety and privacy. Finn had spent so many years learning exactly how to keep his younger brother in the best position among the other miscreants. This really made the best position for the younger boy, even if he hated every second of it.

I had taken to sleeping with the storage when we weren't on shore. There, I could hear if anyone approached when they'd crash into the maze of supplies or frighten the rats into a squeaking frenzy. I had my secret nest back there in my little corner. Though, as I'd become second in command in the kitchen, I could now justify sleeping near the fire with Nik. I could hardly turn down the extra warmth when we meant to arrive in England during winter.

"I'm not giving you my hammock." Nik had clearly followed my stare.

"I wouldn't ask you to." Maybe I could just take it instead. At least for a quick rest after my early rigging shift. My eyelids grew heavy, and I longed for a hot cup of tea and a warm blanket.

"Try not to cook anything, all right?" He stood and began pulling pots and pans from the cupboards.

I worked my way upright to join him at the table and examined the produce before me. "Then what would you have me do in here? I can't do nothing all day." I had to stay busy. If left alone with my thoughts for too long, I often dwelt on the sorrow of my former life. Sometimes, my worries went wild, and I realized what a dangerous life we led *now*—how at any moment, I could lose the people I loved the most. No, I definitely preferred to stay occupied.

Nik tossed a sheathed knife onto the countertop until it bounced to a dull stop in front of me. Then he gestured to the barrel of potatoes at the table's end. "You can stay out of the way, mostly. And peel potatoes. I don't think you could mess that up too badly."

I slipped the small knife from its wrap and pinched the cold steel of the blade between my fingertips, inspecting the smooth hilt. Throwing knives always soothed me during down time, gave me something to do with my hands and a task to focus on rather than face the fears swirling around in my head.

"Don't even think about it. That knife is dull enough as it is." He pulled out a brown bag full of vegetables and rummaged through for what he needed.

"I wasn't going to throw it." The little mongrel always knew my thoughts.

"Then you obviously don't know you can't hold it by the blade if you mean to use it to peel a potato." He chucked an onion peel at me.

I slumped down on a stool and turned the blade from throwing position to peeling position. There had to be thousands of potatoes in the barrel beside me. Begrudgingly, I set to work and prayed for time to pass quickly.

My hands ached after the first dozen, growing red and tender with each twist of the knife. No wonder Nikolaus had such calluses on his fingers. On top of it all, he had to perform his duties in solitude and mostly in the dark. I couldn't blame him for wanting new work.

"So, this is what you do all day? Annihilating onions and undressing potatoes?" I asked.

He sighed. "No, sometimes I pick worms out of bread, swab floors, and sift through piles of spoiled vegetables."

Worms? Why did he have to mention that? I enjoyed my meals without the knowledge of how it came to my plate.

Nik nodded toward his project. "After we get these cut, we'll start the stew. It'll be enough to feed the lot of them for several days. I also have to take Finn his tea multiple times a day, or he'll whine about it. Bout time for that, too."

I ran a potato through with my knife and grinned. If Nik wouldn't talk to me, I could at least steal away to visit another that *would*. "Now, there's a task I'd quite enjoy."

Nik groaned. "You disgust me."

I tossed the last of my peeled potatoes into the pot and dropped my knife on the table. "Perhaps being on kitchen detail with the likes of you won't be so bad after all."

FOUR

As always, I paused at the entryway leading out of the hull. The salty air coated my lips, and my shoulders eased as if new life breathed into me. I never tired of the magical transition from the musty underworld of the ship into the blazing light of day. The cool breeze washed over my skin, and the roaring magnitude of the ocean waves churned restlessly in all directions. How had I ever survived without the sea?

"Bunch of lazy seadogs!" Finn yelled from above me on the bridge, breaking my calm thoughts. "If I see another slacker, I'll throw the lot of you to Davy Jones and let him deal with you sorry excuses. Long, retie those ropes. Fevre, head's duty for the rest of the week for the shoddy job you've done with the cables. Piper, you're a disgrace to this ship and the whole bloody ocean."

I bit my bottom lip to keep from smiling. The men's attention gravitated in my direction, so I couldn't afford to give away my amusement, especially when I should be as terrified of our captain as they were. I used to be, but that didn't last long. I'd seen his rage first hand, and the punishments he administered to an unruly crew. Still, witnessing his deep remorse after the fact hurt me more than the act itself. It went against his nature to be cruel, even when acting the way a captain needed to.

The tea tray swayed in my hands when the wind tried to knock it from my grasp, and I readjusted my position to keep from spilling the piping hot drink all over myself. My back straightened, head held high, as I marched in front of the bridge and made my way to the winding staircase that led up to the helm.

Finn groaned. "Long, will you give up already? Let someone have a go with it that actually knows what they're doing. Holystones and cleaning detail might be better suited to you, old man."

I moved behind Finn to hide from Long's cold stare. Perhaps he thought I'd mentioned his incompetence to the captain. I hadn't. Long's inability to tie a simple knot went on display for all the ship to see.

"Please tell me that's rum," Finn said over his shoulder.

The teakettle rattled when I set it down on the small table that held his map.

"I hadn't thought to include that in your *breakfast*, Captain. My apologies." The man didn't care about the hour, especially since he'd been awake for so long. And with this lot to command, I hardly blamed him for needing a stronger beverage.

"So, Long's got you held up in the galley then? He sent my best rigger to Nikolaus, and now I'm stuck with Leeson up there. I'm not entirely sure he knows what a sail does." Finn reached behind him to take the cup from me.

I plopped a scoop of sugar into the tea before he pulled it away. "I've been instructed by your Mr. Long to stay out of the way. Instead of feeling the breeze on my face high above the deck, I'm now slaughtering potatoes and protecting innocent loaves of bread from worms. It's all wonderfully exciting."

Finn came away from the wheel to set his compass atop his strewn maps and took another long sip of his tea. The gritty sugar crunched between his teeth with each sip.

"Nikolaus must be thrilled to have you," he said.

"Naturally." I grinned toward the stern.

He breathed a laugh. "Well, he likes you better than me these days. He wants to work on deck. Has he mentioned this? Though, why he'd want to be closer to these sorry sea dogs, I haven't the slightest idea."

"Perhaps because he's better at this than all of them combined into one?" If I put in a good word for my younger companion, he might be more pleasant the next time we sat around the table attempting to make conversation over dinner preparation.

"Don't you start on me, too. The last thing I need is the pair of you forming an alliance against me." Finn poured himself another cup and added an extra scoop of sugar this time. Soon, his liquid tea would become a solid cake.

"Oh, no. You definitely don't want that. We'd overtake you and then be tried for mutiny." I rearranged the supplies on my tray to make it appear I had an actual purpose at the helm with the captain.

Finn raised an eyebrow as he glanced over his shoulder at me. "You know I don't hate that you're down there with him."

"I figured as much. But that doesn't change the fact that we both hate it and are unconcerned about our safety when it goes against having a job we can tolerate." As long as I didn't look too deeply into his eyes, I might stand my ground and get somewhere with this. Neither Nik nor I could gain the crew's respect as equals if Finn kept us low in power and mostly hidden from the others.

Finn blew out a loud breath and tapped his forehead to the helm. He paused when he observed the crew at work below him. "Cess dear, if I had the power, I would give you the world. For now, all I can do is keep you safe until the world is mine to give."

My hands nearly lost their grip on the tray when my heart hammered in my chest. He never made it easy to hide my feelings on deck, especially in those moments when I longed to grab his collar and pull him against me.

Below on the poop deck, Long called out more orders as if he knew what needed done. At least two of his three orders were entirely made up occupations. Finn, Nikolaus, and I weren't the only ones working to keep up false appearances on this ship.

Finn held his cup up to his lips and mumbled, "We need a meeting. The three of us. We can't speak freely under their watch."

"When?" I fidgeted with the teapot, keeping my eyes down.

"Tonight. I'll set you up with a reason to come to me." He readjusted his tricorn hat as he flashed me a wink. "Though, I won't be able to keep you as long as I'd like."

I gathered the tray in my arms and bit my lip to fight off my emotions. "Yes, sir."

The moment my foot hit the first step, Finn cleared his throat. "Walk a bit slower, will you?"

When I turned to him, he tipped his cap and showed his crooked grin.

"Captain?" If he insisted on making such advance, I'd topple straight down the stairs to my death.

"Not for that reason!" He bent over the wheel to hide his laughter.

My cheeks caught fire, and it took every effort on my part not to collapse into a fit of laughter—and embarrassment. Suddenly, it seemed as if the sun burned ten times hotter, and the entire crew had turned their eyes on me, even though neither was true.

"I meant walk slowly so you don't miss your setup." He chuckled into the wheel again, still unable to fully compose himself.

I steadied against the railing and tiptoed the rest of the way down, readjusting the items on my tray to buy some time.

On the last step, Finn's booming voice once again scolded his crew for the horrendous efforts exuded. Surely none of them would thank me for distracting the captain with tea, even for just a few minutes. Instead, my presence only irritated them more. A new disgusted expression met me with every tap of my boots across the tattered deck.

"For pity's sake, Leeson. Just get down. *Now*," Finn cried.

Above me, a man threw his leg over the edge of the bucket, his spyglass slipping from his hand and toppling back into the nest. If he broke that thing, I would have some strong words for him later.

I came to a complete halt at the bottom of the steps and waited until Finn's eager footsteps approached from behind me. He brushed past me as if he hadn't seen me standing there at all, though a gentle finger slid across the small of my back to prove otherwise.

"Who sent such incompetence to the nest?" Finn shouted.

The men looked around, no one wanting to accept the blame.

Finn clutched harder to the hilt of his blade hanging on his belt. He picked his second-in-command out amongst the crowd. "You send a man of that size up to do a job like this, and you get this rubbish in return. Long, who on board this ship is better suited for this position?"

Long's hands shook as he assessed the surrounding men in vain.

I couldn't blame him for the hesitation. Ideally, the riggers should be smaller men, and few of them fit that description. If they were as familiar with the pubs as I presumed them to be, their sizes made sense.

"No one?" Finn brushed aside the flap in his coat, hand resting on his belt to reveal the weaponry there. "How about yourself, Mr. Long? Would you care to make the climb?"

"Captain, sir, I am not—"

"I find your excuses extremely boring. Go take the helm. See if you can follow a compass better than you can tie a knot," Finn said.

Long's head lowered, and he walked past the group of men to follow orders in silence.

The others watched with bated breath, while Finn's mannerisms screamed with an authority that intimidated them all—even me a little. His stare bounced from each one of his men, examining their expressions and waiting for a volunteer he knew wouldn't step forward.

"Hastings," he shouted.

I nearly threw the teakettle over my shoulder when he startled me this way. Did he have to yell when he knew I stood right behind him?

"Yes, Captain?" I stepped around him and into sight.

"Do you want your job back?" Finn asked.

If he meant this to be the setup, he should have advised me on a response. Unquestionably, I wanted to be a rigger. But did *he* want that for me, too, or did he mean for me to refuse and come to his quarters for another round of consequences over my insubordination?

My voice squeaked as I answered. "Captain, Mr. Long has assigned me to the galley."

Finn scratched at the stubble on his cheek and let his head roll back on his shoulders. "Hastings, I'll ask you again. Do you want your job back in the rigs?"

He refused to turn and face me straight on. Thank goodness, too. It was hard enough to act as strangers without the threat of eye contact making one of us falter.

"Yes, Captain," I said.

"Get up there and hoist the remaining sails. Stevens, take her tray." Finn stepped aside to grant me access to the rope ladder.

Matthew Stevens stepped into view to unburden my hands, and I took comfort in seeing him amongst the others. He offered a quick smile to urge me onward. At least I knew one of my observers didn't secretly hope I plunged to my death while I completed my task.

I moved to the mainmast and stretched my arms out to the side, warming up for the climb. The mast towered over me, mocking my attempt to prove myself in front of my captain and an angry audience. Finn's attempt at a setup might have only made the crew despise me more, but I couldn't entertain that thought. It might fill my mind every moment after this, but it mustn't *now*.

On our journey to the Caribbean, with just Finn and Nikolaus for company, Nik and I would find alternative ways to climb the mast, aside from using the rope ladder. We spent many nights plucking splinters from our fingers and teasing one another over who would win the next race. But if I wanted to prove my knowledge of rigging, I had to do each step in the process the way Finn meant it done.

I scurried to the top of the rope ladder, my speed still half that of the other men, proving Finn's point that the job should belong to the smallest crewmembers. At the top, I held my palms to the beam and shifted my body weight to mount its broad width. Down below, Finn gave the command for the others to man their stations. The sails needed adjustment to catch the winds, rather than the standard placement the men had put it in for the first part of our journey.

As I inched my way across, I wiggled the ropes free, a task that would have been easier if it had been done right.

"Full sail, Hastings," Finn shouted.

"Aye!" I stood, holding a rope for balance, and made my way to the other end of the beam.

Below me, I glimpsed Long's wrinkled face staring up at me from the helm. Though I couldn't make out his expression, I knew he scowled as if he watched the devil himself take away all he loved.

I shifted my legs around to swing my body in the other direction. The sail cracked in the wind, catching just right, and I clutched a little tighter on the beam for support when the ship lurched, speeding up with the new force. My balance even impressed me at such a height. I belonged here.

Finn waved his hand to draw me back to the ground, and I kicked off the beam to grab the rope ladder and start my descent. The ladder shook in the heavier winds that rocked the ship, but I clung to it, afraid to lose my job all over again if I accidentally slipped and fell.

When my feet hit the deck, Finn nodded his approval. "You

will finish your duties in the galley per Long's command, serve dinner in my quarters tonight, and in the morning, resume your position as rigger. Understood?"

"Yes, Captain," I said. It took all my strength to keep my surprise at bay. After admitting he preferred me in the galley with Nik, I hadn't expected to have my job back mere moments later.

Finn took his leave to return to the helm. Behind me, the grumbles started up again, and I tried in vain to ignore them. I may have proven myself a competent rigger, but I'd also given the men more reason to despise me. My feat impressed no one. Though I'd never expected much camaraderie amongst the crew, I didn't need to create more enemies, especially since the first mate already loathed my existence. Incompetent nincompoop.

All I could do now was keep my chin up, prove my worth as a sailor, and hope these men grew to accept me as one of their own. Oh, and try not to find myself at the wrong end of their revenge schemes. I couldn't forget about that.

FIVE

THE AGONY OF BEING STUCK IN THE DARK GALLEY FOR THE afternoon almost killed me. Nikolaus worked on, ignoring me most of the time, which added to my boredom. He didn't appreciate the shanties I sang while stirring the stew or piling hard bread into baskets for supper. I'd even made up my own lyrics, as I didn't really know any actual shanties.

"I will be so happy when you leave," Nikolaus mumbled.

I tapped the wooden paddle on the pot's rim hard enough that stew broth sprayed the wall. "You honestly prefer being alone?"

"Yes," he said matter-of-factly.

The paddle slipped from my hand and landed on the table beside me—for the third time since I began stirring. I left it lie and reached to tear off a piece of bread, stuffing it into my mouth to keep from throwing an insult at Nik. There wasn't enough work in here to occupy two people for an entire day. In fact, Nikolaus had been a cabin boy so long he'd mapped out his tasks to perfection. Tossing me into his routine just made it more difficult on him. I hated sitting around, though. If only Finn had sent me to the rigs immediately.

"You can thank Finn later for sending me back to the nest," I said.

"He must have panicked when he realized you'd be cooking." Nik bit his lip and spun out of my reach.

I picked the paddle back up and pointed it at him. "You are rotten."

He yanked the spoon from my grasp and began stirring the stew in my place. I sank down on the stool and stacked a few more rolls onto the leaning tower I'd already made. It'd most likely all topple when we went upstairs. But really, would touching the floor make them any worse?

"What do you think Finn wants to talk about tonight?" Aside from escaping my galley prison, I could hardly think of anything else.

"You asked me that already. Many, many times."

I sighed and pushed the bread basket away to avoid any more unnecessary boredom stacking. "He'd better elaborate on where he's been all this time. I'm not satisfied with his latest answer."

"And you're still on about that, too, eh?" Nik asked. "He's done this for years, you know. You'll have to get used to it."

"I'll be 'on about it' until I get a decent answer from him. All these secrets exhaust me." My bread pyramid crumbled when I smashed my fist onto the tabletop.

Nikolaus rolled his eyes and moved on to readying the drinking water.

When the meal hour finally arrived, Nik and I loaded our arms with food and drink for the crew, a task that required multiple trips up and down the stairwell until my legs ached.

I paused along the railing to catch my breath, admiring the beauty of the setting sun. Layers of purple, pink, and orange clouds colored the sky, the ocean swallowing half of the blazing ball of light. But something appeared off about the sunset. For starters, it should have been on the *other* side of the ship.

It took me a long moment to gather my bearings. Had spending the day below decks thrown off my perception so badly? When heading northeast, the sun should set port side, not starboard side. We headed south. I must have been too fatigued from my late-night shift to have paid attention to the sunrise.

I cursed myself for not noticing earlier. A proper sailor would have caught it right away.

"Hastings!" Nik's shouts drew me away from the railing. He stood amongst the crew, gathering emptied bowls and glaring at me to come and help him. Cabin boys, or girls, couldn't afford to study the skyline when they had work to do. I'd forgotten my place.

We rushed around to clean up after the men, then returned to the kitchen to prepare the captain's plates with extra for Nikolaus and me underneath the platters. Though I never would have admitted it out loud, I had missed Nikolaus's cooking while we stayed in Barbados. The island cuisine tasted of dreams and magic, but Nik's food tasted like home.

Nikolaus and I carried the plates up the flight of stairs and arranged everything neatly onto a rolling cart. Once fully loaded, we made our way to the captain's chambers and entered at our own will to set the table and wait for Finn's arrival. I followed Nikolaus's lead to perfection, right up until the door closed behind us, hiding us away from the watchful eyes of the crew. To them, they only saw two dedicated crewmembers diligently serving their captain.

"I'm starving." I sighed as I set the plates on the table.

Nik followed behind me to place cups and utensils. "You just ate some bread downstairs."

"Yes, but I couldn't finish it because I thought of your insect comment."

"The bread has always had bugs in it, Cecily. You haven't died yet," he said.

My hunger subsided somewhat. I supposed even grand adventures out to sea had to have a downside, including the possibility of infested fare.

Finn wouldn't leave his post until everything had settled for the night, so Nikolaus and I made ourselves at home in his quarters to await his return. Nik started a fire in the hearth, while I straightened the sheets on Finn's bed and poured myself a cup of tea.

The sun fell beneath the waves of the horizon, letting the fire's glow lull us into a sleepy daze. I sank into a chair at the table and fought to keep my heavy eyelids open. My chin rested upon my hand as I watched the ocean overtake the light.

"Nik, have you noticed the sun isn't setting on the correct side of our ship?" I asked.

He stopped pouring his tea. "That might be the oddest question you have ever asked me."

"I mean, have you realized we're heading south? What happened to England?" The bell outside the cabin rang the hour, startling me in my seat.

Nik turned to assess the view out the bay window. "Yes, I've noticed, but I've given up asking *why* with my brother. He changes his mind so quickly it's pointless trying to keep up. Besides, why bother informing us lowly crewmembers of his captain-ly orders?"

I rolled my eyes and ignored the jab at Finn. "But this is a rather significant change in plans, and we're—"

The latch on the door flipped violently, and Finn stormed into the room, slamming the door shut behind him.

I stood from my chair with such abruptness that tea splashed over the brim of my cup and splattered my pant legs. "What's wrong?"

He threw his hat into the corner and shrugged his waistcoat onto the floor. His weapons came off next, one by one. He exhaled with the force of an entire day's exertion, kicking at the fallen articles of clothing and sheathed weaponry on the floor.

"Smells good. Let's eat." Finn slumped in his seat and stared at the spread across the table.

"Finn?" I leaned forward, hoping to catch his eye. "What's wrong?"

His lips pursed, and he took in a lengthy breath through his nose. "This crew is a nightmare. We'll be lucky if we even make it all the way to England." He stabbed hard at a piece of meat and turned to regard me. "Are you positive you want to take up the position of rigger again?"

"Yes, she is." Nikolaus shoveled a bite of food into his mouth.

I shot him a disapproving glance, then answered for myself. "Yes, absolutely. Nik and I may murder one another if we have to remain cooped up in such small confines."

"Yeah, don't kill each other, please. You may be the only decent sailors on my ship." Finn scooped a large slab of butter onto his biscuit and stuffed it into his mouth in what appeared to be one quick motion.

Now that he'd arrived, we could eat without guilt, though Finn's mood and Nikolaus's snide remarks didn't make for great atmosphere. "What do you think about Stevens, the minister I brought you? He mentioned he'd sailed before. He has to have some abilities, I would think."

"He's fine enough. Doing cooper work for the time being and making small repairs throughout the ship. Sang the whole time, though." Finn smiled as he reached for the kettle.

"See? He'll be good for morale," I said.

"He'd be better for morale if he could carry a tune." Finn lifted his cup as if to toast our new songbird.

Nik's laugh sent a small spray of potatoes across his plate.

Finn waved his hand to settle the boy, holding back a chuckle of his own. "Regardless, he'll be a contender for quartermaster. If not for his skill, then simply to aggravate Long."

"I like that plan." If Nik or I couldn't be quartermaster, I'd rather it be Stevens than anyone else on board.

Nikolaus wiped his chin on his sleeve and scooted his chair up to the table. He cleared his throat and glanced between the two of us. "Coopers don't make quartermasters. If we're here to solve your crew problem, I have the perfect suggestion."

"You're too young." Finn didn't make eye contact when he spoke, merely taking another loud sip of his tea.

"I hadn't even said my piece yet, you—"

"We've had this conversation enough that I know exactly what you mean to say," Finn said.

I chewed slower on my meat, afraid to make a sound that might draw me in to such a disagreement. It never came to a resolution where either man could be happy, and I had no desire to choose a side.

"You say I'm too young, that I'm safer down below, but you know it's not true. If the ship sinks, we all drown." Nikolaus's fist clenched beside his plate.

How many times had this conversation taken place without me present?

Finn sighed. "It's not about—"

"I don't want to be a cabin boy forever. Besides, you let *her* work on deck," Nik growled.

Finn placed his cup on the table, glared at his younger brother, and muttered something in Finnish. As if the entire room didn't already weigh heavily with tension, Finn had to take his argument to another language so I couldn't even understand him?

"I know more than those other men. More than *her*." Nik's finger hung in the air, pointing directly at me.

As often as Nik and I argued, it never turned hostile. This hurt. He blamed his brother, but he felt animosity toward me, as well. And Finn couldn't possibly argue such a point. Nik knew considerably more than me about every aspect of this ship. I'd been at sea for a year compared to his three. Finn eyed his brother with the weariness of a man long at battle. "Nik, when we get to England, we can discuss this further. I cannot do this now. Not with everything else."

Nikolaus tried to protest, but Finn held up his hand to maintain his silence.

"When we get there," Finn repeated.

Nik seethed but didn't look up from his meal. Both he and Finn shoveled a forkful of meat into their mouths simultaneously. The tension hung heavy around the room, my lungs tight, as I sat tapping my thumbs against my knees below the table.

Our little paradise hadn't come without its qualms. Why *did* Finn allow me to work on deck but not his brother? Asking such a question now might cause the ship to explode.

Finn broke the silence before I thought on it any more.

"I wanted us to meet tonight to make a plan." He rubbed his hands over his hair, his exhaustion growing more and more evident as he sat. Maybe the lengthy trip back to England would keep him busy enough not to focus on his troubles too much. If he meant to sail to England at all...

Nik snuffed. "Oh, yes. Let's make a plan. Let's lay out our entire journey according to what *you* think is best, then change it whenever *you* see fit."

"I am the captain of this ship." Finn's voice caught in his gritted teeth.

I had only just picked up my fork, but it tumbled back to my plate. Should I interrupt? Distract them? Run? This torturous argument could go on all night, as both men held valid points.

Nik leaned hard against the table in his brother's direction. "And you would never make a mistake or steer us in the wrong direction because you know—"

"That is enough, Nikolaus." Finn flew from his seat, hands slamming against the table to quiet his brother. "You are dismissed."

Nik stood and shoved his plate with enough force it crashed into the other dishes on the tabletop. "Easy as that, huh?"

I should have run.

When had it gotten so bad between them? They'd hardly been around each other this past week to demand such a quarrel. I just hoped this didn't become a regular exchange over such a long journey.

Finn kept silent.

"Fine. I'm sure Cecily is eager to hear about this plan of yours, though I could hardly care." Nikolaus shoved his chair under the table and stomped out of the quarters, shutting the door behind him.

Finn cursed softly under his breath and crossed the room to lock the door behind his younger brother. He swore again and wandered to his bed where he collapsed onto the mattress. Most of our food sat untouched on the table, appetites long gone.

"What was that about?" My voice was barely more than a whisper. I removed myself from the abandoned dinner and approached Finn, unsure of what to do after a scene like that. Should I have chased after Nik as part of the kitchen help? Or did my loyalty lie in consoling the captain?

Finn's face rested in his hands, and I sank down beside him, my fingers laced together in my lap. Touching him seemed a bad idea, like embracing a freshly fired cannon. His hands fell away from his face and dangled between his legs as if he hadn't the energy to do anything else with them.

"He is so stubborn," Finn said.

I shrugged. "A family trait?"

My attempt at breaking the tension with a joke went unnoticed.

"If he'd just wait. If he'd just trust me on this." He looked up into my eyes then, his back still hunched in both annoyance and fatigue. "And he has to drag you into this because you've got a job on deck now, and he hasn't."

"Well, honestly, is it fair?" I asked.

"Maybe not. But you're the only woman on this ship, Cess. I need you in plain sight and prefer you out of their reach—even if it means you aren't in the safest occupation on board. I need Nik to stay below because that's how I keep *him* safe. He's too young to be a sailor, and no one else on board could do what he does for this ship. We'd all starve to death. Besides, he does a lot more below decks than anyone knows."

"I see." That answered that.

"This crew is terrible," he said.

I threw my hands into the air. "We've established this many times over."

"They like Nik. They're happy to have a cabin boy that knows how to cook. They'll leave him alone down below." Finn lifted his head to regard me.

I shifted under his uncomfortable gaze. "I don't understand what that has to do with—"

"They hate you. They hate you very much, Cecily."

"That's not a secret." It still stung a bit to hear the words out loud. Between the crew's hatred of me, and Nikolaus's jealousy, I was beginning to feel very unwanted on the *Hellbound*, finding little comfort in the only home I had.

"In addition to keeping you out of their reach, I want to give you the chance to prove yourself their equal. I need them to know you're as much a part of this crew as they are. They've accepted Nikolaus as well as can be expected, but you're different."

I fought in vain to keep my frustration at bay. "Because I am a woman."

Finn nodded.

"So, we find more," I said.

"Not a lot of women waiting in line to sail the seas with villainous pirates, I'm afraid."

"But we exist." The fire cooled on this side of the room, and I shivered in my seat. Finn reached for the crumpled blanket on his bed and pulled it up around my shoulders, letting his arm remain there with it.

"I'm sorry about all this. I wish I could give you more than a rotting ship, surround you with love instead of hate, be more than a plain man pretending to be a captain."

I leaned closer into him and inhaled the sea. "But you're not pretending. You *are* the captain of this ship and anything but a 'plain man.' And I don't need anything else. It doesn't matter how crazy this life gets, it's still better than what I had before. I'll take an adventure with you over that any day."

"That's exactly what I mean, though. The only life you have to compare this to is what you had on the farm. I've taken you from the pits of hell and set you in front of the devil."

I tried to protest, but he continued, "You could have a warm house of your own, a family to raise, and a husband with a respectable profession to provide for your needs. You wouldn't be a wanted criminal, and no one would tell you what to do. Your life would be your own. I wanted to give you that, Cecily. That's true freedom. That's what I've always wanted for you."

My heart fluttered at the idea of calling him my husband, of living in a home of our own and growing old in a safe location, with legitimate occupations, no crew, and...*children.*

I smoothed the wild hairs on his head, my fingers lingering on the side of his face. As much as I longed for all of that somewhere deep in my heart, I didn't need it. I just needed him. "Why are you saying these things?"

"This life is a lot to deal with sometimes." He pressed his cheek into my palm.

"You're not doing it alone." A lump caught in my throat, cutting off any lingering encouragement I had to give.

He nodded mindlessly, his eyes shifting to the floor. Then he fell sideways into my lap. I laughed and continued to run my fingers through his shaggy blond hair. He let out a low moan, as if his entire life had somehow toppled into the depths of despair that very evening. Finn could be rather dramatic sometimes, but I loved him anyway.

I brushed my hands along his arms, down his sides, and across his back. "I'm sorry about Nikolaus. Though, I have to ask..." He tensed under my hands. But I had to know. "Have you forgotten where England is? Because it would seem we're heading south."

He held so still, I wondered if he even breathed. My hands stopped over his collar as I stilled my every action, just in case he answered so quietly I couldn't hear. It took another moment before he shifted, bending farther toward the floor rather than looking at me straight on. Never a good sign with Finn.

"I haven't forgotten. We still need more crew before we make the journey. In case we run into trouble, that is," he said.

"Are you expecting trouble?" I leaned back on my hands, letting the blanket slip off my shoulders.

"It can't hurt to be prepared, can it?"

Getting a legitimate response out of this man proved impossible when he didn't want to disclose certain information. And it drove me mad. "I suppose not, but dishonesty might."

Finn wadded up the abandoned blanket in his lap. "I am exhausted, Cess. Can we fight later?"

Like so many of our tender moments together, this one took a rapid turn in a foul direction. Though, to be fair, the reverse happened just as often. "Absolutely. I'm always willing to fight with you later. But first, tell me where you've been this week, why we need more crew in case of trouble, or why you think we need to go in the complete opposite direction of England to get them?" I sucked in a deep breath to keep my voice from rising any higher.

We both looked to the door, waiting for someone to burst in at my cries. When no one came, Finn stood, moved to the table, and sucked down a long sip of rum.

I waited on the bed, watching his every motion for some indication he meant to answer my question.

Finn had never been known for his honesty. No pirate was, really. But after all we'd been through, hadn't I earned his trust?

"Do you want me to go?" I asked.

He shook his head and turned toward me. "Never."

I stood and closed the gap between us, wrapping my arms around his middle and burying my face in the crook of his neck. He quickly returned the hug, holding me tightly against him.

His breath tickled the wisps of hair around my ears. "I met with some local anglers. They say there have been some cursed ships spotted to the north. I wanted to ensure we wouldn't have a run-in on our voyage. I didn't tell you because I didn't want you to worry."

Oh. That made sense. However, when I took over the crow's nest again, I'd likely be the first to see an enemy ship.

Gadsbobs, that's probably all I'd think about until we made port. Hence, why he wanted to keep me from worrying.

Finn clutched my waist and brought me backward until our eyes met. "I really do prefer we grow our crew, and there's still time before the hurricanes come in from the east. We're going no farther than the southern part of the island. Not to mention we'll need a few more supplies before we set off—as we're two sacks of flour down..."

I smacked him in the stomach, but smiled.

"And as I recall, you like Barbados," he added.

"My favorite of the islands," I said.

He took hold of my shoulders to plant a kiss on my forehead. "If we don't stay long, I might be able to keep you out of danger and—"

I pulled from his grasp to look up at him. "Stop. You aren't responsible for Nikolaus and me, you know. Let us help you instead of fretting over our safety. Trust us a little, all right?"

"And I need you to trust me, too. My word. My judgment. All of it." The fire crackled behind him, the lights dimming steadily as the night drew on.

Could I trust him? He'd pulled me out of the binds of servitude and saved my life on several occasions. I loved him. Dearly. But by nature, he lied. To me and everyone else he encountered daily. He asked for trust in return for distrust. The very idea of it made me want to scream.

"You make it difficult sometimes," I said.

He nodded. "I know, but I presumed I made up the difference with my attractive features."

"Oh, Finn." I hated when he said such things while I was trying to be mad at him.

His fingers slid down my arms, releasing me the rest of the way. The table still held all of our dinner plates, mostly untouched and scattered around from partial use. I contemplated cleaning them up. That was my job, at least for the rest of the day.

Too much cluttered my mind to stay in the room with him any longer, even though it was usually my favorite place in the world. I needed to get out into the fresh air.

"I should get back to Nikolaus." I walked to the table to reclaim my hat and straightened my jacket.

"*Cess.*" The desperation in his voice was the only thing that caused me to pause before opening the door.

A deep sigh caught in my chest when I shifted toward him. "Yeah?"

He didn't look up when he spoke. "I hate to ask this after the evening we've had, but will you do me a favor?"

Finn moved to the doorway in front of me, his hand resting on top of the latch to keep me from leaving. I forced an expectant look, urging him to continue.

"One reason I want more crew is because I don't want to keep all the men we have. It's not just that they're terrible shipmen, but they may not all be of the best character," he said.

"They're pirates, Finn." When he didn't argue, I continued, "What's the favor?"

"You'll be working more closely with them tomorrow. I want your judgment on who to keep and who to send away, if you're able to move amongst them at all. Just stay on deck as much as you're able."

"You want me to filter through them?" It seemed like an odd job to give me, as I wanted to begin the task by tossing Long overboard, and Finn had already told me I couldn't.

"It would be helpful. I rarely get to see their true nature as captain. You might have more luck. You'll see them at their very worst." The next words took some effort for him to form. "And I trust your judgment."

"Right." My heart squeezed painfully.

Finn's breath was heavy as he unlocked the door and opened it for me to go. I didn't know what else to say to him in that moment. He seemed equally depleted of words. Still, I felt a pull toward him as I always did, and a part of me wanted to embrace him again, wanted to assure us both that everything was fine. But was it?

The moonlight leaked into the room through the crack in the door, sending a narrow beam of light between us. The cool evening breeze followed, and I breathed it deeply, not letting it escape in a groan that would give away my feelings. I nodded toward the night and let it lead me away from Finn and back to my quarters below.

SIX

"Would have preferred you remain a cabin boy," Long's haughty voice boomed over me.

"I don't recall being taken on as a cabin boy, sir. Not to mention, I lack some qualifications for that position." I leaned against my mop, giving him the hard stare I'd practiced on Nikolaus so many times before. How I yearned to add him to my mental list of those to leave behind in Barbados. Though, I hated to leave a land I loved such a miserable parting gift.

Long waved an arm, dismissing my comments, and I plunged the mop back into the bucket. The sun beat against the dark wood of the deck, creating a shimmering mirage over the surface. I couldn't wait to dip my toes into the salty water again. Could I really stay mad at Finn for changing plans as we went along? After all, he'd given me this island, too.

No one had instructed me to swab the deck, but with the sails adjusted and the island barely a league parallel to our position at sea, I opted to combat the seagull attacks on our ship. No one else wanted the task, and it gave me plenty of opportunity to move among the men, watching and listening. Unfortunately, it also gave me ample time to examine my captain at the helm.

Finn's commanding stature stood firmly over the wheel, as always. He subtly checked the compass in his hands occasionally and inspected the ship from his perch in perfect time with the shuffling of maps spread across his table. It hadn't passed my notice that his gaze often found me, as well, but I turned away each time before our eyes met for too long.

I once looked forward to returning to rigging to see more of him, but with the events of the previous night, the thought of bumping into him on deck made my stomach tumble. We'd had our squabbles in the past year together. We rarely agreed on anything, in truth, but this seemed unlike those others. Something weighed on him more than usual. It made us all restless.

The effort I put into swabbing the decks sent sweat dripping down my forehead, and the water I pushed around on the balmy wood dried up almost faster than I could keep up with it. I made my way along, scrubbing bird droppings from obvious places and inching closer to where the remaining crew worked. Most of them sat around, as we hadn't much to keep us occupied. My task of eliminating unnecessary crewmembers would have been much easier if I had more than a day to meet them.

"You don't even know what you're talking about. There's been no mention of treasure," someone grumbled near the bow.

That merited some attention.

I moved toward the railing where Stevens pried nails from a slab of wood. He gave me a nod, but returned his attention back to the conversation before us.

Another man with a gruff voice and a thick onyx beard argued, "Where else do you think he keeps his wealth? Barbados, boys. That's where. Pirate captains always have a special hideaway. You heard him say we'll replenish more resources when we arrive."

"What if he did? Captain isn't likely to give over all he has. We haven't been on the ship that long, you know." The fellow spit through his missing front teeth with every word he spoke.

So, Finn told them we meant to head south, and they assumed he held some great treasure on the island? Where had they gotten such a silly notion? Though, surely a man as infamous as the Blood Pirate would possess substantial wealth to support his title...

"We should ask him," one man said with an unsettling confidence. His beard was patchy, almost bare in places. His ears were pierced up both sides, a rather unpleasant looking decoration I couldn't stop staring at.

"You want to ask the captain if he's hiding some treasure in Barbados? Are you bloody mad?" the spitter asked.

A younger man chimed in, "Look. We cannot ask the captain about his treasure. That's the quickest way to get ourselves shot up. We're sailing with the dreaded Blood Pirate, if you'd forgotten. He doesn't take too kindly to anyone getting in his way. You've all heard the rumors."

I took my mop around the outside of their circle to get a better look at the faces of those who spoke.

"Rumors are all it is, too." The pierced man scoffed and threw his soiled kerchief on the floor. "Don't believe a word of 'em. Tales of that nature are prone to certain, shall we say, *exaggeration*."

The younger man grew more offended by the moment. "Then why do you think the Royal Navy worked so hard to cover up the tale if it weren't the truth? He burned down an entire naval ship single-handedly. He's known throughout the seas for his villainy. They say he murdered an entire crew to gain possession of the *Hellbound*. Those aren't all exaggerations. Stories got to come from somewhere."

At least some of the crew had Finn's back. Perhaps the younger fellow could stay. The pierced man had to go if he planned to steal Finn's treasure—well, *imaginary* treasure. Still, I needed to find out more about him and his intentions.

"He's right. Those stories are all true." I dropped the mop into the bucket and joined them in their ring, receiving fewer groans than I'd expected over my sudden appearance. "I lived in Wales. Fled north when my village was burned to the ground by this Blood Pirate."

The others stared at me in a mixture of awe and disbelief. My partial truth may just do the trick. I *did* once live in Wales, and my village *did* burn. Finn, however, was not the responsible party. After a year of sailing the seas, I still didn't know who really *had* done it. I hoped to never find out, though. I preferred to think Finn was the most dangerous pirate on the ocean.

"Then why you sailing with us now, lassie? You got something against our captain?" The gross, pierced man narrowed his attention on me as he spoke.

The younger sailor gripped a knife at his belt to adjust his position in case he had to make a move to subdue my plan for vengeance. A man that would protect his captain from a potential mutinous pirate like me definitely earned his keep on board. Those were the sailors we wanted on the *Hellbound*. Alas, I also needed to clarify my story before he prematurely ran me through.

"Do you really think I would be daft enough to hire myself out to the man that destroyed my village, only to plan some revenge scheme once here? I'm just one person." My lip twitched with a grin, knowing that was exactly what Finn had done four years ago to the previous captain and crew of the *Hellbound*. For Finn, madness sometimes had a way of working out to pure brilliance.

The young pirate settled back down. So, I continued while I still had their attention, "That story with the Royal Navy is true. I'd never think myself capable of matching swords with anyone that can do something like that. Sometimes it's better to join the enemy than fight against it." I pointed toward the helm, a pang ringing through my chest at my words.

The pierced pirate stood, pacing along the outside of the group like a vulture marking its prey. "Is that why the captain brought the likes of you on board? The Fire Wench makes a suitable match for the Blood Pirate?"

I swallowed hard. Where had he heard that name? Only Finn and Nik called me that, much to my dismay. I set one man on fire in self-defense on the naval ship, and they strap me with the name for a lifetime—and apparently spread it around the ship for others to use.

He snickered. "Oh, yes. The captain told us about your past, my dear."

"Did he now?" I tilted my head, waiting for whatever version of the story Finn had given the men and trying not to panic that rumors about my life now floated about the ship.

"He says you've sailed under pirate command before, burning whoever gets in the way of what you want. It's a little hard to believe such a claim of a tiny woman covered in seagull dung, if I may be so bold to say."

Oh, how I hated this man already. "I have had little reason to set the world ablaze this week. And, if *I* may be so bold, it seems as if you doubt Captain Worley's word. Eh, Mr....?"

He removed his hat to perform a dramatic bow, revealing a head of patchy hair that matched his gray stubbly beard. "Abnor Cantrill, at your service. And I've nothing against your captain—"

"*Our* captain," I said. This man would definitely not make the return trip to England. In fact, I hadn't completely ruled out a violent removal. My knives could hit him from any distance on deck. If that didn't work, I could throw any number of things at him from up in the nest and crush him like the pesky insect he was.

"*Our* captain," he corrected with a sneer, "has insisted we work on minimum pay until we reach England, and I didn't sign my life away for the experience."

The experience? He and the others had spent most of the morning basking in the sun. The poor excuse of seamanship I'd observed from them over the past few days hardly spoke of anything demanding more than a peanut in payment.

Stevens laid his wooden plank across his lap and braved a glance at Cantrill. "Captain Worley pays us a fair wage for our work. If you weren't so focused on the treasure—"

"I'm telling you, it's there." The largest pirate stood, his black, rough beard seeming to encompass his entire head in a way that made him appear wild and unkempt.

Cantrill clicked his tongue. "Of course, it's there. You'll have your proof when we arrive. You can see it in the captain's eyes. He's eager to make landfall again. Ain't about finding crew neither."

I followed his gaze up to Finn again, my thoughts beginning to whirl with treasure and secrets untold. How could I protect him from his own men if I didn't know whose story to believe?

"They was saying it back in Bristol. It's the biggest treasure in the Caribbean, buried by the fiercest pirate in the seas. Only seemed fitting we joined his crew and sailed off to find it, wouldn't you say?" The giant hairy man's wide nostrils flared with his every word.

Stevens and I exchanged glances. One of us needed to object, but neither of us moved. Even the young pirate that came to Finn's defense earlier had gone silent. It seemed as if we'd run out of ways to deny the claim.

Excited agreement echoed around the circle of men. I'd never change their minds now. It could be a rather dangerous situation for Finn if they believed these rumors, and he couldn't deliver on the prize. I had to admit, too, I'd grown a little curious myself about this treasure now. The only chance we had was to lead them astray: play along, then ditch them at the first chance. I just had to find another pigpen and a privy.

I nodded. "And all these rumors of treasure, you're certain they're about Captain Worley?"

Cantrill's smile dripped with poison. "Know that for a fact, missie."

Did they mean to take him down before we arrived? I rubbed

my chin to buy a moment's time while I thought up a plan. "I can't help but wonder if the rumor is true of his map, as well."

"What do you mean?" Cantrill asked, and each of the men inched a little closer.

"If *all* the rumors are true, there's a map somewhere on the island." My head spun from thinking up a story so quickly on the spot. "They say it's with a girl, the one who holds his heart."

I had no idea where such a story came from, but the men hung on my every word. The islanders told many romantic tales of legends and lost love, many of which they'd demonstrated in colorful art. Clearly, they'd influenced both my imagination and ability to tell a lie.

"Your business isn't with Captain Worley if you're after treasure. It's with her. Find the girl and you find the map," I added.

Breath returned to me, and I relaxed my posture. Perhaps I should have described her as a mermaid, sent them on an even wilder chase. As long as they hunted her and left the captain alone, it didn't matter.

As bizarre as the plan sounded when it came out, I hopefully accomplished what I needed to: the risky members of the crew couldn't mutiny without knowing the treasure's location. Considering that I would probably have to be the girl in my tale anyway—a rather un-majestic, non-mermaid—it would be up to me to lead the men astray, while simultaneously relieving them of their duties on the *Hellbound*.

Because my plans always went *so* splendidly.

SEVEN

Night set in, marking the close of our journey to the southern part of the island. Finn had instructed us to lower the sails and slow our pace, which kept me up in the rigs with very little sleep. The blazing sunset played tricks on my eyes until I saw ships where none existed, land in the wrong direction, and waves that took the shape of fingers stretching from the ocean's surface.

My foot slipped from the ropes as I climbed down to the deck, and I caught myself with the crook of my elbow. The men moved about to collect their evening meals. The last through the line, I ladled myself a bowl of turtle soup and swirled it around in my mug. It had never been my favorite, but the steam rising from the broth begged me to drink it down in ravenous gulps.

From my position under the helm, I searched for a friendly face, finding nothing more than the same mongrels I'd eavesdropped on earlier in the day. It may have helped to cozy up to their lot and uncover other schemes, but my tired mind craved a friend. No one would notice if I slipped below decks to bother the cabin boy for a bit. If he'd even have me after our last tense encounter.

I tiptoed down the steps to the lower deck as quickly as I could without stumbling, lest my fatigued muscles throw me the down the full flight. Light flickered from the kitchen and muffled voices grew louder as I approached. Who else had come to the galley?

Hesitantly, I peered around the corner to find Nikolaus with his feet kicked up on the table and Stevens slurping his soup across from him.

"Oh, Miss Cecily." Stevens stood when I entered the room.

"I hadn't expected to find you here, Stevens. I needed a break from the beasts on deck. Might I join you both?" I placed my empty mug in the washbasin and peeked over my shoulder to meet Nik's eye.

He shrugged and nodded toward the short barrel of potatoes next to him, the only other seating option besides the floor. My tired bones collapsed where instructed, and I pulled my hat from my head to smooth down my wild hair.

"This may have been the longest day of my existence," I said.

Nik threw a pouch of salted beef that hit my chest and landed in my lap. "An unnecessarily long day. The captain has stopped making all sense in his orders."

"It seems unconventional, but I suppose we must trust his judgment," Stevens added.

Trust. That nasty word had plagued my mind for the entire day. I grabbed a handful of the dry beef and shoved it in my mouth. It gave me something to do if I couldn't argue Stevens' point. As a loyal crewmember, he had no understanding of Nik's or my relationship to Finn. We had to watch our tongues with him in the room.

"Follow it, yes. Trust it, perhaps not." Nik grinned and kicked his feet over the side of the table to stand. "Are they finished up top? I should probably clean up the dinner mess and feed the captain."

"I was last through the line. They ought to have finished." I stretched my arms behind my back and yawned. "Making landfall had better bring a good night's sleep."

"Don't plan on it. And if you stay in here, you're washing dishes." Nikolaus's accusatory finger pointed directly at me, yet he lacked the usual twinkle in his eye that generally accompanied his teasing.

"Nikolaus, are you cross with me?" I asked.

His head rolled on his shoulders. "No, of course not. I'm busy, and *Captain Worley* needs his food." He threw up his hands and started out the door.

"Wait." I hated to think he truly held contempt for me now. He had to know I never meant to leave him behind when I assumed my position in the rigs. Unless his attitude came on because he had to go face his brother again.

Nik didn't turn toward me, but he paused in the entryway. Stevens cleared his throat and adjusted in his seat. I'd forgotten him there and needed to choose my words carefully.

"Let me help you. I can take the captain his evening meal. As I've only recently been dismissed from kitchen duty, he shouldn't question my offer to help with everyone rushing to make landfall again." That ought to help, if I could do nothing else to offer him peace tonight.

"He's eating at the helm. His tray is in the corner." With that, Nik left.

So much for finding a friend amongst the unfriendly crew. To top it off, I had to speak with Finn for the first time since our unusual meal the night before. My heart picked up speed at the thought of being closer to my captain and simultaneously ached when I thought of the tension that hung around us all.

Stevens remained seated, though I hardly felt like holding a conversation now. I forced a smile as I tossed the remaining dried beef onto the countertop. "I don't intend to do dishes."

With a laugh, he stood to place his empty mug into the washbasin, then moved ahead of me into the doorway. He held up his hand, urging me to wait as he peeked around the corner to inspect our immediate surroundings.

What now?

When he turned back to me, his expression grew serious, almost grim. Never a good sign.

"Forgive me, Miss Cecily, but since you're here, might I confide in you about something?" he asked.

I clutched the door latch to steady myself for whatever might come next.

"It's about the earlier conversation on deck," he continued.

Had he heard more from those men while I worked up in the nest? "Is this about the treasure?"

He lowered his voice. "Somewhat."

I glanced past him to ensure we were entirely alone. We couldn't be too careful on this topic. "Speak quickly before Nikolaus returns."

"You seemed quite knowledgeable about the rumors of Captain Worley's fortune. Do you know it lies in Barbados for certain?" he asked.

My head fogged as I tried to remember what I'd said on deck. "I do not know about the treasure for certain. It's merely speculation."

I couldn't admit to making up Finn's lover with the map. Stevens may be clergy, but he was still a pirate.

Stevens bent closer until the fabric of his hat touched mine. I stilled and held my breath. What was the meaning of all this?

"Miss Cecily, I know that many other pirates keep their gold hidden throughout the Caribbean, particularly in the southern islands. They hold a pact between them, have formed a governing body of sorts. While this system is meant to provide a ring of trust for captains and their men, there are those who do not honor the system." Stevens' voice shook more with each word.

"I don't understand. What does this have to do with Captain Worley?" His knowledge of the outside world struck fear in my heart.

Stevens swallowed hard. "I fear traveling to Barbados now will put us directly into the path of these rogue pirates. I joined this crew to flee the islands. If I'd known Captain Worley meant to head south, I never would have..."

Footsteps on the deck above pounded over our heads. Anyone could come down the stairs and find us like this. Surely, everything about this meeting screamed of suspicion. But I couldn't let him go now. This man before me gave me more outside information than Finn ever had. It was both intoxicating and horrifying.

"You think we're sailing straight into danger?" I clutched his shirt sleeve to ensure he didn't run off without giving me answers.

His hands quivered where he held them folded against his chest. "I've prayed every day for God to take away my fear. But it remains. If my former captain finds me after I've abandoned..."

His voice cut off and what sounded like a sob caught in his throat.

"You *deserted* your duty?" Though the *Hellbound* had not experienced such a loss, Finn had impressed upon us our loyalty to our ship and his command as captain. If one broke this rule, the consequences would be severe. And if Stevens' former captain proved as ruthless as he'd said him to be...

Stevens said nothing more. His eyes distance, lost in a painful memory.

I bent in closer. "Who was your captain, Stevens?"

He bit his lip hard, his focus somewhere far off behind me. "Benjamin Hornigold." His answer came in the form of a breath barely below a whisper. Then he found the strength to look me in the eye. "He founded the Republic of Pirates."

Republic of Pirates.

The room grew warmer, though the stove in the corner had died out without Nikolaus to prod it back to life. Finn had never mentioned the Republic, though he may not know such a thing existed. Certainly, he'd want to know what all dangers lurked in the Caribbean. He'd hoped to prepare for the open waters of the

Atlantic, but had he prepared for a fight in the southern islands we might not win?

Stevens took a ragged gulp of air. "I'm sorry. Speaking of him gives me as much fear as if he stood in this very room. I have nightmares he will come for me." He clasped his hands together and closed his eyes.

Nothing about the quaking man before me spoke of dreams to pillage or live a life at sea. "Why did you join his crew in the beginning?"

His eyes remained closed, and he pressed against the doorframe for support. "He brought me on board by force, demanding a need for a minister. He believed his sins would be absolved if only he had someone to readily forgive him. But only God in Heaven can forgive, and this man's sins are great. I have spent my days begging for my own forgiveness, Miss Cecily."

Did Hornigold seek men that had betrayed him? Would he bother searching the seas for one man?

The *Hellbound* carried a deserter of another man's ship—a powerful captain from the sounds of it. What had I done by bringing Stevens on board?

I stepped backward and reached for the table to steady myself. Finn had asked me to sort out the crew and determine those who posed a threat to the *Hellbound*. How could I tell him the one that brought the most danger to his ship came at my request?

EIGHT

When I worked on deck, Finn treated me as one of his crew. If he spoke, he commanded. If he looked, his brow furrowed. But under the cover of night and shaded by his tricorn hat, his face softened for the first time that day when he saw me coming up the stairs.

"Nikolaus must really be angry, yeah?" he muttered when I reached the top.

"He's busy with the crew, and I offered to take this task so we could discuss the favor you asked of me," I said.

His voice usually soothed me, no matter how I felt. Tonight, the very sound of it filled me with guilt. I knew what he didn't, and I couldn't tell him.

He dropped his compass into his pocket and turned to remove his maps from the table so I could place my tray.

"You did not volunteer for any other reason?" He reached first for his fresh cup of tea but kept his focus on the meal I'd brought.

"I..." How could I answer? At any other time, I might offer him a wink or a flirtatious smile. My heart held no joy tonight. "Are we on track to make landfall soon?"

His head bowed. "Yes. Possibly within the next few hours. Take the helm, will you? I'm hungry."

"Of course." I moved around him, careful not to make contact. Even with the shield of night, the crew could still notice the suspicious shadows interacting in the moonlight. Though, even if we'd found ourselves entirely alone, I couldn't have touched him. I'd brought a hunted man on board our ship. I'd endangered my entire crew, my captain.

I clutched harder on the wheel's spokes and examined the shadows of men below me. A few had fallen asleep propped against a barrel or pile of ropes. It'd be a miracle if any of us had the strength to complete Finn's mission on land.

Behind me, Finn ate his meal in silence. How I wanted to turn from my place at the helm and wrap my arms around him, to will everything go back to the way it once was. No more fighting. No lies. No scheming crew. And definitely no dangerous waters filled with the possibility of death.

"You have news of the crew?" Finn's voice startled me from my thoughts.

On shore, I'd have to lose Stevens with the rest of the men I meant to lead astray. A kind soul like that didn't deserve to suffer such a fate at the hands of a former angry captain. But my family came first.

"I do. There are a few not worth a wooden nickel, though I have had little time to investigate the full lot. We've been hard at work," I said.

"I have worked you all harder today. Time is of the essence to accomplish our task before the hurricanes arrive. For that, I'm sorry." He set his fork on his plate and moved to take a handle on the opposite side of the wheel from where I held.

I let go, ready to return to the rigs for another sleepless night on post.

"Cecily, *minun ankkurri*." Finn's gentle, familiar tone kept me in place at the top of the stairs. As I glanced over the crew once more, no one seemed to observe the pair of us towering above them. No one heard what he'd called me, and no one knew how weak it made my knees when he said those exact words. I still didn't even know its meaning.

It took all my strength to face him. Under the brim of his hat, I his blue eyes pleaded. Tendrils of his fair hair had fallen around his ears. He hadn't even bothered to push them back.

"I didn't just come to help Nikolaus." I closed my eyes and grabbed hold of the banister to steady myself. "You're so far from me during the day."

"You're so far from me *now*," he said.

A lump rose in my throat. "Let's turn the ship around. Throw the rotten men overboard and sail to England alone. We don't need to return to the islands. With the hurricanes coming—"

"Cecily." He took a single step toward me, unable to close the gap the way I wanted him to. "I assure you we won't be long."

I nodded, tears brimming in my eyes I tried to blink away before he noticed. "I should get back to the nest."

Footsteps pounded up the stairwell, and I stiffened, turning my face toward the moonlit waves to shield my emotions.

Finn's tone changed to one of authority. "Yes, Hastings, you'll report to me from the nest, as we go ashore at first light."

Long appeared, his breath labored after the short climb. He stood at attention before his captain and ignored me, as usual.

"Yes, Captain," I said.

Finn held up a finger to indicate he wanted me to stay while he addressed Long.

"Captain, the men have prepared the longboats. We are ready to drop anchor at your command." Long clasped his hands behind him, the soldier's stance—still not enough to straighten his arched back.

"Excellent. Once we anchor, you may rest." He then yelled for

Nikolaus when he spotted the boy gathering remaining dishes on deck.

Nik skipped every other step as he ascended the stairs to meet us. He ignored both Long and me, standing at attention before his captain. While the three of us had been to hell and back again as one, we now seemed as if we sailed on different oceans. If Finn, acting as our captain, hadn't requested I remain, I would have excused myself from their presence just to escape the wretched feeling.

"I'll need all hands on deck for our arrival, all areas of the ship secured," Finn said.

Why had he called the three of us together? A first mate, a cabin boy, and a rigger? Surely, Long must have thought it strange, though his face didn't show it.

"When we get to shore, have the men make camp and split into groups to search for crew in the villages." Finn examined the bow when he spoke again. "Hastings, you will remain with Nikolaus and share in his duties on shore. You may choose any other men you'd like for your team."

I opened my mouth to object to the assignment but remembered Long. It made sense now. We couldn't argue his commands if he had a witness present. We had no choice but to follow, or Long could charge us for insubordination.

My fists balled, and I bit hard on my bottom lip. Nikolaus issued a tense nod toward Finn. Would this command only make things worse for the three of us? His constant desire to strap Nikolaus and me together for our safety and keep us apart from the others made it impossible to become a true part of this crew. He allowed us to choose our team, however. Though, I had a strong feeling if we chose the "wrong" men, he'd interfere with that, too, or simply force us to stay to the beach and prepare food or give us some meaningless task.

Finn waved toward his table as if the entire reason he'd called

Nikolaus was to clear away the dishes. He bowed his head to me, and I ran down the steps in haste. I scaled the rope ladder in a matter of seconds, even though it took every last bit of energy I had in me.

Inside the bucket, I gathered my spyglass and examined the island in the distance, searching for answers or forcing the distraction. I didn't know which. At such a late hour, I could barely make out the tall jungle trees as more than a dark shadow. How I'd love to get lost in the jungle's warmth for a few hours, listen to the monkey's shouting in the treetops, the birds singing their island songs. Right now, I just needed to feel the soft, warm sand between my toes. I could almost taste the fresh oranges that dripped down my chin with each bite.

The island could heal us. If it didn't kill us first.

I sank to my knees and propped my elbows along the nest's ledge as I examined the black ocean in all directions. On our first trek across the Atlantic, I often saw things from my perch that didn't really exist. I'd blamed cabin fever for the phenomenon and always waited a few minutes before I announced any sightings to Finn. If I spotted something, it was usually a merchant ship. Finn and I had established a series of hand gestures to demonstrate what I'd seen. He could steer away from danger without any of the crew knowing.

Besides, Finn had no interest in merchant ships as most pirates did. Letting the crew know as much could spark a mutiny if they realized the amount of wealth he passed up along our way.

Not that it mattered now. The men already had their eyes set on Finn's fortune. It wouldn't be long before we made camp on the island, and Cantrill and his men went off to hunt for the young maiden that possessed the captain's treasure map. I let my mind wander further into the story and how romantic waiting on the island for my sea-dwelling lover could be—if he had entrusted me with the only key to the treasure desired by men around the world.

What better faith could you put in another person than that? Finn trusted me with his spyglass. That was about all.

A sigh slipped from my lips, carried off in the breeze. If only my thoughts had gone with it.

NINE

WITH ALL SAILS SECURED, I HAD DONE MY PART TO KEEP THE ship in order and somehow stayed awake through it all. Not that I'd get much rest anyway, knowing what lurked in the surrounding waters.

The decks remained quiet for such an early hour, with the rest of the crew packing up their cots and supplies below decks and awaiting the captain's commands to go ashore.

Finn knew the island well enough to find places to make camp at each stop, and the villagers left them well enough alone. Few people had the nerve to tamper with pirates' belongings—even other pirates. That could be a condition of the governing body Stevens' mentioned. Did the Republic of Pirates negotiate property throughout the islands?

The Republic still sent shivers down my spine. The union of pirate crews and captains alike, all working together? We might as well burn the world down now.

From my perch, I took in the sight of the palm trees waving their branches in greeting. Large boulders clustered together sporadically to dot the landscape, while other rock formations climbed high above the trees throughout the island. The fiery sunrise made the sand crystals glisten like diamonds. It was hard to believe something so beautiful held so much potential for danger.

I squinted to see farther down the way to the place we'd camped before, though the sun still hadn't reached far enough for a clear view. I recognized the tree that marked our spot. It stood taller than the others surrounding it. Nikolaus had said once its wild flowering made it look as if the tree wore a governor's wig. The image always made me smile.

Clouds hovered low above the tree like an early morning fog...

No, not clouds. Smoke.

Finn wouldn't have sent someone ahead to start a campfire. They'd never have beaten us there. I checked the boats below me just in case—all still readied, none missing.

I fumbled with my spyglass, barely balanced on my knees, and aimed it toward the beach. Something burned at our usual campsite. In fact, I counted several places where the smoke rose to meet the light of the early morning sun.

My tongue twisted inside my mouth. I had to tell Finn. He would know what to do, and, if nothing else, he could at least confirm what I saw.

"Ffff–" I cursed myself. I couldn't use his name. All the warmth left my body when I managed a single, shrieking cry of, "Captain!"

A few men popped out from below decks, Finn bursting from his quarters, his coat still unbuttoned around his waist. Even from my place high above him, I could see the worry in his expression. I held the spyglass out in my hand and pointed toward the shoreline. He rushed up to the helm to grab his own scope and let his weight press heavily against the stern railing.

One by one, the crew lined the deck, many of them gathered to see what had turned the captain a ghostly white. I couldn't bring myself to look again, focusing instead on studying Finn's body language from my perch.

Below, the questions began. I heard them much more clearly

without the sails cracking in the wind all around me. We all wanted answers.

"Long, load the boats! James, the weapons!" Finn cried.

He still meant for us to go ashore? My mouth fell open, the rest of me paralyzed from the burden of his words.

"Stevens, Morgan, prepare the cannons for backup!" he shouted again.

Men rushed around to plan for whatever lay in wait for us. Others stood stunned near the paling, straining to catch a better glimpse. No one spoke a word now.

I stumbled out of my bucket and talked myself down each rung on the rope ladder. As part of this crew, I needed to join their defense efforts. If they fought, I fought.

Halfway down the ladder, I heard the men mumbling to one another.

"There on the beach. Plain as day," one said.

"Never seen it before. Where's it from?" another asked.

I twisted around on the ladder to look toward the shore once more and retrieved my spyglass from inside my coat. Something dark moved on the shoreline that held the entire crew's attention.

Where I expected to discover a person walking amongst the remains, I found instead a black sheet whipping in the breeze.

A flag. A single black flag, bearing a skeleton with a spear. It stuck firmly in the sand in front of our campsite, as if claiming domination over the territory. My heart sank deeper into my stomach.

I knew that flag.

"Finn." I forgot myself in that moment and ran across the deck, searching through the men. "Captain!"

"Cecily?" Finn dropped the sword not yet attached to his belt, and it clamored to the deck. He rushed to my side, taking my arms in his hands to straighten me. The look on his face shattered all that had built up between us.

Why couldn't we just run away again? We'd fought the Royal

Navy together as one with so many lives lost in one night. I didn't want to fight another battle like that for a million years.

I gasped for breath. "There's a flag. On the beach. The flag. Look."

He took the spyglass from my hands. His posture shifted when he found it on shore, and I knew he recognized it, too. We saw it once in Ireland three months ago when Finn had delivered the captives to a life of freedom.

"Isn't that..."

He bit down hard on his lip, gaze fixed on the shoreline. "Yeah."

"Do you know who it is?" I dug my fingers into the thick fabric of his overcoat as I searched his face.

He swallowed hard, shaking his head as he stared into the distance.

"Finn, who is it?" I begged.

He stared at the beach, still shaking his head. "Never actually saw him that day, but he must have seen me."

I yanked harder on his sleeve. "*Who?*"

"Captain?" Long appeared at the top of the stairs, his forehead scrunched to reveal all the lines of age and concern. He didn't seem to care that Finn and I were in the middle of our own conversation —or that I held the fabric of Finn's coat so tightly in my grasp.

My hands fell to my sides, and I straightened as much as my nerves allowed.

Finn moved for a better look, or at least the best he could get from our position. His eyes squinted, but not as a result of the scorching sun, more from disbelief or confusion. Suddenly, he appeared every bit a young man, dressed in pirate's clothes, the weight of the ocean sweeping in on him.

He handed the spyglass back to me and nodded. "There are no ships or longboats in sight, and the fire has long been out. Whoever did this has left this part of the island. For now, we take a smaller, armed crew ashore to search the area. When it's safe, we send for

the others. We aren't able to go farther south without crossing terri-
tories. The responsible party most likely meant to send a message
rather than start a battle. Long, choose your best men and meet me
at the boats."

Long nodded, wasting no time in passing along the orders. As I
watched him go, I caught sight of Nikolaus elbowing his way
through the men, no doubt with questions of his own for his
brother.

Finn followed his first mate, ready to lead his crew. Long would
never choose me to go ashore as a fighter, but he was thick-skulled if
he thought I'd stay behind.

Not waiting for permission—nor needing it in my opinion—I
ran down the short corridor and burst into the captain's quarters,
retrieving a few more knives from his drawer. Strength surged
through my veins when I strapped them to my belt beside the
others. I could defend myself if need be. Living life as a pirate,
however, meant self defense would become a regular part of my
existence. At least when I threw the knives, I could keep my opponent at bay and never have to look him in the eye. I hoped to never
have to kill again the way I had on the naval ship, so close to my
victim, his screams still fresh in my mind.

Back on deck, the boat lowered into the water. Men piled into
the second, and I raced to get in line, but a fierce grasp spun me
around.

Finn held tightly to my arm, his eyes alight with fire. "Get in
my quarters and stay—"

I yanked my arm from his hand. "I'm part of this crew, too."

"You don't even know how to wield a sword, Cecily. Just stay
here with Nikolaus." He spoke through gritted teeth.

"You're right. I'm terrible with a sword. But I can throw a knife,
and my loyalty to this ship's captain is greater than anyone else
here. And you know that." I stood taller to prove I wouldn't back
down.

Nikolaus darted across the deck toward us, strapping a sword onto his belt as he came. He stopped when he saw the inferno in Finn's eyes, but made no indication he meant to stay behind either.

Finn growled low under his breath. "I am the captain of this ship, and I—"

"Then consider this a mutiny, *Captain*." I looked to Nikolaus, whose mouth twitched into a smile for the first time since he'd turned against me.

"We're going." Nik shrugged and pushed past Finn on the way to the longboat, as if fear had never been an option.

Finn's chin dropped to his chest. He mumbled something in Finnish that sounded like a prayer—or a long string of swears.

I sucked in a deep breath and marched past him, letting my shoulder crash into his in the same way Nikolaus had done. The three of us held a lot of rage, but we needed to save it for whatever waited for us on shore.

TEN

Finn's commands toward the rest of the crew grew more colorful after Nikolaus and I made it clear we planned to ignore him. The others minded his command, so he had that to fall back on at least. He took volunteers to fill another boat besides the two he originally wanted. If he had no way to make us stay, he would arrange for us to be in a separate boat from himself, even if it meant risking more of his men to do so.

He jumped over the railing and into the lowering boat. The action made certain we couldn't follow. Nikolaus and I filed into the next boat, our weapons strapped in place. Nik sat next to me on the bench, something I hadn't expected, though I didn't draw any attention to the fact. Regaining my relationship with Nikolaus before he was ready, the stubborn little fellow, would be like trying to coax a wild fox to eat out of my hand.

I watched him out of the corner of my eye, his jaw set hard as he stared toward the shore. His fingers fluttered over the hilt of his sword, ready to draw even before we hit the water if necessary. I'd never really seen him armed, which made him appear somewhat a stranger. He grew up at a rapid pace, capable of so much more than I wanted him to be.

The remaining men gathered around us on deck, ready to lower us to the water's level. I watched the shore, my attention darting back and forth between the campsite wreckage and the second boat eagerly rowing toward it: Finn's boat. We should be with him. Not trailing behind while he rides ahead to face the unknown.

"Miss Hastings?" An eager voice pulled me out of my trance.

Stevens hung over the railing. I hadn't much chance to speak with him since our terrifying conversation in the kitchen. All I saw when I looked into his eyes was a hunted man, a substantial risk to my family.

Had his former captain done this? Was he the same man that attacked our crew in Ireland?

The blood froze within my veins.

Nik elbowed me in the ribs and nodded toward the ship's ministering cooper.

"Yes?" I asked.

"Let me come with you. I will help as I'm able." He wore a dull sword on his side and had a pistol-shaped bulge on his breast. More odd behavior from a man of faith. The nuns in Barry never wielded weapons.

The men around me chorused with demands for Stevens to just get in the boat already, and he quickly obeyed before he missed the opportunity entirely. The boat lowered the rest of the way and released with a thump. We clutched the bench bottoms to keep from toppling into one another, while the men with the oars rowed toward the shore.

"Don't look like they've found anything," a man up front said.

"Captain is splittin' them up. Don't seem fair," another added— Cantrill. I could have guessed he'd be the one bickering.

"And why not?" Nikolaus spoke up, balanced on the edge of his seat. I hadn't seen him interact much with this crew. His voice sounded almost foreign in that capacity.

"We just joined ship. If someone is after the captain, it be nobody's fault but 'is own, boy." Cantrill's chin hair hung to his torn shirt collar.

Were none of these men loyal to their captain? The previous crew had fought beside Finn until their last breath. These men disgraced even the laws of piracy.

My eyes narrowed. "You're part of his crew; you bear his burdens. That's what it means to serve under a captain."

Nikolaus inched farther toward the direction of our challenger. "You pledged your allegiance to Captain Worley when you stepped foot on board the *Hellbound*, and you'd do well to keep your bleedin' mouth shut."

At least, I had the reassurance that if these men turned on us, Nik would still fight beside me—even if only in verbal combat.

Cantrill smirked, an odd reaction to being put in his proper place by the cabin boy. Then he placed his elbows on his knees, his words directed to me alone. "Wouldn't take nothin' to leave 'im here. Go back to the ship and—"

"How dare you..." Nik didn't finish the thought, instead leaping from his seat to lunge at the swine, ready to defend his captain to the fullest. On instinct, I threw my body between them and twisted Nik's arm to hold his wrist behind his back, careful to maintain control of the knife I'd slid from his sheath and held tightly in my grasp. I had to keep Cantrill somewhat on my side, but if he made any attempt to harm Nik, I'd turn on him rather quickly.

The boat wobbled, robbing us of balance. It took me a bit to gather my bearings and ensure nothing had actually happened. Beside us, Stevens had also stood, his arms outstretched between the combative parties. He held no drawn weapons.

My face fell to Nik's shoulder. "Easy," I whispered. "Save it for when we get to shore."

Cantrill's laughter roared above the others. I wanted so badly to cut him.

A low growl slipped between Nik's lips when I released him,

and he spun back toward the island. I clung to his shirtsleeve for balance against the white-capped waves of the shoreline. Finn had vanished from sight. The three of us slowly sank to the bench once more, Cantrill's harsh laugh satisfied with the turn of events. He could go swallow a jellyfish tentacle for all I cared. Finn's safety was at stake. That mattered most now.

Only minutes remained until we reached our destination, but it felt like hours stood between us and our target. Finally, we came to an abrupt stop as the bottom of our boat dug into the sand, and I jumped into the hip-deep waters.

"Stay with me," I said to Nikolaus. I needed to keep my wits about me and couldn't manage as much if both Finn *and* Nikolaus disappeared from my sight.

Nik nodded without a fuss this time and withdrew his sword. I knew Finn's lessons with him had gone infinitely better than they had with me. Granted, they'd worked on the skill far longer than I had. I'd never seen Nikolaus in true combat, though I had no choice but to trust his abilities now. Somehow, the thought brought me no comfort.

The men kept their blades drawn, and I let my fingers hover over my knives, ready to extract them at any moment. I nodded toward Stevens, and he followed Nik and me toward the jungle's edge.

"Do you see anything?" Nikolaus whispered when we stepped amongst the charred trees.

I shook my head. "Nothing but embers."

Distant voices drew our attention down the beach, and we ran toward the commotion. Stevens followed, bringing up the rear while maintaining a safe distance behind. On the shore, men gathered together, Finn at the center of their anxious cluster.

"There's no one around. No ships down the shoreline." Finn caught sight of Nikolaus and me, his posture easing. "They're gone."

"Should we return to the *Hellbound,* Captain?" someone asked.

Finn observed his ship bobbing on the waves. He held all of our lives in his hands, more so now than ever before.

"Long, send word to the others on board. We'll remain here for the night." Finn turned a circle, making sure he had everyone's attention, his eyes lingering on some of us longer than others. "Keep alert at all times. No one is to stray far from camp. Be ready to fight at my command."

He couldn't be serious. Staying when such a threat on our lives was absolute madness. We could undoubtedly sail the seas with this many men. We did not *need* two bags of flour to survive. If only I could see his mind, or throw him to the sand and demand the answers I craved.

The group broke apart, some heading straight to work on cleaning up the mess that was our camp, while others secured the longboats and few supplies that made the short journey from the ship. Long selected a few men to go back to the *Hellbound* and prepare the remaining crew to come ashore. I kept watch over him as a wolf watched a rabbit until I knew for certain he hadn't sent Cantrill or his like-minded mates to claim our ship. Of all the men in our motley crew, I trusted them the least.

When I found them preparing the campsite, I breathed easier. As easily as I could with all hell breaking loose.

Nikolaus wandered toward the trees with a basket to collect fruit for the morning meal. Though Finn preferred I stick close to our cabin boy, I assigned myself to the cleanup crew, heading straight for the flag staked deep within the sand. With all my might, I yanked out the post and fell to my knees, holding the banner across my lap to examine the evidence. I wished then that the former men of the *Hellbound* had been even less merciful and destroyed the other ship entirely when they had the chance that day in Ireland.

It had never occurred to me that this enemy captain and his

crew would seek us out for retribution. Once the men put together a fire, I would gladly throw the flag into it.

I balled it in my hands and kicked sand as I stood. At my feet, a streak of color caught my attention. If a memory hadn't sparked at the image, I might have never noticed such miniscule objects. I dug through the sand until my fingers wrapped around the small beads: red, white, and yellow. They were modest, meant as a decoration. These adorned sailors' braids or beards from time to time, but this color sequence... I'd seen it only once before, long ago and only for a split second.

My hand closed around the beads, and I stared off in memory of that horrific night. I heard the screams all over again. Flames engulfed the village, and Mrs. Collins, the wife of my former master, looked at me for the last time. Blood flowed from her chest as she collapsed into the dirt.

I saw the villain only for a moment before the world went dark. I had no name for him—just a face—eyes like death, gold-toothed grin shaded by a dark flowing beard, spotted with beads of red, white, and yellow.

Finn, I wanted to cry out.

The pirate who haunted my dreams for years was real. He was real, and he hunted us. He'd followed me from Wales to Ireland to the Caribbean.

I searched the camp for my captain, hands trembling against my stomach. My thoughts clouded, body unsteady enough that I sank to the ground once more.

Just when I thought I may vomit in the sand, someone knelt beside me. Stevens rubbed his shirtsleeve across the sweat that beaded on his forehead. I gave him my full focus, thankful for any grounding in the present as I continued to clench the beads in my palm.

"Is this who you're running from?" Anxiety bubbled through my insides, and it took everything I had not to spill out my fears in a shrieking frenzy. "The man that flies this flag has haunted me for years. He burned my village in Wales. He attacked the *Hell-bound* in Ireland. And now, he's destroying the island home I love."

"It's not..." Stevens closed his eyes and moved his hands in the sign of the cross. "...not Hornigold. He flies a red banner."

I pulled my hat from my head and threw it down next to the flag. As the sun rose higher throughout the morning, my hair matted to my head with a mix of salt and sweat.

"Then who could it be? Who else lurks in these waters?" One danger provoked enough fear, but many bloodthirsty enemies?

"I couldn't tell you." Stevens glanced around the campsite to ensure no one could overhear our conversation. For extra caution, he gathered the courage to stand in front of me but lowered his voice. "My former captain kept me below decks. I know he commanded other ships, though I never knew who sailed them."

It was hopeless. Finn made the connection to Ireland, but did he truly know who it was? A name might only make the villain more terrifying.

"Forgive me, Miss Cecily. Forgive me for casting my fear to you." Stevens' hands trembled as he folded them and muttered a prayer.

I waited for him to finish and summoned the courage to ask him what had consumed my mind since we last spoke in confidence. "Does taking you aboard my ship put our men in danger?"

He only bowed his head lower. "I share this concern. I have faith that a man as great as him wouldn't trouble himself to hunt down a lowly clergyman."

"So, I have not endangered my home, my crew, my *captain* by allowing you aboard the *Hellbound*?" An unwanted tear slipped down my cheek, dragging bits of sand with it.

"If I have, I will go now. I would not wish that on you—any of you," he said.

The ocean breeze whipped my fallen curls around my shoulders. In the distance, men continued to clean up debris, while others took the boats to and from the *Hellbound* to gather supplies. I didn't see Finn.

What would my captain advise? Stevens would leave if I asked. I wouldn't even have to lead him astray, something I already felt a little guilty about. Stevens was an honorable man. I saw that the moment I met him. I couldn't fault him for wanting to escape his former life.

I looked toward the heavens. "Captain Worley would never ask you to leave if it meant putting your life in danger. He, like you, is a good man."

Relief washed over Stevens' face. "He is. Thank you, Miss Cecily. I appreciate your discretion more than you know."

I slid the sandy beads into my pocket. My body ached from fatigue and hours on end working the rigs. Stevens knelt once more and began gathering some wooden planks beside me. Then he paused, his hands still atop the pile of wood. "In the way of discretion, might I ask you something?"

My first instinct was to say no. My head swam with so many lies I couldn't risk any of it slipping out. Alas, my wretched curiosity wouldn't allow my silence, and I nodded.

Stevens inched closer still. Visions of our conversation in the kitchen crept into my mind. I should have said no.

He stuttered as he spoke. "Forgive my forwardness, but Captain Worley. Is he... Well, I mean to ask if..." His shoulders dropped, and his voice squeaked with nerves. "Are you in love with the captain?"

"What?" My head tilted like it may fall from the rest of my body, my voice betraying me as nothing more than a whisper.

Of all the things he could have asked me, that one had not crossed my mind. I'd have sooner been prepared to give him the recipe for Nikolaus's stew or divulge my preference for throwing knives over firepower.

He held out his hands to subdue my panic. "I only meant to ask if you were married?"

"Married?" All balance betrayed me, and I fell sideways into the sand.

Stevens reached for me but quickly righted himself. He seemed both alarmed and entertained by my heightened reaction, his eyebrows beginning to twitch simultaneously with the corners of his mouth.

I glanced around to inspect the area for observers. "No marriage. No love. Cripes! Why are you asking me this?"

"It's just... Well, he speaks with you differently than the others," Stevens said.

"I'm a woman." I stood, though my legs still trembled beneath me.

He mimicked my action. "And he's a man."

"I do not see the connection." My free hand flew to my hips as I studied the horizon.

Stevens breathed a laugh. "As I said, you have my discretion, and I apologize for the abruptness of my question. A few of the men have speculated—"

"Speculated?" My cheeks burned in the morning sun. The men had been watching me this whole time and formulating their ideas as to my relationship with Finn. That couldn't be good.

"They have cast their suspicions but have also noticed how often you get in trouble." He raised an eyebrow, his expression revealing no judgment. "That keeps them guessing."

I smiled then. Stevens didn't mean to rat me out to the others. We both had our secrets. "He says I'm his most insubordinate crewmember."

"And yet, you haven't been dismissed," he added.

"Not yet, anyway." I bent to retrieve the flag. Part of me wanted to get out from under this humiliating interrogation. The other part desperately wanted to release a pent-up lie I'd held onto for the last year.

"And the cabin boy, Nikolaus, I believe?" He knelt to gather the pile of wood.

Oh, no. "Yes?"

"What is his relation to the captain? I can tell Captain Worley cares a great deal for him. The boy is so fiercely loyal, and they look so similar," he said.

"Nikolaus is the most faithful member of the crew." Nik's identity was not mine to confirm. However, I highly suspected Stevens didn't need my confirmation.

"It seems as if God led me to your crew for a reason, even if I once again find myself in the lion's den. It is a much greater honor to serve under such a captain as Worley. May I overcome my fear and endeavor to be worthy to serve him—and his family." Stevens bowed his head and turned toward the campsite.

The entire conversation replayed in my head at a rapid speed. "Stevens?"

He slowed and glanced over his shoulder to regard me.

"If you tell a single soul about this conversation, I will cut you down where you stand, minister or not," I said.

He grinned. "I have no doubt you would, miss."

ELEVEN

As the sun lowered over the water, the crew settled. Many of them had fallen asleep by the bonfire—Cantrill and his men included, thank the Lord. The weight of the day's work left us all empty and exhausted. Nikolaus, too, had drifted off, sword in hand. I wanted to stay awake to watch over him, but with Stevens close by, seemingly on high alert, I opted to wander off on my own for a bit.

Dangerous pirates or not, I craved the healing powers my island could give. Armed with my knives, I tiptoed through the jungle of palm trees and took in the song of the chirping insects that awoken to the night. The path I tread still showed wear from the last time we made camp here, guiding me through the tree maze until the jungle swallowed me whole.

After a small hike, I heard the swirling water, and my heart leapt. The brown rocks towered high, creating a cavern over the cool, clear pool below. Trickling waterfalls hummed from the interior of the cave. But I knew I had to save my exploration for another day. I couldn't stay long, not with the captain requiring our vigilance or knowing what else lurked around the island. A single, stolen moment of solace would be enough to get me through the remainder of our stay.

It took only seconds to peel off my boots, hat, and vest, piling them onto an enormous boulder. I didn't even bother with the rest of my attire as I sat on one of the poolside rocks and let my body slide off the smooth surface into the crystal waters. For a moment, I stood relishing in the scene's beauty before sinking down fully underneath.

I emerged to the night sky that exploded in an elaborate array of starlight. The moon, nearly full, danced across the ripples I created in the water. Where the cave ended, the trees gathered to enclose the space, making it the perfect hidden escape on the busy island. As the day washed away, so did my fear and exhaustion. I'd never get to sleep with so much dried sweat and sand matted to my skin. I might as well enjoy a relaxing float instead.

"I thought I might find you here."

The voice startled me out of the water, though the transition took more time due to the weight of my wet clothes clinging to my body. My hair hung even heavier, whipping over my shoulder when I turned toward the rocks along the surface.

Finn knelt beside the pool, his hands testing the water's temperature, his furrowed brow testing my reaction to his presence.

"How did you get away without being followed?" I peeked over his shoulder, just in case.

"Escaping pirates is my specialty." He chuckled to himself and sat on one of the smoother rocks to remove his boots and stick his bare toes in the water. "And most of them are asleep. Hopefully not the ones on watch."

"Welcome, then. The rest of the world doesn't exist here. Might as well enjoy it." I wrung my hair out in my hands and waded closer to lean against the rock beside him. The cold stone curved just right on my back, relieving the aches that came with over-working my body this past week.

Finn stared into the reflecting light on the pool and sighed. His nearness brought so many feelings these days. Love. Hurt. Fear.

"Cess, do you ever regret this life with me?" He tilted his head to see me, but spoke fast enough that I didn't have time to answer. "It's something I've wondered more often as of late. I gave you the choice of staying here in Barbados once, having a life of your own. Yet you chose to sail with me. Do you wish you hadn't?"

He had told me that was his plan when we first met—to grant my freedom on the islands, far away from the oppressive life I'd led in Wales. It was only after Nikolaus made it clear Finn secretly hoped I'd stay on the ship, choose him over the islands, I realized I wanted the same. More than anything. It seemed as if I'd made the harder choice, leading a life of danger, insecurity, and loneliness at times, especially this past month. But regret wasn't a term that ever crossed my mind. Not when it came to him.

"No. I don't. Not once," I said.

He hunched over, his body unable to hold the weight he bore. "I'm so sorry, Cecily. I'm sorry for all of this. I feel as if I've made life worse for you instead of better. Worse was never, ever my intention. I want you to know that."

"Finn, I would choose this dangerous and horrifying life with *you* over anything else the world could offer." I smiled when I lifted his hat from his brow to ensure his gaze met mine. "So, never say such ridiculous things to me again."

He laughed with a sort of relief and took hold of my hand. I released the brim of his hat, my skin tingling at his touch.

His eyes held a note of worry as he brought my hand to his mouth and slowly kissed my palm. His lips inched downward to my wrist, while my fingers rested against his cheek. My body followed along behind, unable to accept the distance between us any longer.

I expected his expression to change, perhaps a smile or twinkle in his eye like he used to get when we were alone together. But nothing altered, except the firmness of his grasp, like I'd slip below the water's surface forever if he let me go.

"Can I just..." He let his hands do the rest of the talking as he drew me closer still. His hat fell away from his head when our bodies collided. With my face buried into his neck, I fought back tears and tried to focus on his pulsating breath in my wet hair to keep me grounded in this moment, rather than dwell on what the world had in store for us next.

He slid from his seat and wrapped his arms even tighter around my middle, lifting me from the pool floor, and pressed his lips to my jaw. We melted together into the water. He kept me in his lap but brought his hands up to cup my cheeks. His eyes held so much behind them. My heart raced faster the longer I looked into them.

Then he kissed me. And nothing else mattered.

A twig snapped nearby, and I slipped out of Finn's arms. In a quick second, he stood with his dagger drawn and dripping, his free arm outstretched to keep me behind him. But no one was there, only a curious parrot hopping through the trees.

The cold rush of reality knocked the wind out of me—or maybe it was the force of that kiss. Finn groaned and sank back into the water. Everything came back to us in that one moment. There was no escape from it, no matter how much we needed one. This was our life. The one I'd chosen.

Finn's chin dropped to his chest, and his shoulders softened. "I don't want to do this anymore. I hate feeling like we're being watched, like we're being hunted everywhere we go."

"We'll figure this out. Just like we always—"

"It's not that simple. Not this time." His fist pounded the muddy bank beside him.

"What do you mean?"

"These are pirates, Cess. *Real* ones. Not just some kid in a captain's hat commandeering a ship."

"You aren't just some kid with a hat, Finn. What's going on? You're acting so unusual lately." I waded closer once more and sunk down to meet him face on.

"I don't deserve to be the captain of that ship, Cecily." He spoke quietly when he would normally match my tone. "I never meant for it to get this far. I watched those men destroy my home and rip my family apart, and all I could think about was revenge. And I got it. After that, it seemed like the easiest way to take care of Nikolaus. We didn't have to beg for food anymore or sneak into barns just to sleep.

"I heard about how the Caribbean islands were a haven for pirates, so I went. I stupidly came here, and I never should have..." He stopped himself when I leaned forward, eager to hear what weighed so heavily on him when he'd never expressed such regret over his work. My fingers laced his, and I gave them a reassuring squeeze.

He bent his forehead to touch mine. "I got swept up in this life, but it's too much."

I shifted around so that one knee supported me on either side of him. "I don't understand. Why all of the sudden? What is it about the Caribbean? And why come back if you knew there would be trouble? You make no sense to me at all, Finnigan. You know I'd fight beside you no matter what the reason, but you aren't telling me what that reason is. And frankly, it makes me want to slap you."

He released a breathy laugh and took both my hands in his, pulling them to his lips. "I have missed you so much."

"Don't you dare try to get out of answering my question." I used both our hands to poke him in the chest.

"I'm not trying to. I promise," he said.

"Then tell me what's going on. *Please*. I can't stand this anymore. It's like you're going one way, Nik's going another, and I'm standing in between the two of you just trying to hold pieces together." I dropped my head to his shoulder.

He placed a gentle kiss against my hair. "You'll be so mad at me."

I sat up, feeling my face twist into a new emotion I couldn't even explain. My thighs tightened around his legs to keep from falling from his lap when I placed my hands on my hips. "I'm already mad at you."

"This will be a different kind of mad. Trust me," he said.

My head rolled back, and I swore toward the starlit sky. This man. This infuriating human had to be the one to hold my heart. I couldn't have been rescued from the farm by a well-established gentleman who told me everything and walked with me through a simple life. No, it *had* to be him. It would *always* be him.

His thumbs brushed over my knuckles. "Do you remember our first week together? When I couldn't tell you everything going on. To keep you safe?" His words held a certain urgency that kept me hanging on for more, but I'd also started to wonder if drowning him might be a better idea.

"Not 'safety' again, Finn. I told you its run its course, and now I'm even more seriously contemplating your bodily harm. Tell me where you're going with this."

He smirked. "Your weapons are way over there."

"I wasn't planning to use weapons," I mumbled.

"Oh." One eyebrow shot up when he realized I didn't share his amusement.

"You're trying to tell me this entire past month has been because you're keeping me safe? You've been lying because whatever secret you have, whatever purpose you have here in Barbados, jeopardizes my safety. And yet we're *here*. In Barbados. In total and complete danger. Only, you know who's after us, don't you? You know they're still around here, but we set up camp anyway."

"I thought I could fix it before anything came of it." He stood with a wave of water pouring from his wet clothes. I slid from his lap, but his hands around my waist kept me from going under.

My fist hit the water, splashing us both. "How can you fix this? *What* can you fix? Let's just get away from here? We can leave the entire crew behind, get out of the Caribbean, and be done with this. *That* is how you keep us safe. That's how we make sure *you* are safe."

"It won't work," Finn said.

The resolve in his voice sent a chill through my veins. "Why not?"

"Because they'll never stop." He swallowed hard.

"Who, Finn? Who won't stop?" My heart raced, fingers trembling beneath the water's surface.

He stared into the pool for a long moment. A gentle wind rustled the treetops, and I focused on the sound until I could force away the tears.

Finn took a slight step toward me, his voice only a whisper. "I took gold from another captain to pay my men all these years."

I processed the information slowly. He'd stolen money. That explained how he afforded a big crew without overtaking the merchant ships.

"How much?" I asked.

He looked up at me then. "A lot."

"And we're here because—"

"Because I need to fix it so he stops following us." He had to force each word from his mouth as if speaking the truth physically hurt him.

What could I say in response? This pirate tracked us to get his money back? It made sense, though it didn't make it any less terrifying. That same blackguard had been in my life entirely too long, and now I knew for sure he *hunted* us.

"But you keep telling the men we're here for more crew." My mind could hardly form my thoughts into words.

"We really will need them if we come under attack. If we don't beat the storms, we'll need as many hands as we can to sail," he said.

My body grew weary, the day and the conversation catching up to me all at once. "We'd ask them to risk their lives, but we can't pay them?"

"Which is why I don't want to do this anymore. I'm not worth anyone risking their life over, but I'd risk the whole island for *you*—

for Nik." He plucked his dagger from the bank and ran his fingers across the mud that colored the blade.

The great Blood Pirate had gotten in too deep. Would the entire crew of the *Hellbound* be forced to join him in the depths? Would *I* follow him there?

I closed my eyes against the night. "You're our captain, Finn. It's not about Nik and me anymore. Whether or not you want to do this, you have to. We all have to. We sail or sink with the *Hellbound* —with its captain. Get yourself together."

With that, I climbed over the pool's edge, gathered my effects in my arms, and ran back to camp without him.

TWELVE

A RESTLESS NIGHT'S SLEEP BROKE WHEN THE MORNING SUN climbed over the horizon. My arm fell across my face to block out the light, but returning to sleep wasn't an option. Not to mention, I had little desire to remain still and let my thoughts dictate my anxiety.

Beside me, Nikolaus cursed and rolled over, face down on his blanket. Had he even noticed my disappearance last night?

Stevens sat propped against a tree trunk, whittling away at a long stick. Judging from his haggard expression, he hadn't slept much either. He stared hard at me, as if wanting to pass along an unspoken message. When he nodded to a group of pirates near the fire—Cantrill doing most of the talking at the group's center—I figured it out.

The huddled men, all of whom I'd put on the list to abandon on this island, spoke in quieted voices. While one talked, another would glance about the campsite. If they planned something, I needed to intervene before their scheming got out of control.

When I searched out Finn on the opposite side of camp, a wave of relief washed over me to see him safely in conversation with some of his other men. Nikolaus, too, had crawled from his makeshift bed to go receive morning orders. With the pair of them accounted for, I feigned a desire for breakfast and made my way toward the fire. Even though the thought of eating sent my knotted stomach into a whirl, I needed to keep up my strength amid the unavoidable chaos that had become my life.

As I approached, voices hushed.

"Heading into the village today, gentlemen?" I sat on a charred log, summoned my friendliest of smiles, and snatched up a piece of bread.

"Should we?" Cantrill poked a stick into the dying embers to nudge the flames back to life.

The others leaned in with his question, and I struggled to remember all the details of the stories I'd made up for them. It seemed my days had turned into nothing but one humongous, drawn out lie—some I knew the truth to; others I didn't.

"I just wondered if you still had your sights set on finding that treasure." I let my voice drop to a whisper and peered over my shoulder to Finn. They inched closer, seemingly granting their trust as I played the part of lookout.

Cantrill narrowed his eyes on the opposite side of the fire. "Nobody stashes treasure in a village."

"Not the treasure, you idiot. Aren't you looking for the girl?" Had we built enough rapport that I could insult him without getting murdered? They could insult each other all day, but for it to come from a woman they disliked might warrant a gunshot wound to the chest. "I assumed Captain Worley had chosen this campsite because of its proximity to the woman he loves. Why else would he have stayed when such a threat lingered?"

Actually, that made a lot of sense.

"And you're sure she has the map?" Cantrill asked.

I lifted my chin to convey my confidence. Finn had an epic battle of his own to fight, somehow having to return a large sum of money to an angry pirate. The least I could do was to prevent a mutiny in the meantime. It was the only way to help so we could get away from this place once and for all.

Though, if Finn just needed money, and I could somehow pay his debt for him...

"You're certain Barbados holds the treasure?" I asked.

"'Course I am. Bet my life on it." Cantrill threw the stick he'd used to stoke the fire into the burning pile, sending sparks high above our heads.

They believed wholeheartedly that such a treasure existed. Too bad the woman with a map was a lie. That would have been convenient—unless it meant Finn loved her, too. That was less convenient.

"Enjoy the hunt, boys." I held my wicked grin, bidding them a good morning with a tip of my cap. I just hoped my claim about the girl would be enough to keep them occupied until we returned to the *Hellbound*. Who knew how long Finn needed to succeed in his business? Or if it were even possible.

I returned to my cot and sank to my knees, stuffing the hardened bread into my mouth while I cleaned up.

"What were you doing over there?" Nikolaus knelt beside me and side-eyed the rough group still huddled around the fire.

"Planning," I said with a mouthful.

He winced. "Does Finn know? Your plans are usually terrible."

I threw my wadded up blanket at him, a sense of relief washing over me when he smiled. The Nikolaus I knew was still in there somewhere, and one day, we'd all be back to normal. One day soon, I hoped.

"So, have you heard any rumors of treasure on this island?" I kept my voice low, lest I collect any more suspicions.

"It's the Caribbean. There's gold in lots of places. Why?" He finished packing his belongings and stood as he shook out his long hair to retie it behind his head.

I shrugged. "Just curious."

Nik kicked his belongings to the side and laughed. "You've

been on a pirate ship long enough, now you think you need to hunt for treasure?"

"Shut it." I shoved him over into the sand.

Behind us, the men gathered around their captain for daily orders. I stuffed whatever I could grab into my knapsack and straightened my vest. Nikolaus and I stood at attention and rushed to join the others.

Finn's voice boomed over his crew. "Today we journey to the village. We find ourselves greatly in need of men, especially with the threat of an unknown enemy haunting the seas." He gestured to the camp around him. "Place yourselves in pubs, in the streets, in the marketplace. Find any willing, able-bodied men to join us on the *Hellbound*. At the end of the day, bring your men to the north-side tavern, and I will make the final selection. We will return to camp before nightfall. As we cannot sacrifice more than a day's time for this task, everyone must work diligently."

He paced in front of us, his back stiff, playing up his height to its greatest advantage. When he ran out of commands, he instructed us to begin our mission. Weapons clanged as men hastily sheathed their blades and loaded their pistols, just in case. And we marched together toward town.

As we walked, I kept stock of the crew. Stevens moved ahead in the group to remain closer to Finn. I couldn't hear their conversation, but Stevens smiled on his part. Finn wouldn't have let him walk so close if he'd hated the man. If only he knew Stevens understood our truth. Or was that what Stevens had moved up there to say?

I scratched the back of my neck as sweat dripped from my hairline. I had to establish my priorities. Stop Stevens from telling Finn I'm a windbag with a loose jaw? Remain close to Nikolaus in case we needed to protect one another from an attack? Or stalk the treasure-hunters who had no commitment to following orders from a captain they didn't respect?

Then again, I kind of wanted to find that fortune for myself. That could take care of all our problems at once.

I really should have gotten more sleep.

My slow pace put me toward the back of the group. Instead of focusing on any of my objectives, I watched my feet to ensure I didn't trip and fall on my face.

Someone grabbed my arm and pulled me farther behind the group. I almost let out a shriek but caught sight of my mutinous 'friends,' their expressions urging me to keep quiet.

"What?" I yanked my elbow from the man's grasp.

"What else do you know?" It was one of the pirates from earlier in the morning, a rather ugly sort, all fleshy and pale—nothing terribly intriguing about him in any way. Though I couldn't recall his name, I knew it matched his appearance somehow.

"Your name again?" I asked.

"Dull."

Ah. That made sense.

I scanned the eager faces awaiting my answer. "Know about what, Mr. Dull?"

"The girl, twit. We're nearly to town," he spat.

I'd have to make something up to keep them occupied. Thinking so quickly on such little rest proved difficult, however.

If only Nikolaus could hear me now, scheming and making up nonsense.

"They say he returns to her twice a year, bringing new riches and affirming his love for her. She's the only one he trusts with the location of his treasure. The only one with the map," I said.

Norris, the largest, hairiest member of the group, clicked his tongue. "And why would he trust a woman with something like that?"

"I beg your pardon, sir, but women are incredibly trustworthy." I scoffed, trying to hide behind my chasm of lies.

"Where do we find her? What's she look like?" Dull asked.

Criminy. I couldn't come up with a description. Knowing my

luck, I'd describe someone perfectly without intention and inadvertently hand over some unsuspecting female to a band of ill-intentioned pirates.

I had to keep the women of Barbados from harm—one more thing on my ever-growing list. "If I knew, I'd tell you."

Cantrill snickered, showing his rather alarming, twisted mouth of teeth. "We could let the captain lead us to her."

Lovely. Now they'd want to follow Finn around the island. As if I needed more dangerous men stalking my captain than what already lurked around every corner.

"And when the captain sees you're not searching for new crew as per his orders?" I raised an eyebrow and tried desperately to keep it from twitching.

"He'll never see us. We'll keep our distance." Cantrill nodded toward his men.

I tipped my cap and walked on ahead. If they kept their distance, maybe they'd pose less of a hazard. If Stevens stayed at Finn's side, Finn would have extra protection in case things got out of control—something that was entirely too possible when I took charge of plans.

THIRTEEN

The noise of the lively village roared as we approached. Inside the small town, vendors sold their handmade goods and baskets of fresh produce. I longed to stop time just for an instant and rush toward the nearest food stand to taste the island delights that once brought a sense of peace and safety when we first came. Would the fruit juices now flow bitterly as the island turned against us?

Finn paused and began separating the men into groups to begin their search. He placed me with Nikolaus, unsurprisingly, and dismissed us all at once. I almost missed the side glance Finn shot in my direction. In an instant, I felt his arms around me, his lips pressed against mine, the butterflies that took flight in my belly. He had so much power in those eyes. But I needed to keep my head clear.

"I miss the sea breeze already." Nikolaus wiped his brow with his kerchief and wrapped it around his forehead, securing it just below his ponytail.

I had braided my hair and tied it up in a bun at the back of my head in hopes it'd help keep me cool, but it hadn't mattered. The jungle blocked the ocean air and forced the heat upon us as if we walked through an oven.

"Let's just get this over with." He started onward, and I followed close behind, while simultaneously trying to take in all the sights. It all served as a reminder of Finn's comment last night. He had given me a choice to live here, too, as one of these people.

I tried to picture myself working at one of the trade tables, picking fruits from the surrounding trees for my daily meals, and sleeping in one of the huts I admired so. Even though it formed as nothing more than a painting in my imagination, the loneliness still crept in. I couldn't live in this beautiful place without these two men in my life. Couldn't be happy if a part of me was missing.

"Finn said you're eliminating half the crew if you get your way," Nik said over his shoulder.

I sped up to walk at his side. "We wouldn't have to if there weren't so many corrupt souls on board. I'd love to blame Long's judgment in Santo Domingo."

"Which ones?" Nik asked.

"Um, well, Norris and Cantrill and their following. There are a couple I've worked with rigging that are rather worthless at sea, Jepps and Latos. And Long, obviously."

Nik laughed. "Do you have the authority to ditch the first mate?"

"*Acting* first mate." I nudged him with my elbow.

"Is that so you can take his job?" He nudged me back, but it wasn't in the same teasing manner.

"As it turns out, I'm not qualified for that position," I said.

Nik rolled his eyes. "Since when has Finn cared much about qualifications? Smalley, a man with no ambition, is boatswain. Stevens, a minister, is cooper. Finn won't even trust anyone else enough to appoint a navigator. And then there's you up in rigging when you didn't even know what a rig was a year ago. But the one man on board that could do all of it to perfection with his eyes closed? Galley."

I grabbed Nikolaus's shoulder and turned him toward me. "Is first mate what you really want?"

"I don't want to talk about it." He tried to walk away, but I clung to his arm, keeping him there.

"The three of us need to stick together if we're going to survive the devils that await us on this island, and your whining is getting you nowhere." I sucked in my lower lip. I hadn't meant to speak so crassly.

He swatted my hand from his arm but didn't move away. "Any job on that ship is better than being a kitchen boy. I've been doing that for four years, Cecily. I'm trained with a sword and have memorized every inch of that vessel. He won't trust me to do anything but what I already do. But *you* get to go up into the bloody rigs."

He had a reason for his frustration, undoubtedly, and I stared into his eyes to see a boy desperately trying to become the man he longed to be.

"I'm sorry, Nik." I wished I had some say in the matter, but I knew if Finn decided to keep Nikolaus belowdecks, there was little to be done about it. "I never meant to take anything from you."

"I know you didn't." He rolled up the sleeves on his loose-fitting shirt.

"Maybe as part of our search for a new crew, we can find another cabin boy, so Finn'll have no choice but to change your occupation," I said.

He smiled at that. "It won't work. He's stubborn as an ass."

"Oh, so much worse than that." I breathed a laugh and read-justed my sweaty collar.

Nikolaus reached into his pocket, drawing out a handful of coins. He held them outstretched like a peace offering.

"Where did you get all that?" I pushed them around in his hand but didn't take any.

"I stole them from Finn's desk. You hungry?" he asked.

The brothers grew more alike by the day, which could be why

they hadn't been getting along. Bunch of headstrong thieves, they were. "Almost always."

We could hunt new crew *after* we ate.

As if in an unspoken race, we darted through the center of town, squeezing in and out of the busy bodies until we met again at a small fruit stand.

A woman greeted us in her thick accent. The bright patterns of her head wrap rivaled the color of the fresh produce she sold. She took our coins and fed us a breakfast of juice squeezed right out of an orange and into a bowl of berries and homemade cheese, sprinkled with fine sugar. Each bite melted in my mouth, the sugar and seeds crunching between my teeth in the most delightful way. I wished Finn could enjoy it with us the way we had before.

Our stomachs full and spirits lifted, we turned to face the crowd and move on with our task. We stood out amongst the others, but no one seemed to care. Piracy was about as common as cocoa around here. Though the people were many, convincing any of them to leave the island and join the pirates they usually traded with would be a sizeable task.

"How many do we need again?" I asked.

"Probably a good thirty men if you release even half of what we already got." Nikolaus's gaze shifted around the vendors, most likely focused more on dessert than seeking our next crewmates.

Why did so many of our current men have to be so wretched? It really made my life difficult. "Fine. Let's get to it," I said.

Nikolaus followed behind me, moving in the direction of my head tilts and pursuing each of the choices we found. I kept my hair tucked into my hat and let my shirt flow freely about my waist—the coolest combination I could come up with.

We approached several men who looked strong enough to complete the work and less villainous than what we already had. Only two agreed to meet us at the tavern later to interview with the captain. Not the amount we'd hoped for. Perhaps the other men had more luck. If each group brought two men, it might amount to something—unless our wretched fellows brought equally wretched prospects.

The afternoon heat grew more intense. Nikolaus and I prepared to call it a day and head back when our bodies had no more sweat to produce. That and I had to make sure that the mutinous bunch hadn't arbitrarily kidnapped some girl and forced her to hand over a nonexistent treasure map.

"Hey!" someone called from behind us.

Nikolaus and I spun around to see the face of the one so bold as to shout at us.

A young woman stood alone, a long green skirt flowing down to her bare feet. A high slit in the fabric revealed a dagger strapped to her outer thigh. She grinned wickedly to reveal the contrast of her white teeth against her ebony skin. As she moved closer to us, her fingers brushed her upper leg—a warning that she would withdraw the dagger at any moment.

"You," she said, pointing to me. "You're a woman."

An urge to grab at my knives in self-defense arose. Instead, I held my arm out to keep Nikolaus from producing a weapon of his own. "Same as you, it would seem."

She smiled again, her gray eyes darting to Nikolaus for a moment before returning to me. "You're lookin' for pirates?"

"We're looking for a crew," I answered.

"Of pirates." Her head tilted in a way that sent her tiny, dark braids dancing over her shoulder. "Never met a girl pirate before."

"This is stupid. Let's head back." Nikolaus waved his hand to dismiss her. In an instant, the girl lunged forward and caught his arm, twisting it into an odd angle. He yelped in pain, but she held on, her eyes searching him with a hungry expression.

"Let him go." My fingers brushed over my knife.

Still, she glared, holding Nikolaus in place despite his protests. His eyes found me, as well. He either meant for me to attack her and save him or let me know he planned to murder her the moment he wiggled free.

She released his arm with a laugh. "This your man? That why you've been wandering the village whisperin' and carryin' on?"

Nikolaus stood up straight and glared at her. He definitely meant to murder her. "You're lucky I don't cut your tongue out for saying such drivel."

"Nikolaus!" That was nearly worse than murder.

"The name's Josette." She crossed her arms instead of offering a hand to shake. "And I want in."

Who was this force of a woman? "Want in for what?"

Nik still seethed beside me, his breathing so loud it almost made me chuckle. Which would have just made things much, much worse.

"I wanna be part of the crew. What else would I be talkin' about?" She winked at Nikolaus.

I'd told Finn I wanted to bring more women on board, but I hadn't thought through to the possibility of actually finding one brave enough to join me in this madness. The whole idea seemed impossible.

And amazing.

"Why do you want to be part of our crew?" I asked.

"Why did *you* wanna join?" Her arms remained crossed tightly over her chest, and her head bent with accusation.

Nikolaus turned his full body toward me, his face displaying just how much interest he had in hearing my explanation. *Join* seemed like such an amusing term for it. If anything, I was dragged on board as a prisoner, fell in love with both the ship's captain and his mission, and continued to lie my way through the realms of piracy, hoping to stay alive.

Oh, I had an answer. "Freedom. I wanted to get away from the life I had."

"Then, we really aren't so different, you and me," she said.

Nikolaus looked between the two of us, waiting for a decision, a fight, *something*.

I stepped closer to her. "Can you sail?"

104

"I'm a quick learner. And I can fight. But that much is obvious." She looked Nikolaus up and down and bit her lower lip to suppress a giggle.

A low growl escaped him. This woman knew exactly how to dig at Nik. In that moment, I couldn't decide who would win if the pair of them fought. They both held a roaring fire inside them. It was best not to even entertain such thoughts, but rather prevent the situation altogether.

On the upside of things, Finn said he wanted fighters. I'd found one.

I reached out a hand for her to take. "Josette, come to the tavern near the end of town in one hour. You'll meet the captain then."

Nikolaus threw his hands up. "You cannot be serious. She's hardly sane!"

"She's *perfect.*" I flashed a quick smile before spinning on my heels to escort Nik away from his new nemesis. "Besides, if nothing else, she'll keep the others in line."

"She's a woman." He dropped his head when my eyes narrowed at him.

"And?"

He sighed. "Your kind give me a headache."

"I think that particular one will give you a whole lot more than a headache," I said.

He rubbed his shoulder where Josette had twisted it behind him moments before. The poor soul. He'd met his match. Now, we just had to see what Finn thought about the matter.

FOURTEEN

ALL OF BARBADOS HELD A UNIQUE BEAUTY—EXCEPT THE tavern on the edge of the main road. To my knowledge, it had no name, but somehow didn't need one for people to find it on the map. Men with pipes puffed away, mostly farmers taking a break after a long day in their fields. I generally enjoyed the scent of smoking pipes from a distance, but when the smoke remained the only air to breathe, it nauseated me.

The patrons spoke loudly over each other, talking of crops, the weather, sometimes even family. On our first journey to the islands, we disguised ourselves as villagers and sat amongst the others, listening to stories and making up tales of our own until we practically suffocated from laughter and smoke inhalation. I'd always cherish the memory, the feeling of normalcy, and a life far from the danger that came with the infamous lifestyle.

Tonight, Nikolaus and I claimed a corner table, tucked away so we could watch the room without drawing too much attention to ourselves. He clearly enjoyed the time away from his duties, and I rather liked being away from the mutinous mutts for the afternoon. Soon, they'd join us in the tavern and bring down the mood. That was, unless they had kidnapped a woman in the village or turned on Finn and Stevens, which I really didn't care to think about for long.

When Finn finally walked in the door, I relaxed my concerns of an early onset mutiny, then took a long swig from my mug. Finn stood tall in full captain's gear, his mouth tight as he scoured the busy room and took over a table near the center, Long at his immediate side. Stevens sat on the opposite end of the room, keeping watch over everything. The entire mood changed when a captain entered the tavern. No matter their position, everyone showed a reverence for the man who commanded a ship.

The pretty waitresses flocked to the captain's table, his status taking priority over all the other patrons in the room. His looks didn't hurt his situation either. He was much more pleasant in appearance than any other pirate I'd sailed with. Or any man I could imagine, really. And from the flirtatious way they touched his shoulder, they shared my opinion. Each one giggled as they spoke or leaned down low and *strategically*, playing up their generous endowments.

Finn brought his hat lower on his head to shade his expression and kept his attention toward Long and the dealings at hand. That only made the girls try harder, their squeals piercing through the chorus of conversations drifting through the room. I downed the rest of my drink, coughing heavily into my arm when I swallowed.

"You all right?" Nikolaus patted me hard on the back, making my coughing fit much worse.

"Fine." My attention lingered on the good captain and his pretty female attendants as my imagination took over. I thought I'd made up the stories about him having an island love, but he'd been here many times before we met...

"You look like you're going to kill someone," Nik added.

"I hope I don't." I stood but kept my palms pressed against the table for support. The room seemed tilted, and my stomach began to churn. The smoke made my head pound.

"You want to go back to camp?" He scooted his chair away from the table—and me—as if expecting me to explode at any moment.

I shook my head. "No. I need to talk to Finn."

"That seems like a *great* idea." He chuckled to himself and got up.

"Are you really going back to camp right now?" Maybe I *should* go with him. I didn't feel like walking such a distance alone or with anyone else in our crew.

"Soon. I'm escorting some new men after they meet approval, and..." He hesitated as if he either couldn't remember what he meant to say next, or he didn't really want to tell me. "I have someplace I need to be, but I can take you to the camp with the others."

"Someplace to be?" I asked.

His eyebrows rose high on his forehead, and I couldn't keep the smirk off my face at how ridiculous he looked.

"Never mind. Forget I said that. Just...do you want to go back or not?" he asked.

"No, I want to stay. I may come with Finn," I said.

"Well, good luck with *that*." He forced a sheepish grin and scooted around me, being anything but careful about bumping into me.

I thought I had more to say to him, or perhaps I forgot to say goodbye. Alas, he vanished, leaving me at the table with my thoughts. It didn't matter. I just really needed to get to Finn. My foggy mind knew nothing other than that right now.

With each step toward his table, my legs seemed to turn to wood. Not that different from being out to sea, only it smelled much worse in here. My head throbbed from lack of sleep.

"What do you want?" A gangly human formed a wall to block my path, knocking me backward into one of the tavern's support beams. It only took a moment before I realized Long stood before me. His arms crossed over his chest, and he looked down at me as if I were a spot of seagull dung on his shoe.

"I need to speak with the captain. Let me through." My tongue tied itself in knots. I rammed into him again. Twice. But he didn't budge.

"Nobody speaks to the captain without going through me first." His breath reeked of alcohol and something else much stronger in odor, which made my stomach roil. Vomiting might solve many problems. He'd get out of my way, for one thing.

"I have important business." One hand still clutched the beam behind me so I didn't fall.

"I'll pass it along. The captain's a little busy tonight." He glanced over his shoulder as another buxom woman bent down next to Finn and whispered something in his ear. I thought I saw him blush at her words but couldn't be sure.

"It doesn't matter." I could hardly remember what I responded to when I said that. "Get out of my way!"

He laughed hard enough that the excess skin on his scraggly neck flapped. Too intrigued to look away from the bizarre display, I stopped fighting for a moment. That was until he reached out and grabbed my collar.

I stepped back just enough to get momentum, then lunged forward and punched the older man square in the nose. My hand exploded in pain when it connected, but the blood that dotted my knuckles was not mine—and it made me smile.

Long roared and dove toward me, but he got caught up in the arms of another, while I fell back into the awaiting grasp of the beam I'd found stability before. The dumb piece of wood had proven my best ally on the whole infernal island. Shouts broke out around the room and brought me upright once more as the occupants of the tavern encouraged a fight.

"What is going on here?" Finn's outstretched arms maintained the space between us.

Stevens held Long at bay, despite the old man's squirming.

"She struck me!" Long wasted no time throwing out the blame.

I shrugged, since he wasn't wrong.

"What have I said about fighting amongst the crew?" Finn

yelled with such anger that the rest of the tavern quieted. When we didn't answer his question, he grew even louder. "What did I say?"

"Fighting isn't tolerated." I spoke through gritted teeth. While I'd never engaged anyone in this way before, I really did know how Finn felt about his men fighting. I'd seen him punish men with his whip for such behavior.

"And you'll do well to remember that." Finn released our shoulders, gaze switching between us as he spoke. "Long, get back to the camp. I'll deal with you tomorrow. Hastings, out back *now*."

The room grew silent, my ragged breaths ringing in my ears. I moved toward where Finn pointed, but avoided contact with his fiery stare. My foot caught on the edge of a stool and tripped me enough that I toppled into the corner of the table with a loud crash. As punishment for its betrayal, I kicked hard at the chair to send it crashing to the ground with an equally loud clatter. The men hollered behind me, their drunken enthusiasm returning at the show, but I tried to ignore them. My focus remained on the back door and on what Finn might say—or *do*—once we got outside. The room seemed so large now, so consuming, and I was no bigger than a beetle.

When I beat my fist against the wooden door of the backroom to open it, I realized just how much my hand really hurt. Regardless, I swallowed my yelp. Finn's boots thumped on the ground behind me, his heavy breath equally loud as we moved out of earshot from the others inside the pub. Soon, the door clicked, leaving us alone in the abandoned alley.

I leaned against the building, fully giving up my attempt to stand on my wooden legs. Finn paced in front of me, rubbing his forehead as he often did when something upset him. It seemed I had become the source of that gesture more and more often as our time together went on.

"You punched my first mate." He stopped pacing and turned toward me—rather close to me, too.

"Yes, because he is a rat-faced pirate, and I despise him," I said.

Finn rested his hand on the wall behind me, and I quickly noted how the fire had subsided in his eyes, unless my mind played some kind of trick on me. "We all despise him, Cecily, but—"

"Why would you let him be the first mate, anyway?" I leaned closer into him like an invisible force drew me forward. "Even an acting first mate is way too much power for one—"

"He's just rotten enough to pass for a real pirate in our midst, which is important, considering what wretched pirates we are in the first place," he said.

My head fell back hard against the side of the building, and I groaned. "I was only trying to get to you to talk to you about something. He stood in my way, so I made him move."

"By right, he's allowed to prevent you from coming to me. You know we can always find other ways to communicate when he's not around. You have to stop causing trouble with him, Cess. With any of them. I'm expected to keep you in line, treat you as the others. How am I supposed to do that *and* maintain our secrets? Or keep you from harm? I can't protect you every time, and you're making this *so* difficult."

Behind him, the shadowy jungle sang its nighttime song. I stared into the darkness and tried to allow my mind to mimic the calm void. It was no use. My knuckles ached where they'd collided with Long's face. Tomorrow, they'd bruise if they hadn't already.

"Cecily?"

I shook my head, hardly caring what consequence he gave me, as long as I could sleep after. "Punish me however you sit fit, Captain, but can you do it tomorrow? I'm exhausted."

"*Todella, nainen?*" He growled and dropped his hands at his side. "*You* exhaust *me*."

"Then we both need a goodnight's rest, eh?" I crossed my arms over my chest and let my body slide down the tavern wall until my rear end hit the ground. The splintery wood scratched at my shirt the whole way, ready to tear the fabric or pierce my flesh. It didn't matter. Everything already hurt—my body, mind, spirit.

Finn squatted beside me, using his hand to support him against the tavern wall. "I really should have seen all this coming when I came for you in Barry."

I squinted at him in the darkness, trying to read his expression. "Seen what coming?"

"You starting fights. The enormous pain in my ass that would come with keeping you safe," he said.

"What about starting fights? You won me in a bet. I did very little fighting in the matter." My life had never been particularly *safe*, nor had I put up much of a battle against him in Jones's Tavern when he won his game of Liar's Dice against Mr. Collins. My mind had been in too great of a shock to protest.

Finn shook his head. "Not that night. The ones before it. I'd gone there many times after I discovered you sitting on a bag of flour one winter evening."

"Many times? Nik said you'd been there before, but I'd only seen you once. Maybe once, anyway—enough to recognize you when you challenged Mr. Collins. We hosted so many pirates and anglers alike at that rotten tavern; it's hard to know faces."

"But you remembered mine." Finn's teeth shone in the moonlight.

I couldn't help but smile back. "Yours is hard to forget."

Finn's fingers brushed over my shoulder and slid down my arm until he took my hand in his. "As is yours. But it was your spirit that caught my eye first." Finn squeezed my fingers. "That first night I saw you, you hit someone, too."

My eyes went wide. The last time I'd hit someone at Jones's Tavern had to have been years ago.

He continued without waiting for my reply, "That's right, Hastings. Some bloke made a ruckus trying to get you off your flour bag, and that's when I saw you." Finn's smile broadened, and he laughed. "You were so livid."

"You didn't offer your help?" I used both our hands to swat him in the stomach.

He tried to quiet his chuckle. "I stood to interfere, but you cracked him across the jaw. He toppled into my table, and you sat down on your flour sack again."

"I remember that. Mr. Collins did not deal kindly with my fighting at the pub." The memory of the punishment made me shudder. "I can't believe the man didn't hit me back."

"Ah." Finn released my hand to raise his finger. "That's because someone caught him with a pistol to his back and threatened his life if he tried again."

I shifted against the wall to better see his face. "You did?"

He nodded. "I watched you until Collins dragged you out the door. And I couldn't protect you any longer, but something inside me went with you that night. I came back over and over until I had a plan strong enough to ensure you left with me without raising suspicions of my crew or drawing too much attention to us in your village." He released a long breath. "Though, I'd be lying if I didn't say I spent many nights imagining what it'd be like to run Collins through with my blade and steal away with you."

I enjoyed his phrasing more than I should have. In fact, I dreamt of running off with him frequently.

"Why are you telling me this now?" I asked. He should have been punishing me. Should have left by now to keep the crew from getting suspicious or coming to find him.

"I don't know. Maybe just so you know how much you mean to me—how much I need you to be safe and stop tempting harm." He stood and straightened his hat, inspecting the area once more for danger.

If only he knew how many outlets for harm I juggled at that very moment, all to keep him from his own demise. Is this what love comprised? Two people risking their lives to save the other over and over until both died an untimely death from exhaustion or the enemy's hand?

Or was this only an occurrence in piracy?

"I won't fight Long again." I might *possibly* be able to keep that promise.

"Thank you." Finn stretched his neck to the side until it popped, and he straightened his overcoat. "I should get back before they come for us. I'll send someone to get you back to camp, you drunken wench."

"Oh, shut it." My head spun again.

He tapped his finger to his chin and stared at me for a thoughtful moment. "Limp or something when you get back to camp, would you, love?"

"Aye, sir." That would have been a good enough conclusion to our chat had I not remembered why I needed to speak with him tonight. "Wait. I wanted to tell you something. That's the whole reason for my fighting." I reached out and snatched hold of his coat, not wanting to let go, maybe ever. "I've got you three new recruits."

"Three is better than none," he said.

I pulled a piece of parchment from my pocket. "Nik took their names, so you'd know which were ours. I meant to give it to you before Long got in the way. The last name is my favorite."

Finn plucked the torn parchment from my fingers and squinted at the list in the dim light of the overhanging lantern. "Josette? Is that a woman?"

I smiled, probably more zealously than necessary. "She's got more fight in her than most of your men combined. I like that about her."

"Of course, you do." His lip twitched into a partial grin.

"And when you assign this new crew, I have some suggestions for what to do with them," I said.

"We can discuss this another time, Cess. I really—"

"Make Nikolaus your new first mate for a start." The ale had kicked my courage up a notch.

"What?" The suggestion seemed to catch him off guard, but he hadn't totally cut me off. He bent closer, as if to ensure I spoke with a right mind.

"You'll have the numbers after tonight. Just move Nikolaus up, and put someone else in his place," I continued.

"He's entirely too young for that position."

"I think we're all a bit young for all the malarkey we've gotten ourselves into, wouldn't you say?" I reached up and tapped my finger to his chest in between the weapons strapped there.

As my hand fell back to my side, Finn caught hold of it. "What's going on with you tonight? Besides the obvious intoxication and general disregard for my rules."

A lifetime of wild memories and new and horrifying information whirled across my mind. I had so much to tell him and nothing to say all at once. Certainly his heart weighed as heavily as mine did, if not much more so with the weight of the ship and all its men on his shoulders.

"I found something on the beach." The words spilled from my lips before I really knew what I said.

He started to say something but changed course, as if abandoning his prepared speech at the last moment. "What?"

"When we were cleaning up yesterday, I found something." I dug into my pants pocket with my free hand. The colorful beads I'd retrieved from the sand clanked against each other in my palm. "I think I know who burned the camp."

"His name?" His tone wasn't what I expected for the magnitude of the proclamation. He released my fingers and plucked the beads one by one from my palm to examine them. "The bastard from Ireland?"

"Yes, but it's more than that. I've seen these exact color patterns twisted in the beard of another pirate once before—long before Ireland." The terrifying images played through my mind again. "It was the same man that invaded my village. The man that killed Mrs. Collins."

His brow furrowed. "And you think the man that did that is the same one who burned our camp?"

"*And* nearly killed you in Ireland."

I expected to earn a reaction from him—shock, horror, realization. But definitely not this: he laughed.

Somehow, that was much more unsettling.

"The man that burned your village is the same man that destroyed our camp." He laughed harder, placing his hat over his mouth to muffle the sound.

"Finn?" I wiggled my feet underneath me in case I needed to run off and get help, sure that insanity had finally claimed him. He grabbed my arm to keep me in place.

"The man that burned your village is the same man that destroyed our camp," he repeated.

"You said that already…"

The laughter ceased. Only silence remained behind his hat where he'd buried his face.

"And you know who he is," I whispered, barely able to get the statement out. Would I finally hear the name of the man that haunted my dreams all these years?

Finn slowly lowered the hat until I could fully see his face. He wouldn't meet my gaze, but nodded.

He closed his eyes when he finally spoke. "His name is Edward Teach. But you might have heard him called Blackbeard."

I collapsed against the wall again. How could that possibly be? The men had mentioned the name before. He sounded dreadful.

He *was* dreadful.

"You knew the whole time. Why didn't you tell me?" I squeaked.

"I didn't know he was the one that burned your village. I didn't even realize it was his ship in Ireland until after the fact. That fog shielded their vessel from us. If any of the other men recognized it, they never said as much." He swallowed hard, an almost painful sound accompanying the action.

"And now he's hunting you?" I asked.

Finn's deep blue eyes caught the only light in the shadows as he stared back at me. "It would seem he wants his treasure back."

FIFTEEN

I don't know how long I sat there, staring into the dark jungle, listening for footsteps that didn't exist, and allowing my imagination to play one horrifying scenario after another in my mind. The weariness kept me in place, weighted to the cold stone. My eyes fluttered from exhaustion until I bordered on unconsciousness.

Blackbeard wanted his treasure back.

That's whose fortune Finn took?

Someone kicked hard at my leg, and I yelped. The force shook the fog from my mind and sent me into a trembling state of alarm. My knives were in my hand before my brain even called them into action.

"If you meant to stab me, you'd have better luck aiming in the right direction," came a thick island accent.

I groaned and turned around. "Josette?"

"Captain's a man of his word, it seems. Done quite a number on you. And you were the one lecturin' me on fightin'." She clicked her tongue and tossed something into my lap, startling me all over again.

When I felt the mushy skin of liquid across my legs, I brushed it to the side. "I'm not drinking this."

She knelt down and opened the container. "It's water, and I don't recall givin' you a choice."

"Oh." I wrapped my shaking fingers around the offering and took a sip. The chilled drink slid down my throat, relieving the dry ache from breathing in the sultry air all day. The twinge in my knuckles eased just from holding the cool skin, as well. "Thank you."

"Welcome." Instead of leaving as I expected her to, she looked around, then slid down the wall next to me until we sat side by side.

"Um." What else could I say to her? She wasn't anything like the smelly men I usually had to listen to, carrying on about whatever nonsense came to mind. Even so, she scared me more than they did.

"I'm waitin' for you to get up," she said.

"Why?" I rubbed my head and tried in vain to put the evening into perspective. I'd talked with Finn. That really happened. And all that we said...

"You'll be takin' me back to the camp. At your convenience, by all means. I've got all night." She stretched her arms over her head and yawned. "Captain said you were in need of an escort and thought we'd be able to figure out our way together since I don't know it, and you're too beat to walk."

"Right." My stomach grumbled with nausea. "My name is Cecily, by the way. And you met with the captain already?" I had to have sat out there for hours. At least, it felt that way.

"I did. Strange fellow, that one." She covered her mouth quickly and glanced around for eavesdroppers. "Probably shouldn't say that, should I?"

I choked back a hoarse giggle. "I won't tell him. Besides, it's true. He's been unusual the entire time I've known him, at least." In the darkness, I could sense her smiling. "But he approved you for the crew?"

"He took one look at me—one long, *strange* look—and nodded. Didn't make me sign nothin'. Asked no questions. Just kept nodding as he scribbled somethin' down on his paper."

"Scribbled something down?" I asked.

She fidgeted next to me. "I didn't see what it was. I don't read, anyway. He just welcomed me aboard and told me to come back here for you after I'd gotten something to fill my belly. Shoulda heard the ruckus in there when he gave his approval. Don't think they were all that happy with another woman joining the crew —'specially not that bloke whose nose you busted up. Seems they don't care for you much."

"No. They really don't." At least, if my plans worked—and I really couldn't count on anything—I'd lose my biggest problems before we boarded the *Hellbound* again. If Finn came around, Nikolaus would be the next first mate and, therefore, the one handing out positions in the crew. While that boded fairly well for me, Josette hadn't made the greatest impression on him earlier. He'd likely give her his job of peeling potatoes just to keep her locked in the galley and away from him.

"You were brave to strike the old man in front of the captain." She stood and patted the dirt from her legs, then offered a hand to me. I took it, dizzily coming to a stance and using the wall for support. "Figured that'd get you killed by now, but look at ya out here all alive."

"You were there? I didn't see—"

"Tucked away in the corner, I was. Watchin' it all. Wanted to know what sort I was gettin' mixed up with before I signed on."

"And?" I stepped away from the building and stumbled. Josette put an arm around me to keep me upright, her grasp gentle but firm. I took another long swig from the waterskin. When was the last time I'd had a drink of fresh water? I hadn't eaten since that morning, having totally forgotten to grab something inside the pub before I got myself kicked out.

She shook me straighter onto my feet. "I 'spect I'll manage all right on board. I 'spect I'd manage with worse, even."

"What do you mean?" I started toward camp, dreading the agonizing walk when my body could barely hold its own weight. At least, I wouldn't have to go it alone, and the moon lit the jungle enough that I had a rather good sense of our direction.

"I'd have joined any ship if it meant I could get off this island. We're really leavin' tomorrow?"

"Supposedly, but why—"

"You'd better just focus on walkin'." She bit into her lip as she looked straight ahead. Whatever her reasons for wanting to abandon the island, she kept quiet about it. Surely, she hadn't sailed as a minister under some other infamous pirate the same as Stevens had. The likelihood of me finding two runaways that posed a risk couldn't be that high. Then again, I had the worst luck about these things.

My legs grew stronger with each step, my mind clearer. Soon, I wouldn't need her support at all, but I was grateful for it none-theless. Having Josette around already made for an improvement to the *Hellbound*. "Thank you for helping me."

"I'm just glad you aren't dead. Figured that might have been the case when the captain took you out back like that. When he told me to make sure you could walk back to camp, I just assumed he broke your legs."

"Not this time he didn't." I left it at that. Though I felt as if I'd received a beating this evening, it had not come from the captain's hand.

"Well, then. I best stay on his good side," she said.

"Please do." I let her see my smile then and released her shoulder completely. The crew became a friendlier place in this single evening. "I'd like to keep you around."

She scoffed. "That cabin boy sure don't want me here. He gave me the awful-est look when he was leaving. Scrawny fella like that better keep his eyebrows to himself if he don't want me tearing them off him."

The image of her tearing anyone's eyebrows from their face made me pick up the pace. Either Josette and Nik would rise to the top of the rankings on the *Hellbound* simultaneously, or they'd kill one another in the pursuit.

Josette hummed to herself and glanced around the jungle. "Not sure he knows the way back to the ship, come to think of it. Or *you're* going in the wrong direction."

"What do you mean?" I asked.

"He headed in the opposite way. Looked sneaky if you ask me. I don't trust him." She pulled a long stick from the ground and whacked at hanging branches as we passed through.

Nik told me he had some place to be...but Finn also instructed him to lead the crew back to the ship. *Sneaky* might have been the word for it.

My head still hurt terribly. Why must all the men in my life be either mysterious and stubborn or downright murderous? Even the minister I collected held dangerous secrets of his own.

"I'm sure he just ran an errand for the captain or something like it." Or perhaps he, too, had gone after Finn's nonexistent island love— unless she worked in the pub, serving drinks. Any of those women would have happily kept Finn's treasure map in return for his *company*.

I grabbed a stick and swatted hard at the trunk of a tree. We couldn't make it to the ocean fast enough for me to cool off from this miserable heat and chill my boiling blood.

"You all right?" Josette asked.

"Fine. I'm just ready to leave this all behind." I'd only just met the woman and couldn't confess my distaste for flirty barmaids, but she would undoubtedly understand my hatred for the mutinous crew. "We've quite a few men on our current crew I'm hoping to lead astray before we sail, as I have no desire to spend another moment on board the *Hellbound* with them."

"Captain's orders or your own?" She snapped her stick in half and chucked one side behind her.

"He won't miss them or their defiance."

"Aye," she said. I already had her on my side, it seemed.

Between the two of us, we might actually get rid of at least one of my problems. There remained the issue of Finn potentially having Blackbeard's treasure and being hunted for it. "Josette, do you know of any treasure on this island?"

"Treasure?" She laughed and threw the other half of her stick so hard it stuck in the mud. "If I'd found any of that, I wouldn't need the likes of you for an escape, now would I?"

"I—I don't know." Just because she hadn't found it didn't mean one didn't exist.

"Well, if one's there, I sure would like to find it." Her shrill laugh echoed off the trees.

"As would I, Josette. Desperately." I listened for the sound of the waves breaking on the shore to indicate the end of our journey. I needed to rest, to quiet my mind for even a moment, but I heard nothing. We still had a long journey ahead of us—in so many ways.

SIXTEEN

ANY ATTEMPT MADE FOR A PEACEFUL NIGHT'S REST shattered with the recurring nightmares of my village burning, Mrs. Collins dropping to the ground in a pool of her own blood, and me screaming as the madman looked into my eyes. But this time it differed from all the other nights I dreamt of him. Now, he had a name: Edward Teach. Blackbeard.

I'd thought nothing could make me more afraid of that man, but giving him a name exemplified my terror. And realizing I might see him again if he caught up with us? I wanted to bury myself in the sand and give up now.

My unease heightened when I awoke fully to another's face a few inches from mine. I bit back a scream as I stared into the dark eyes that focused keenly on me.

Josette's smile overtook her. "You don't look so bad today. I 'magine you'll be all right."

I sat up and rubbed at my sticky face. Josette still grinned maniacally at having delivered such a fright. She may have given off the impression of a trustworthy crewmate, but her intensity was tough to digest before breakfast. Perhaps our friendship might be better suited for the afternoon hour.

"Where's Captain Worley?" I asked.

"Over there talkin' to that serious chap. I forget his name. Bevins or some such thing. The one that sings like an old nun and acts as if the captain turns air to gold."

I held up my hands to stop her rambling, my head pounding. "Stevens. Matthew Stevens. He's clergy. Or, I guess, a cooper now. What are you supposed to be doing today, Josette?"

"Annoying everyone with her questions," Nikolaus whispered behind me.

Josette glared at her young accuser, then drew her focus back to me. "What do you do on the ship?"

It took me a long moment to remember what my occupation was on board the *Hellbound*. "I'm a rigger."

"What is that?" she asked.

"Maybe you should help the rest of the crew load the boats. That'd be a good place to start." I massaged my fingertips through my hair, hoping to straighten out my mane while manually organizing my thoughts.

Without another word, Josette ran off to help the other men with the supplies.

"You didn't tell her you were in charge here, did you?" Nik threw his pack into the sand.

My lip curled. "Why would I tell her something like that?"

"You make up a lot of nonsense. Figured the way she asked you for instruction meant she thought you had a lot more power than you do in this crew." He raised a blond eyebrow, and I considered Josette's threat to rip them off him.

Sure, I'd invented a good amount of stories for our new members, but claiming power hadn't been one of them. "Not this time. And she's part of us now, so you'll have to learn to accept her."

"I refuse. If you can actively lose men to the island before we sail, I can lose her." He turned away from me and headed in Finn's direction.

He could *try* to lose her. Not that she'd let him. With Josette's will matched to mine, poor Nikolaus didn't stand a chance.

My pack put together once more, I leapt up to chase the cabin boy and help him gather some breakfast for Finn. Food remained the sole opportunity for communication time between us and our captain, so I didn't mind helping.

On our approach, Stevens removed himself from the captain's side to give the three of us our privacy, an action that seemed to go unnoticed by both Finn and Nikolaus.

Nik stopped short in front of Finn, his hands resting on his skinny hips. "Stop letting Cecily have a say in the crew. We end up with muck-spouts. And you really think we need another woman on board? As if Cecily's not bad enough already."

I shot him a look. "I'm *right here*, Nikolaus. Besides, you're not giving Josette a chance."

"Because she's bloody mad," he shouted.

"And for good reason." Finn's interjection stopped the argument short when he pointed to me. "You weren't joking about her being a fighter. She's a runaway."

"She's a what?" I sank to the ground to meet Finn face to face.

"Knew it straightaway. She introduced herself with a lie and seemed more eager than most to set sail. She kept her collar pulled up around her neck, but it didn't fully hide the marks there. We both know what those are from. Could be slave trade or forced marriage. Both are rather common around here. I suspect she fought her way out to the fastest means of escape."

I winced. "That would explain some things. Though, you didn't hesitate to give her a place knowing she could be hunted?"

"We're already hunted. I'm certain she'll hold her own here. Not many people are as brave as she, if my guess is accurate as to her situation and her age." Finn gave Nik a sly smile when he noticed the boy's expression change with the weight of the information.

"Her age?" Nik knelt and fumbled through Finn's belongings to appear busy.

Finn smirked. "I suspect her to be somewhere close to Cecily."

At that, Nik sat up straight, a wooden dish clutched in his hand. "She must be older than that."

"A life like hers can add age when there aren't years to match. If we can get her off this island, she'll have a better chance. But I think we ought to let her go once we get to a safe village. We don't want her stuck with piracy if she has other options." Finn's gaze flickered up to meet mine.

Of course, he would use Josette to prove a point. He couldn't accept that he had forced nothing on me. My eyes narrowed. "Unless she doesn't *want* that…"

"How soon are we sailing?" Nikolaus interrupted, keeping his voice quiet. The subject change proved excellent medicine for my increasing heartbeat.

"I haven't announced the official word, but I hope within the hour. We can't risk lingering much longer." He shifted toward me, tugging his hat low to shade his face from view. "You're still certain of the ones you want to leave behind?"

I nodded when he turned back to me. My thoughts had never faltered in that area. The men on my list posed a substantial risk and a waste of our time on board.

"Then I will send them on an errand before I make the announcement." He stood ready to go on about his plans. "Just stay together, will you? No matter what."

"No matter what?" Nikolaus grabbed Finn's arm to keep him in place. "Why no matter what? We aren't doing anything. And why am I always stuck with her?"

"I keep better track of you when you're together." Finn shrugged, then must have thought of a better explanation. "And I need you watching each other's backs."

Nikolaus turned up his nose. "I can take care of myself, though. You taught me how to use a sword. I wouldn't mind the chance to try it out sometime."

"I taught you to defend yourself. Don't go looking for trouble, understood? Don't be like *her*." Finn nodded at me, then tightened the strap of his baldric, his mouth tight.

"Again. I am still here," I said.

Nik rolled his eyes in one of the most dramatic fashions I'd ever seen.

Finn brushed past us to avoid answering any more questions. Nik and I returned to our area to clean and pack up for the journey, while the others tended to their own tasks. As I examined the crew and mentally counted each body, something didn't add up. Several of our men had vanished. Truthfully, I'd hoped those missing might disappear at some point anyway, but not yet...

"What's wrong?" Nikolaus moved to my side, trying to follow my focus.

"I don't see Cantrill and his men." I searched out Stevens next, hoping he might hold some answers, but he worked with Josette on the shoreline, loading the boats with supplies.

"Maybe Finn already sent them on?" Nik asked.

"I don't think so. He wouldn't allow them on his ship alone." I squinted to search the crew once more. "Long isn't here either."

Nik held his hand to his brow to block out the early morning glare, but came up empty on his search as well.

"I'm going to have a look around, all right? I'll be back," I said.

"I'll go with you." He dropped his satchel into the sand again.

I shook my head. "No, I don't think that's such a good idea this time."

"But Finn said—"

"You didn't seem to care what Finn said mere minutes ago." I shot him an accusatory look, which he returned in his own way. "Besides, if Finn knew what I was going to do, he'd want you to stay here, too."

"Something tells me if Finn knew what you were going to do, he'd want *you* to stay here." Nik folded his arms across his chest and shifted his weight to one side. He had a point, albeit one I intended to ignore.

I patted down the sides of my trousers to ensure I had my knives. "And this way, only I will get in trouble, and you are in the clear."

"You're impossible." Nik grabbed his sack up once again.

"I'll be right back. If you need something, talk to Stevens. I'm pretty sure he knows who you are, and he'll keep you safe if anything happens while I'm gone."

Nikolaus's eyes grew wide. "Wait. What have you told him?"

"I didn't tell him anything. He figured it—oh, it doesn't matter. I'll explain it all later. Just stay here and keep watch in case they return."

With that, I ran along the tree line toward the side of the beach where Cantrill had camped. Often, I would stop to listen closely within the jungle and keep my eyes wide open in case anything appeared through the trees. But all remained quiet, which wasn't entirely reassuring.

Not until I'd decided to head back to camp did the movement catch my eye. Where the trees met the sandy beach, figures shifted, and I situated myself as close to the action as I could without being seen.

There, gathered together in the sand, stood Cantrill, Norris, and Dull. Before them, Long's arms flailed as he spoke in his usual gruff murmur. When had he joined the likes of them? He may be a beast of a man, but he'd never struck me as mutinous. My reasons for abandoning him were entirely different from my reasons for ridding ourselves of the other three.

The mutinous trio spoke at once, their gestures appearing rather aggressive, voices rising and falling as if they wanted to be quiet, but their tempers wouldn't allow such a thing. I sunk to my knees, using the tree's trunk to hide my body, and slipped into the overgrown weeds beside it for a better view.

Cantrill did most of the talking, or arguing, as it was. Long shook his head more violently as he went on. Suddenly, he stopped flailing and went still as he regarded his company. He took a single step backward, his knee twisting in a way that made me think he meant to flee the scene.

The other four men laughed together. Then Norris shrugged and flipped a dagger up into his hands, lunging forward until the blade crushed through Long's chest. My hands flew to my mouth to stifle a scream, and I sank lower to the jungle floor, unable to hold myself upright.

Before me, the men didn't stop chuckling after the kill. I was right not to trust them, yet it didn't make it any easier to watch them at work. They took Long's life as if he'd been nothing more than a pesky fly on their boot.

Together, they dug a hole with their bare hands then shoved the lifeless body of our former first mate in, kicking sand back into place over him. With the tide coming in, it wouldn't be long before the ocean claimed the offering for Davy Jones.

Their chatter continued as they turned to leave the sight of the gruesome murder. I remained in place, paralyzed with fear. I could hear them clearly now, as they sauntered guiltlessly along the edge of the trees.

"No time like the present," Norris said.

Cantrill grunted in agreement. "We're on borrowed time. Has to be now or never. Long's disappearance won't go unnoticed this close to sail."

The irony pierced through me. I'd hoped they'd all disappear before sail. Sending the men into the village on an errand without telling them had become the usual standard for ditching the crewmembers we didn't want to keep. What errand could occupy a band of murderous brutes?

"What about the map? Won't get any farther without that."

Norris's deep, guttural voice made my throat hurt every time I heard him speak.

A loud smack indicated that someone must have gotten cracked upside the head. "That's 'cause we didn't find the girl, you idiot."

"How do we know Hastings story isn't a total lie? She wasn't too eager to join us in our search," Dull mumbled.

I held my breath at the mention of my name.

It was Cantrill who spoke again. "She's loyal to Worley. I promise you that. Should have killed her with Long."

The others laughed; my stomach roiled.

Dull's voice broke through the chortling. "Might want to be sure about the girl with the map first before we kill the only person with the story."

"Dull, you daft imbecile! She probably *is* the girl. You've seen the way Worley looks at her," Cantrill growled. "She told that story to throw us off the trail."

"If not, I bet the cabin boy would know something. He's always at the captain's side," Norris offered.

My heart turned to dust inside me.

"You know how Worley protects him. How *similar* they look," Norris continued.

I couldn't breathe the thick air anymore. Had they figured it out the way Stevens had? Nikolaus resembled Finn more each day. Their relation couldn't remain hidden forever.

"Kill Hastings and take the boy." Cantrill said aloud as if to test the idea. "But we have to make sure Hastings's story holds first, find out if she's his map."

Norris grunted his agreement. "There's no time to be sure. The captain will be here soon enough. If we've got nothin' to show for this, then we're dead men, too."

"Captain didn't make this one easy on us, did he?" Dull laughed like they shared drinks in a tavern rather than spilled blood on the beach. "Be easier if we could make Worley show us the treasure himself."

Cantrill scoffed. "And set the whole crew against us before the others arrive? We need to be quick."

Others. Bile burned the back of my throat. They wanted Nikolaus and me, both of our lives on the line for the sake of this invisible treasure. And what other captain did they refer to? As if we didn't share the same one?

Trembling overcame the nausea, and I lay there in my jungle bed, wishing we'd never come to this island. We'd faced unknown dangers before our feet even hit the sand.

I had to warn him, had to get to Nikolaus, so he knew, too. He needed to get away, to hide until we figured something out. But the villains had started their trek back to camp, their voices fading into the jungle. My only chance was to beat them there.

With legs wobbling like a bowl of cream, I willed strength to return and carry me the rest of the way. I burst from the jungle in a frantic search, trying to ensure I'd made it back before them. I had, but only just barely. I could hear them in the near distance as they came up from the beach.

Finn and Nikolaus stood together near a longboat, making last-minute preparations to set sail. But I'd never make it across the shore to warn them in time. If I could intercept the villains, lead them off on the chase, the others could load the ship and be gone before they figured out what I'd done.

At least, it'd get Finn and Nik off this island...

It was my only chance to save their lives.

Josette caught sight of me, her head bobbing as her gaze traveled up and down my frame. "What's with you? You're pasty as cotton."

"Josette," I huffed and drew her even closer. "I need you to help me."

She took my arm, panic seeming to root deeply in her at the realization that something was definitely, very wrong.

"The captain's in danger. Stay on his side, no matter what happens today," I said.

"What's going on? Why is the captain in danger?" She took a small step back. Would she run and report my hysteria to Finn?

She stilled and waited.

"I have a plan." I could only issue short bursts of my thoughts before breathlessness and fear redirected me. "It's my worst one ever." Tearless sobs racked my shoulders, and I dropped my face into my hands to regroup. "But it's all I have. Just stay with him. Protect him. *Please*."

"Yes." She shook her head, as if the information refused to seep into her mind. "I'll stay with him. But what are you—"

"Please," I begged again. "If he asks, tell him I'm already on the ship."

She nodded once more, and I ran off to join the enemy.

SEVENTEEN

THE OCEAN BREEZE BLEW STEADILY, FORCING ITS WAY INTO MY lungs. Thank God, because I couldn't breathe on my own. I wasn't even sure my heart had beaten since I walked away from Josette. Though, if I dropped dead on the spot, it might actually help our situation.

Cantrill's grin widened when I approached. "Ah, Miss Hastings. We were just talking about you."

I forced a smile of my own, though my lips stuck awkwardly to my teeth with the sudden dry-mouth that joined the multitude of other symptoms I'd acquired.

"You were? I'd ask about the nature of your conversation, but it must have been all good, judging by your jovial manner." Every word felt like poison. These men wanted me dead, and I spoke to them as friends.

"Of course." When he held out his arms, the other men encircled me to block my path back to the rest of the crew.

"I..." They gave me no chance to act my part. These brutes had one objective, and nothing I said or did could come between them and their goal.

Their fingers fluttered over the weapons on their belts. It would be complete foolishness to pull them out now in front of the other men that *did* support Finn, but the thought of it made it difficult to focus on my task. I hadn't felt fear like this since the Royal Navy overtook the *Hellbound* and claimed Finn for their trophy. This ending would not be the same.

I stood straighter, lifting my chin to face Cantrill straight on. "Did you boys have any luck in the village? Did you find the girl?"

"It's funny you would ask such a thing." Cantrill stepped forward, his finger pointed to my face in amused accusation. "We meant to ask you something similar."

"We're not so sure there *is* a girl, really." A waxy-looking face leaned in from the side: Dull.

"No? That's unfortunate." My muscles twitched under my skin as I used every ounce of my energy to hold still in their presence.

Cantrill paced in a full circle around me. "Is it? We followed Captain Worley all day yesterday and never once saw him with a girl. Sure, there were some fine wenches at the tavern, but he hardly seemed interested in a single one of 'em."

"Very unusual for a captain long at sea..." The tallest of the group, Norris, chuckled with a deep, throaty sound that fit his dark, hairy exterior and crooked nose.

"Indeed." I took a deep breath I hoped gave the appearance of profound thought, when really I just needed it to keep me from passing out. We couldn't linger here. If Finn caught sight of me surrounded by these men, he wouldn't hesitate to intervene. "Why do you think you didn't find her?"

"Perhaps we could take a walk on the beach, and you can enlighten us." Cantrill opened his palm to show the way he wished me to go.

A sweaty, tattooed hand coiled around my shoulder, attempting to guide me toward the shore. I shrugged enough to break the grasp. They didn't need to push me. I was willing to go with them.

"It's odd, isn't it? That his first visit ashore wouldn't be to his girl." I moved in the direction of the jungle, ready to run. As long as my lungs held up, I could take these men far away, maybe even hide.

Maybe I didn't have to die if my legs brought me enough strength.

"The girl isn't our concern anymore. We want to speak with *you,* Miss Hastings." Cantrill nodded toward the ocean, probably imagining me buried next to Long in the sand.

I shivered, despite the blazing tropical sun beating down on us, and took a few more steps. The men moved together before me to ensure I couldn't get any farther away.

"Then I think the girl remains your primary concern." I waited for my words to have an impact, though the men only paused with baffled expressions and a hint of annoyance. I continued, "I told you we wanted the same things, and that is why I vowed to assist you if you gave me a cut of the treasure. I didn't spend the last few weeks on a rotting ship with a band of sweaty pirates just to go back and do it all over again. I want that gold, and I want to be done with this wretched crew."

Cantrill's eyes were mere slits as he glared at me. "Your lies mean nothing to us anymore."

I approached him, close enough to his face that he might feel the power of my breath. Energy surged through me when the first bit of confidence in my plan surfaced. It was still stupid and reckless. As usual. But Finn had commanded Nik and me to keep each other safe. I planned to do my part.

"As I'm sure you've guessed, I am that girl," I said.

Hope flickered amongst them, and they muttered questions to one another, as if I weren't able to hear every word.

"But he mentioned nothing about a girl," Dull said offhandedly.

"Maybe the captain didn't know." Cantrill at least turned his body away from me, though it was of no help to his cause. "But he'll certainly be pleased to hear it."

135

"Could be another one of her lies, too." Norris, with his crooked nose and furry face, growled under his breath.

The gold ring in Cantrill's nostril flared, and he turned back to me. "Forgive me, milady, but I'm having some trouble believing that a captain as famous as Worley would have chosen a scrawny little girl like you as his mate. No offense, of course."

His wicked grin made the insult plunge deeper inside me. In truth, I'd wondered the same thing recently. Why *had* Finn chosen me? He meant to leave me in Barbados on our first journey here, but I wanted to stay with him. In fact, he'd brought this matter up more often than ever before...

Tears burned in the back of my eyes, but I willed them away. "What proof do you need? I am who I say I am. I'll lead you to the treasure *now*."

"Suppose you *are* his wench, and we take you with us. The captain isn't just going to let some rogue shipmates run off with his lady fair, now, is he?" Cantrill glanced down the beach to where our crew loaded the longboats. I could only assume our meeting continued to go unnoticed by the busy captain. "And suppose you're *not* who you say you are, and you can't help us find the gold..." He pulled a dagger from his belt and let his fingers run the length of the weapon. "We really need that treasure, love."

And I really wished I could give it to him. If I had the location of any amount of gold, I would hand it over so they would leave us once and for all. But I had nothing. All I could hope for was that my wild hunt would keep them away from Nikolaus and Finn and give the rest of the crew a chance to get off the island before Blackbeard also appeared to wage another war...

Heaven above. Why hadn't I put it together before?

"Blackbeard's your captain," I whispered.

A low laugh rippled around the small ring of men.

"Right you are, miss," Cantrill hissed.

A familiar howl hung in the air, and all at once, the clamor of swords and battle cries echoed across the camp. I almost forgot about the immediate threat on my life when I watched the newly hired crew surround Finn and Nik.

I screamed until Dull covered my mouth with his waxen hand. The greasy side of his face met my cheek, and he lifted me from the ground, walking me toward the center of camp. His cold dagger rested on my throat, but still I screamed into his hand and kicked, refusing to walk on my own will.

A battle ensued, those loyal to Finn taking up arms. We outnumbered them, but they still immobilized Nik and Finn at the center with a ring of pistols, their swords taken. The butts of heavy guns hammered into their backs to force them to their knees.

The ring of men opened to let us pass through, and Dull forced me to the ground in front of my captain. Dull kept his hold, sinking to the ground with me, leaving no space between our bodies.

"You're in luck, Captain Worley." Cantrill ran his fingers over the pistol in his hands. "We're not allowed to kill you."

"You're with Teach." Finn's focus remained toward the ground, his voice strong and full of hatred.

Cantrill clapped his hands together—slowly. "You know, your lady friend here just came to the same conclusion." When he paused beside me, he took hold of my chin to force my gaze and winked. Dull pressed the blade harder to my throat to keep me from retaliating.

Finn's eyes lit with all the fire of hell when he raised his head. "You take your hands—"

"There's no point, Worley. You've lost any power you once had over us, but no matter. We won't be staying long." Cantrill waved his arms around their circle to make a display of their control. "We'll need a little more, shall we say, leverage before we leave, however. For starters, we're taking the girl. But we'll have the boy, as well."

Cantrill clutched Nikolaus's arm and yanked him to his feet, Nik making no attempt to escape the grasp. His body moved like clay under their direction. Finn bit into his lip as he stared at the sand.

Dull followed Cantrill's lead and pulled me up, but I stomped hard enough onto his foot he released my mouth, only for a moment.

"Not him!" I screamed and fought the hands that held me. I couldn't let them take Nikolaus, couldn't leave Finn to die at Blackbeard's hand. None of us could stand on our own against such a force. I never meant for any of it to get this far.

Dull struggled to regain his grasp, but Norris was quick to lend a hand. He cracked me across the face, stars commanding my vision. I sank to the earth, making it easier for them to bind my hands behind my back. My ears throbbed, and everything seemed so far away now, as if I watched it from behind a thick shroud.

Someone yelled my name. Nikolaus, or Finn perhaps. They sounded so similar these days.

The pirates bound Nick's hands. Finn faded into the distance as we moved away, his head sinking low on his slumped shoulders at the center of the ring, unable to follow.

My plan had failed. I couldn't save any of them.

We all belonged to Blackbeard now.

EIGHTEEN

THE JUNGLE FLOOR BIT AT MY LEGS WHEN THEY DRAGGED ME over fallen vines and splintered logs. A numbing ache enveloped my arm where Dull held me and directed my every movement like I was his puppet. Above us, birds sang a haunting lullaby in the trees. They didn't know the danger that lurked below them. They watched a death march, and still they mocked us with a song.

At some point, I nodded in a direction for them to go. I hardly remembered doing such a thing, but I had to keep them moving. The longer I stalled, the longer Nikolaus and I might live. Once they realized there was no treasure that was it for us.

"Where to now, girl?" Cantrill hacked away at the overgrown leaves in front of us with his hatchet. There was a spring in his step that made me wish he'd slip and fall on his own blade.

"Keep to this course," I choked. A lump the size of a grapefruit lingered in my throat that kept any other instruction captive.

This next set of directions proved sufficient for the time being. I made quick glances toward Nikolaus to ensure his safety, which seemed stupid, considering we were anything but safe.

Nik met my gaze often. At first, I would look away immediately when he did so, too ashamed of how badly this plan had failed. But the longer we walked, the more I wanted to keep the contact. God only knew what he must think of me now, leading rogue pirates on a nonsensical mission. He showed no judgment in his eyes.

Sweat trickled down my temples as we marched on until the noonday sun beamed high above our heads. Cantrill broke our trek and gave the order to find food. Norris took to tying Nikolaus and I to a large tree, while the others issued vulgar warnings they would make good on if either of us tried to escape.

Nik's steady breath beside me brought the faintest hint of comfort, though it caused the sobs to shake my body all over again when my thoughts got the best of me.

"What'll happen to him?" I whispered. A million suspicions swirled around in my head, all violent, horrible things. "I'm so sorry, Nik."

"Sorry for what?" His voice came out flat, emotionless.

I strained to see his face. Was he serious?

"Sorry for *everything*. I didn't mean for them to come for you. I thought—" I gasped for air between the suffocating sobs. I'd stopped shedding actual tears miles ago. "I thought they'd only need me and leave the two of you alone."

"So, another 'Cecily plan' that went swimmingly, eh?" He lowered his head to hide the smirk that appeared on his lips.

"Aren't you scared?" Something was definitely wrong. Nikolaus had gone mad. The island heat and chaos of our lives had finally caught up with him. Nothing else could explain it.

Nik took in a deep breath as if to say more, but the others had returned, cutting him off. Cantrill led the group, their ever-present sneers growing my hate for them by the minute.

"We were just talking." Cantrill rubbed his hands together. "Kind of a nuisance dragging the two of you around the steamin' jungle. Slows our pace, too." He cocked the pistol in his hand and held it out for us to see. "We figured, between the two of you, one of you would have the map to the treasure. And since our Miss Hastings seems to be the one to pull through for us..." He aimed the gun at Nikolaus.

Ice propelled through my entire body, air sucked from my lungs. I wiggled against the tree, the ropes keeping me from moving into the path of the gun. A contrasting fire lit in my chest, and I wanted to scream, to rip free of those ropes and spread that fire until everything around me erupted in flames.

"Stop!" My shriek caused the birds to cease their songs. "I didn't tell you *everything*."

Cantrill didn't put his gun down, but his attention, along with the others', shifted to me.

"Yes, I lied about the woman being in the village, but I didn't lie about my relationship with..." I searched frantically for what to call him "...Captain Worley. And you've obviously guessed who Nikolaus is. If the captain trusted me with the map, don't you think he trusted Nikolaus, as well?"

"Precisely." Cantrill shrugged. "Which is why we only need one of you."

"He has gone to great lengths to protect us. You really think he'd let us know every detail of his treasure if it would make one of us disposable?" It came out before I fully thought through it, though it definitely sounded like something Finn would do.

Cantrill twirled the pistol in his hand, bringing it back to its upright position. "What is that supposed to mean?"

"He didn't tell me the entire route. Maybe he told Nikolaus more than he's told me." I nodded in Nik's direction, silently praying he'd play along with my new ridiculous plan.

When Cantrill regarded our cabin boy, Nik met him with narrowed eyes.

"There's a reason he always made us stay together," Nik agreed.

It took immense willpower to keep my jaw from dropping. He'd made an excellent, and true, point—one they couldn't possibly counter. These men had always seen Nik and me together when Finn gave orders.

Cantrill's head rolled back on his shoulders, his frustration with our scheme evident. "Prove it."

"We head east until we come to the river. Follow the river inland until it meets the rock formation," Nikolaus said, matter-of-factly.

My head turned slowly in his direction. He'd never gone along with my plans so easily. Yet, this time, he had the next step in it covered before I'd even thought it up.

"It's not an easy journey. Especially at night. Might not want to linger." Nikolaus glared hard at Cantrill, watching as the gun lowered in the man's hand.

"Convenient for you to know the path now that your life depends on it," Norris growled behind his leader.

Nik's shoulders crashed against the tree trunk, but he kept his chin raised. "Well, it's the truth. Cecily doesn't know the rest of the way."

"Nik," I breathed.

Cantrill laughed in his gruff manner and readjusted his pistol in my direction. While *my* plan saved him, Nik had handed me over to Death.

"I wouldn't do that." Nik's tone took on more authority than it had moments ago. "She does, however, know how to get inside, past the booby traps and all. Finn never told me that part, unfortunately."

What? As if I was some human key to this invisible fortune? Why did he speak so surely of himself?

My head spun.

Cantrill released an audible sigh and slipped his pistol into its holster. "Your captain digs at my nerves. I look forward to repaying him when we meet again."

He looked to Dull and nodded. Dull untied our ropes and pulled us to our feet.

"Move." He dug an elbow into my back that sent me stumbling forward.

On my hands and knees, I searched the men to meet Nik's gaze. He offered a quick, crooked grin before the others could notice, and his chest sunk when he exhaled. He probably hadn't expected to see the end of that one either.

I marched along with their ushering, sweat beading on my brow like oil over water—water being something I wanted desperately at that point in the trip. It wasn't long before I heard a steady roar ahead of us, and my tired pace quickened. The others picked up to a run, with Nikolaus and I dragged close behind.

There, just like Nikolaus had said, a small river coursed through the island, waters rushing from one end to the other. We fell to our knees before it and lapped it up in noisy, desperate gulps. I longed to give into the powerful current, let the eager waters carry me away toward the sea, leaving my worries behind.

"And we follow the river inland?" Norris asked between gulps. It was perhaps the nicest inquiry I'd heard any of them make.

"Until the rock formation?" Dull added. His skin glistened from the water he'd flung onto his face, making his complexion appear as fresh clay. How had the midday sun not melted him into a slimy puddle?

Nikolaus nodded, watching as their intentions reappeared with the presentation of their weapons. "Good luck navigating the maze."

"What maze?" Cantrill stepped forward, and I sucked in a breath, afraid all over again for his life.

"The rock formation." Nikolaus's voice sounded solid and confident. Somehow, he continued to channel all his fear into raw power. "I can get you to the first marker, but she's the one that knows the entrance. Finnigan's a bit of an ass when it comes to sharing details. Even with me."

As I watched him, I questioned the truth in it. Did I even know these brothers at all? Nikolaus presented himself as a wild card in this adventure. I couldn't trust this band of pirates, but maybe I couldn't fully trust Nik either.

Cantrill lowered his gun and swore. They all longed for the entertainment of bloodshed before the sun went down for the day. A fact that made my stomach more than a little queasy. But Nikolaus had bought us a little more time—time I wanted to use for planning a way out of this mess, even though it seemed a hopeless endeavor.

Dull sauntered into position behind me, and I waited for him to shove me onward. Instead, he lingered. His wet shirt tickled along my exposed collar, his breath hot along my earlobe.

"Lucky little girl," he whispered and slammed the heel of his hand between my shoulder blades.

NINETEEN

Just before nightfall, the brutish bunch stopped to make torches so we might continue on in the dark. Nikolaus's face bore the swollen redness of their eager questioning, despite the amount of assurance he gave that we were on the right track. Even I believed him, and I still had my doubts about the existence of the treasure we sought. But he stuck with his given instructions, leading us alongside the river no matter how many times they hit him for clarity.

I limped along behind him. My shrieks did nothing to stop any of their attacks, bound hands preventing me from blocking them. Dull held tightly to me. His scorching laugh sent the tendrils of my hair curling up against my neck like frightened snakes. If I stopped moving, his hand found the tender spot on my back, and he'd shove me along. By now, it felt as if my ribs would break free of my skin at any moment with the forceful touch. Even walking had become more difficult with every step. Would this wretched night ever end?

"For the last time." Nikolaus spat out a mouthful of blood. "We're almost there."

"And it's nightfall, boy. *Almost* isn't good enough." Norris raised his hand high to draw another blow.

"What do you expect of him?" I cried out in hysteria. My side spasmed with the force of my scream. I couldn't take it if they hit him again. Nik's eye had swollen shut. "He's telling the truth."

"Stow that, Cecily." Nikolaus knew what I was doing, but if he meant to use this situation as another way to prove his strength, I was done with it.

"If he says we're almost there, then I suggest you shut your rotting trap and walk," I growled.

Dull's hand found his favorite place on my back, wrenching upward in a new direction that sent me to my knees. I gasped for air, but his foot hit me hard in the stomach, flattening my body further against the ground.

"Don't put up much of a fight, do you, deary?" Cantrill raised a thin brow in my direction.

Dull grabbed my arms and tugged me to my feet before clutching hold of my chin and commanding my attention to him. "Let's hope your precious captain puts on a better show."

There was no air to breathe. What did they do to Finn back on shore? Surely, Blackbeard had arrived by now, but did his need for revenge run so deeply? His only aim was to crush his enemy, obliterate the man that had slighted him in Ireland. Finn had to be outnumbered tenfold by this point. I hadn't allowed myself to think such things to any length of unbearable detail. I couldn't let these men plant those images in my mind.

I cocked my head and spit with as much force as I could. Dull stepped back in disgust to wipe his face clean. The guttural snarl that followed let me know he wouldn't tolerate such an offense, and I could barely hear Nikolaus protesting behind him.

"It's there," Norris shouted as he ran through the trees and rejoined our group, breathless. "It's there. It's right up ahead. The rock formation."

"I bloody told you." Nikolaus's voice cracked.

Dull turned toward his companion, Norris's reappearance saving me from whatever heinous punishment he'd had in mind. For now.

"What are we waiting for?" Cantrill smiled, his teeth glowing by the light of his torch.

Dull took hold of me again to march onward, his sticky hands like paste around my arms. My staggered footsteps carried me along, inching myself closer to Nikolaus held captive in Norris's grasp. As wretched as these rats were, I loathed the thought of meeting the man that had control over *them*.

The blaze of the torches, just three, dimmed as shadows rose around our small group, followed by relieved sighs and expressions of awe. We'd made it to the rock formation, a sight more magnificent than I could have imagined. Less than mountains but greater than the boulders surrounding my cave pool, the rock grouping seemed to weave endlessly as far as I could see. Nik had been right about its location.

Was he right about what lay at the center of the maze, too?

A strange puff of air caught my cheek, and I broke my mesmerized stare to see Nikolaus at my side. With his bound hands, he'd chosen to blow on me to get my attention. Strange, but effective. His urgent expression kept me from dwelling on the manner of his actions.

When his head twitched toward the rocks, I remembered what he'd told the others: *I knew the directions from here.* I went rigid in Dull's grasp. How could I make up the entrance to a cave I didn't know existed?

"Looks like we're in need of further instruction." Cantrill hadn't lost his wicked grin. Instead, it seemed to have grown with the anticipation.

Everyone shifted to face me. They hadn't forgotten Nikolaus's claim as I had. I cleared my throat, still tight from the shrieks and swelling of moments past. When I looked to Cantrill, I caught the slightest movement out of the corner of my eye. Nikolaus had turned his back to me, his bound hands wiggling enough to catch my attention. His fingers appeared to be moving in a pattern.

Forward, right, left, right.

I paused a moment, keeping my examination of his movements as unnoticeable as possible until I was certain he repeated the same pattern.

Forward, right, left, right.

He had been here before. Multiple times if he held this level of surety. This had to be the place—all the trouble Finn had found himself in, the money he'd taken from Blackbeard. All of it was real. All of it was just up ahead.

I swallowed hard and tried to play along. "This way, *gentleman.*"

Where I expected some opposition, they followed in utter silence. Cantrill even hustled to my side with his torch to light the way. His hands never touched me, which allowed me full access to the maze that rose up around us. All the answers I'd hunted for waited just around the corner. And most likely, so did death.

The giants surrounding us unsettled me in all fresh ways. If my luck proved true, we'd make it this far alive only to have these giant boulders crush us moments before arriving at our destination. Well, that actually sounded more pleasant than torture at the hands of these brutes if we made it through this phase. Still, I hated to think what might lurk in such a place, not quite a tunnel and only barely open to the sky. We wandered downward, straight into the pits of hell.

My pace remained slow because of the constant spasms in my back that kept me from getting ahead too quickly. It'd also prevent any runaway attempts, too, I figured.

A large rock blocked the path, and I thought of Nikolaus behind me.

Forward, right, left, right.

We needed to go right. I led them in the new direction, each step growing my anxiety.

Another fork in the path stopped us. I directed the group to the left. No one questioned me, an eerie silence overtaking the group. The pirates neared their desired finish line, while Nikolaus and I awaited one of our own.

My body grew heavy, and I leaned against the rocks as I moved, unconcerned about the rough scratching that accompanied each step. It was just nice to feel something, find distraction from the total agony of everything else life had delivered in the past few days.

"Circle around that rock," Nikolaus muttered from behind me after the last right turn I'd guided the group through.

No one responded, only followed the instruction. His quick instructions indicated an end to the arduous journey. And there, just around the large boulder, was the mouth of a cave: small, but sufficiently sized for a human to fit through with ease. I turned behind me to examine Nikolaus. He really had known all along. The questions whirled in my head with no chance to ask a single one.

The others erupted in a joyous, and possibly relieved, cry. I took a step back toward Nikolaus. He looked up at me through his tumbled mess of hair, eyebrows raised in what seemed like expectation. Our captors' presence kept me from yelling or inquiring, but he seemed to understand from the look on my face all I wanted to say. He simply shrugged, his mouth twitching into a quick half smile.

Even after all of this, the pompous little ass still maintained satisfaction in successfully keeping secrets from me. What was wrong with him?

"This it, boy?" Norris grabbed Nikolaus hard by the arms, lifting him off the ground with his powerful grip.

"Of course, it is," Nikolaus deadpanned.

Norris's guttural laugh shook his whole body, his mouth opening wide enough to pull in his surroundings as he dropped Nikolaus. Nik lost his footing and crumpled to his knees. The hatred in his one good eye aimed directly at Norris. I, too, didn't think I'd ever been so disgusted by anyone else on earth, and I'd been raised by Mr. Collins.

"How about you lead the way, lad? Since you're supposedly aware of booby traps." Norris spun Nikolaus around and removed his dagger from his belt, slicing the rope around the boy's wrists. Nikolaus barely had time to shake out his pained hands before Norris thrust the torch into his palm and pushed him to the front of the group.

"Take her with you." Cantrill laughed and shoved me into Nikolaus's chest. He caught me with his free arm so I wouldn't stumble with my hands still bound. My side exploded in pain all over again, and I pressed my forehead to Nik's shoulder to hide my wince from the others' view.

"Better to have two bodies for shield than only one." Dull laughed.

This was it. If we went into this cave, there was no coming out. And what of these booby traps? Nothing about that sounded pleasant in the least bit. We were bait, tied and served on a platter.

"Come on," Nik said to me more than anyone else. I looked up at him, and he murmured more quietly than before, "Follow my step, and you'll be all right."

His unexcited manner didn't help my already racked nerves. Some situations required panic, and this seemed to fit all the requirements of that. Still, he stared into the darkness ahead of him, and I followed with no other choice. Anxious, villainous giggling spurred me on from behind.

I stepped over some jagged rocks, careful to keep my balance and walk in precisely the same places as Nik. The gentle trickle of water that leaked in from the cave walls didn't help me much by covering the stone and mud floor in an oily sheet.

"What's this?" Norris grabbed Nikolaus's arm to keep him from walking any farther and bent down at his side. Nik knelt with him when Norris dragged him down to use the torch light.

Nik didn't fight it, keeping even closer to the swine than he needed to.

When Norris extended the light out in front of him, a flicker caught my eye, too. He held something in his outstretched hand: a golden coin. His deep, crazed laugh returned as he flicked the coin back to his companions for examination.

"Looks like we're on our way, boys," Cantrill hissed.

My gaze flashed back to Nikolaus. All this time, he'd known about this treasure, he and Finn. Neither had trusted me with this, even after living with them for the past year. There really was no end to the lies.

Nikolaus started moving again with no prompting, and I scurried behind to keep up with his light. If Nikolaus knew this place, at least he would know the safest route through it.

"Bloody..." Cantrill brushed past me, yanking Nikolaus's torch out of his hands so he held two instead of just one. He lifted the lights high to illuminate the open space we'd found ourselves in: the belly of the cave.

There, in the wide cavern, were piles of gold, gemstones, and chests of all shapes and sizes. I took a step out of the way, hearing the clink underfoot, only to realize I stood on a carpet of silver coinage. I'd never seen finer things in all my life. It was magnificent, breathtaking, and still rather infuriating to behold.

"You knew about this?" I whispered when Nikolaus moved to my side.

The others erupted in victorious cheers. Norris had fallen to his knees, scooping up handfuls of gold and letting them trickle down his outstretched arms. Dull and Cantrill walked dazedly through the room, as if unsure of what they wanted to touch next.

"I did," Nikolaus said.

"But why... I mean, how..." My mind had stopped working properly to form a solid thought.

"How do you think Finn could afford a crew? It's not like he plunders his wealth from other ships." His voice wasn't as hushed as before, though the others remained too engrossed in the discovery to even look our way. "I don't think now is really the time to discuss this, do you?"

"No. A year ago was a much better time." My fists clenched behind my back.

"Whatever. Just hold still." He slowly inched closer to me, careful not to make any sudden, obvious movements. There was no time to ask what he was doing. The cold blade slipping between my palms answered my question. In a quick twitch, the ropes fell away from my hands and dropped onto the bed of coins at our feet.

"Where did you—"

"Got it off Norris's belt." Nik nodded toward the corner of the room, and I tried to keep up with his ever-changing thoughts. "Weapons. We've got to get to them."

"You mean to fight?" My voice was barely audible.

"Well, yeah. You have a better idea?" he asked.

I had nothing. Nothing at all. I shook my head.

"If you want, you can just get a hold of one of those torches and do what you usually do, Fire Wench." Nik's confidence remained as strong as it had throughout the wretched trek.

I rolled my eyes. "That happened one time. Stop calling me that."

Could he seriously be mocking me in a situation like this? There was so much going on—so many bad things.

"Cecily." His hand encircled my arm in the gentlest way he'd ever touched me. It stopped my every thought in its tracks. "It'll be all right."

I never wanted to believe anything more.

TWENTY

THE CHIMES OF TOUSLED GOLD GREW DEAFENINGLY LOUD inside the cavern, the sharp cries of laughter adding to its echo. Through all of it, I could still hear the faint trickle of water dripping from the sides of the rock walls and the speedy thump of my heartbeat drumming in my ear. My senses had sparked to life, and I followed Nikolaus, one half step at a time.

At first, it seemed as if we hadn't moved at all, but we needed to remain steady and calculated no matter how slight our progress. If the others spotted us before we got to the weapons chest on the other side of the room, we lost all hope. They wouldn't be able to hear us, even if we knocked over a rather expensive looking platter of sorts—which I very nearly did in my trembling state. But our presence in the chamber couldn't go unnoticed forever.

"Do you want a sword or a gun?" Nikolaus whispered to me as we approached our target. I merely stared at him in response. I couldn't swing a sword and actually do any damage. I *might* be able to fire a pistol, but there was no guarantee I'd hit anything. Besides, in this cave, the gunpowder would be too damp to fire if I could get it to work in the first place.

We would die for sure.

He pinched the bridge of his swollen nose, which had to hurt, and mumbled something in Finish. "Just look for knives. Or better yet, stay behind me and keep quiet."

"I am not staying behind you." My voice was as close to a scream as one could manage in a whisper.

"I know how to use a sword. You don't. If we're going to beat these pirates, we have to act like pirates. And you're more of a..."

"A what, exactly?"

"A not-pirate. We don't have time for this." He took hold of my forearm once again and guided me along beside him down the wall, the icy water like prickly quills against my backside.

"A not-pirate? Seriously?"

Nik paid me no mind.

Soundlessly, he plucked a sword from inside a tall urn and began rummaging through another chest. I assumed the part of lookout, an easy task since the pirates had illuminated themselves with torchlight. Though, if they realized what we did and attacked, we stood no chance from this short distance away.

"I love this place," Nikolaus muttered.

I leaned in closer to hear him; the comment seeming as odd as his every other action in recent hours. "The weapons?"

"*So* many weapons." He shifted against the ground, his hand flying into my stomach to deliver something wrapped in cloth. I knew the feel before I even finished removing the layers: knives.

I smiled for the first time in as long as I could remember—until Nikolaus's elbow caught me in the arm again and wiped the grin clean away. The others had begun restlessly moving about, their fretful voices mumbled together until it became clear they had remembered their captives.

And we weren't exactly where they left us.

"Take this, too." Nikolaus shoved a pistol into my hand. But he hadn't given me any powder, ammunition, *anything*. I couldn't even count on it working after sitting in a damp cave for who knew how long.

Dull had just made his way to the exit in search of us when Cantrill's ugly stare fell in our direction. "There they are!"

All the torches swiveled to our end of the cave.

Nikolaus darted away from me, running toward Cantrill with his sword in position, while Norris shouted with a deafening cry as he ran at me. I extended my pistol, hoping it might frighten him to a stop. When my attempt failed, I did the only thing I could think of: I threw it.

Norris's oversized body ducked, but not fast enough. He fumbled to catch the weapon against his chest, his obvious surprise making the feat impossible. The giant beast caught his oversized foot in a crevasse in the cavern floor, tripping him on his way toward me. I ducked out of the way and kicked on instinct, striking the side of his head as he fell. Blood pooled from his nose.

I scrambled backward, wedging myself between the stone wall and some oddly shaped statue. This had worked when Stevens and I fought Frans and Eggert. I had no choice but to try it again, even if I earned another stupid nickname that rivaled Fire Wench.

My feet pressed into the heavy stone, and I shoved with all my might, sending the statue toppling forward toward Norris. He tried to get out of the way, but the heavy stone pinned him to the ground, and a ghastly crack erupted from his legs. Norris shrieked and fainted away when he tried to sit upright again, but the gruesome sight didn't hold my attention for long.

The clanging of steel rang all around me, and I looked up to see Nikolaus swinging his sword through the air with a grace and agility I'd only witnessed from one other person: Finn. I'd never seen Nik fight, never hoped to be in a situation where I had to, but now that I knew what he could do...

I climbed over the rocky cave floor, tiptoeing toward Norris's limp frame to retrieve my knives from his belt without startling him back to consciousness. With double the amount of blades in my possession now, I grew more confident in contributing to our escape.

Across the room, Nikolaus fought Cantrill, the clamor almost hurting my ears with the echo inside the cave. Dull fought a battle of his own with pulling his gun from its holster, his hands still clinging to the golden trinket in his other hand. His attention flashed from the surrounding ruckus to the treasure in his palm and back again.

The opportunity was mine. I stood, ignoring the strain in my back, and threw the first of my daggers, putting a gash near his wrist. He stumbled backward, but didn't drop the gold, despite blood trickling down around it.

The moment I released the blade, my side split like it did every time Dull beat into my ribs. I slid to my knees, clutching the spasm around my middle. My knives clattered to the floor, but I couldn't let Dull get an edge over me.

I snatched up another blade in my left hand, held my breath and threw. Stars burst in front of my eyes. The knife barely reached my target, but sent him stumbling backward enough that he tripped on a rock and toppled the rest of the way back. The cavern rumbled around us, and Dull let out an ear-splitting scream.

He reached forward to grab onto something—anything. But it didn't matter. The ground gave way underneath his weight, and he vanished. Could that have been one of the booby traps the men all feared, or would this entire cave collapse at any moment?

Cantrill caught sight of the motion and spun around wildly, knocking Nik off his feet. I scrambled for the next knife when Cantrill turned toward me. He was our only obstacle left. His full sword would reach farther than I could hope to defend with the smaller blade. He charged and swung. I rolled, kicking out and barely missing his legs. He laughed at my struggle and raised his arm with a second attempt. My fingers fumbled with my blades. Knife throwing wouldn't do any good if I couldn't put some distance between us. My throbbing back seized and made sure I wouldn't be going anywhere too soon.

I held my breath and clenched my fists around my blades.

But Cantrill's sword never fell. He lurched forward, mouth falling open. At his middle, a blade split through his waistcoat, blood pooling around the wound. Nikolaus retracted the sword to let the skewered pirate fall into death.

"Nik," I gasped. "You killed—"

"Yeah." He wiped the blood from his blade on Cantrill's jacket.

"I didn't... I mean, you..."

He held out a hand for me to take and pulled me gently to my feet, the strain surrounding my spine pulsing as intensely as the shock I felt. He'd pushed me away at every turn, kept me at a distance in his irritation over my position on the *Hellbound*. Today, he saved my life by taking another.

"Finn always told me that there were some good things that can only come by way of the bad. I think saving my family falls under that category." He rubbed his torn sleeve across the beading sweat on his forehead, his sword still in the same hand.

Tears sprang to my eyes, returning in full force and unstoppable, as I slowly reached forward to wrap my arms around him. He didn't force me away this time. Instead, he let his head rest against mine, his shaky hands unsteady on my back. Everything seemed to crash over me like a wave of terror and relief mixed into one.

He'd saved me. My friend, my protector. My *brother*.

"Get yourself together," he whispered into my hair.

The sobs kept coming. "I can't."

"We have to go." He drew me back then and fastened his sword to his belt. "This isn't over."

We might have escaped danger, but maybe the rest of our crew... "Finn—"

"Yeah. Come on." Nikolaus walked past me. He didn't speak of what we both knew might have happened in our absence.

Our climb out of the cave took effort we didn't know we still had in us. Nikolaus's hands shook, his legs unsteady underneath him. The splintering pain in my back kept me hunched, unable to move at a steady pace, but together we made it out of the cave.

Night blanketed the sky. Without the torches for light, we had to feel our way through the large, stone structure. Birds yelped from their branches, setting us further on edge with every blast from their beaks. We clung to each other, as if some unseen force meant to take us away into the despair of our circumstance.

"How are we going to get anywhere at this hour?" I whispered more to myself than to my company.

"We can't. This end of the island is too dangerous. We'll have to wait for daybreak. Can't be far off now, though." His voice reflected the trembling of his body, broken at each word. "Let's find a place to rest until sunrise."

As he inched forward, I followed. The rock maze continued on forever, but we eventually discovered a ledge high enough to keep us safe and wide enough to fit both our bodies. With our last burst of energy, we climbed up the rocks and collapsed against the hard stone bed.

TWENTY-ONE

THE SUN WOKE US EARLY THAT MORNING, THE TRICKLING
sound of the nearby stream reminding us of our insatiable thirst. I
stretched my arms over my head to test my range of motion. The
spasm that shot between my shoulder blades sent me curling back
into a motionless ball.

Nikolaus turned to see me assessing my injury. "Are you good
to walk?"

"I'll be fine. It feels better today," I lied and attempted another
stretch. "How do you feel?"

His eye was still swollen, cheek raw, but that wasn't what I
wanted to know. He'd made his first kill and at only thirteen...

"I'll be all right, too," he said.

I patted him on the back, trying not to linger when we couldn't
afford to lose any more time. With that, we made our descent, stopping only briefly for a long drink of water and to gather some fruit
from the nearest tree.

Nik squinted his one good eye against the morning sun. "I think
we should keep close to the beach. That way, we can watch for

ships and still hide amongst the trees if we need to. I think there's a shortcut from here, but I don't trust myself to remember it."

"A shortcut to camp?" I asked.

He popped a bit of avocado into his mouth and kept moving. "No, not camp."

"But Finn—"

"Won't be there."

"How do you know that?" I hustled to keep up with him while brushing overgrown plants away from my legs and gingerly holding my side.

"Look. We can't afford to think the worst, so we have to go off what we know, all right?" His head held firm in the direction he meant to go, like a wolf tracking a scent.

"Which is what, exactly?" I reached for his shoulder and turned him around to face me. "Tell me what you know, Nik. You clearly knew about the treasure, and now you know some shortcut through a treacherous jungle. Just tell me you weren't somehow involved in this mutinous plan." My voice rose as I considered the possibilities. "Tell me you weren't."

"Why would you even accuse me of something like that?" He pushed my hand from his shoulder. "Do you really think I would sell my brother out to Blackbeard? Or even give away the treasure if it meant costing him his life?"

I growled and moved ahead of him to continue on whatever ridiculous path he'd chosen for us. "I don't know what to think. You've both been so secretive that I'm just waiting to find out what will spring up next. You were mad at him this whole trip, and none of *this* has seemed to surprise you, so—"

"Don't you dare go any further with that." He caught up to me, the two of us taking our pent up aggression out on the greenery underfoot, rather than on each other. "You want to whine and complain about secrets, go ahead. I would never betray him, and if I went against him *ever*, it would be to *save* his life, not end it. Don't you ever question my loyalty to my brother. I don't care how big of an idiot he's been."

My lips pursed, holding back the slew of thoughts ready to burst out. So much had happened in such a short amount of time. I'd barely been able to process a thing that had happened.

"Well? Go ahead. Argue your point like you always do. I can't wait to hear it." Nikolaus kicked at a log on the ground to force it out of his way.

I let my hand rest on my cramping sides, while my hair fell over my shoulder to hide my face. There wouldn't be an argument. I had nothing left to give to it. There was a treasure I didn't know about. Big deal. Blackbeard had a bounty on us. So what? If Finn was dead, why would any of that matter?

God in Heaven. If Finn was dead...

"Cecily?"

I gave up trying to conceal it. Fresh tears slid down my cheeks. I couldn't walk, couldn't move another muscle. My wobbling legs nearly knocked me to the ground, but a nearby tree caught my fall.

Nikolaus went silent beside me. I sucked in a loud breath, but it only sent a wave of pain through my ribs and made the sobs worse.

"I'm sorry," Nikolaus said at last. He sounded as pained as I felt, and I dropped my hands from my face to look to him.

"It's not you." My curls were wet with tears and sweat, and I flicked the clinging strands from my eyes. "What if he..." It was all I could get out before the lump in my throat cut off the rest of my words.

"I know." He took hold of my arm and pulled me along. "Which is why we're not going to think about it."

My legs had turned to stone, my feet dragging with each step. "Nik, if—"

"I told you we're sticking with what we know." His voice cracked, and he cleared his throat, pausing only a moment. "What I *know* is that Blackbeard is a man of show. Presentation is his best strength. It's why everyone fears him. There's a village that provides the quickest access to the treasure down this beach if we keep going south. He has to be there. It's where Finn would have led him."

I nodded, whether or not he could see the acknowledgement. But what about the rest of the crew? If Blackbeard sought only Finn, he wouldn't have let the others survive if they stood in his way. My heart palpitated inside my chest as the thoughts continued to creep up one by one, and I had to force them back down, afraid to lose it all over again. What about Josette? Stevens? All the new crewmen who signed up only to never set foot on the *Hellbound* and meet their doom in the sand?

Nik examined the skies. "It won't be long before the storms begin."

I groaned. In all that mess that had become our lives, I'd forgotten about the hurricanes. As if we needed something else to add to the ever-growing list of troubles.

"About the treasure..." Nikolaus blew out a long breath. "Finn didn't want you to know about it."

"I think that's fairly obvious." A small laugh squeaked out from between my lips I hadn't known myself capable of.

Nik glanced over his shoulder so I could see his good eye squinting back at me. "No, I mean, he had a reason."

I shrugged. "Doesn't he always?"

"Well, it's different this time. When he first took over the ship, he came back to get me and gathered the smallest of crews. That was back when Needham was still first mate."

A sad smile crossed my lips at the memory of the strange little man with the perpetual, and rather alarming, grin. I first saw him at the pub with my adoptive father, or slave master, as seemed more suited to his title. I thought I'd meet my end at the hands of Needham—not witness his.

Nik continued, "When we first sailed, we went from island to island in the Caribbean, trying to find the place that suited us best. Most of these islands are swarming with pirates, and we had some close calls before we found Barbados. While visiting another island to the north, Finn, Needham, and I went to explore. It was another beautiful isle, not too different from this. And we started seeing odd signs in the jungle—things just didn't seem to fit. That's when we got curious and dug around. We found most of that back there in a gigantic hole, hidden by a moveable tree stump. It was...crazy, really.

"With the help of the rest of our crew, we got the entirety of treasure back to the ship and went south to Barbados. It was less inhabited by other pirates then, so it seemed like the safest place to keep it. Then we found that cave, which was easy to booby trap."

"So, he hadn't been looking for treasure in the first place?" Finn seemed anything but a treasure hunter. At their young ages, it had to have taken them by surprise.

"No. Didn't even know it existed. It sure seemed an answer to our prayers, though. With that much wealth, we'd be able to survive: buy food and clothing, pay a crew, keep up the appearances we needed. And we wouldn't have to pillage or take down any other ships to do it. At least, Finn didn't want to do that part."

"Did he know it was Blackbeard's when he found it?" I asked.

"If he did, he never let on. He probably figured it out not long ago, if I had to guess. He got more nervous as time went on, but never talked to me about it. He never tells me anything." Nikolaus veered to the left to find a break in the trees.

Together, we took a quick surveillance of the beach. In the clearing, I saw what he meant about the gray sky preparing to rip apart and wreak havoc on the island. The usually blaring sun only glimmered faintly between the clouds now.

Nik sighed. "Everyone from that original crew is dead, except me and Finn. We're the only two left that know about the treasure. We thought it was safer that way."

I reached for the sleeve of his shirt. "But I wouldn't have told anyone. I would never—"

"You can be so daft sometimes. That's not at all why." Nikolaus's shoulders dropped.

Finn always had his reasons. For everything.

A memory rushed across my mind, Finn's body pressed against mine, guiding me backward through his quarters. He'd tied me to a post and asked me to trust him. He hadn't wanted me associated with his crew when the Royal Navy overtook the *Hellbound*.

He hadn't wanted me associated with the treasure's theft when Blackbeard came for his coin...

"The enemy can't force information out of you if you don't have any knowledge of it." Nik's eyes narrowed, but a smirk played on his lips. "Not that it stopped you from trying."

My spirits lifted in an instant. Of course, I'd tried. My love for my captain was nothing short of reckless, and I didn't see that ever changing. He could always try to keep me a step behind for my protection, but it wouldn't matter. I'd catch up to him every time.

TWENTY-TWO

ALMOST TWO DAYS OF HIKING THROUGH THE JUNGLE IN THE steamy heat made me think my peace of mind would never return. I took more and more breaks to dip in the ocean and cool off, regardless of Nikolaus's frequent protests. The stops didn't seem to bother him as much as he let on, though, as he always quickly plunged in behind me. The sky grew darker by the hour and soon, we wouldn't need the ocean if the clouds opened up.

"I think we're getting closer to the village," Nikolaus said.

The words were a beautiful melody to my ears. I sighed in relief, the hope of civilization propelling me from the water. As I rang out my shirt from my most recent dip to cool off, I stretched my back. The pain had eased enough I could walk without limping and take deeper breaths without my lungs exploding.

Nik's swelling had gone down around his eye, replaced by the expected purple and yellow bruises. A few cuts dashed across his face, though the frequent cleansing of the ocean waters seemed to keep them from infection.

None of the past few days felt real. But even now, it all paled compared to what we had waiting ahead.

The island wrapped its leafy arms around us again when we entered the jungle. As we walked, I focused my attention on pulling myself together: twisting my hair up onto my head, tucking my shirt into my trousers, and readjusting the sleeves to better suit the stuffy temperature. My stomach rumbled—this time out of hunger and not because I needed to be sick again. Our bodies seemed to reject a diet made up of almost entirely berries and bananas. At least the nuts stayed down, though the taste left something to be desired.

It was midday, I suspected. We'd lost track of the sun in the thick clouding. The rain spat from the sky, casting an even greater shadow through the trees. If we had to walk another day, we'd need to create torches for light throughout the waking hours, yet I had no idea how we'd keep them lit.

"Did you hear that?" Nikolaus stopped, his hand bringing me to a halt beside him.

"Hear what?" The waves churned louder at sea, but I heard nothing else. Even the rustling trees couldn't compete with the waters.

"Listen."

I held my breath to keep from making any sound at all. The birds had quieted, though not entirely, and the raindrops tapped along the leaves above us, creating a steady drumbeat. Then I heard it: a rustling in the trees. It was hard to tell exactly where it came from.

"Stay close to me," I whispered, taking Nikolaus by the arm and slipping a knife from my belt.

Nik had already drawn his sword, my offered protection unnecessary, as he indicated with an irritated look. But what were we about to fight? Pirates? Angry villagers? A rabid monkey?

A branch snapped, and so did our attention. Ahead of us, a figure fell from a tree branch and landed catlike on the green jungle floor. We raised our weapons soundlessly, neither of us taking our eyes off the person before us. I almost dropped my blade when the mystery figure lowered her hood.

"Cecily?" She laughed.

I would have run to her if my feet weren't stuck in place with disbelief. "Josette!"

"Josette?" Nikolaus repeated, his mouth falling open.

She plunged her sword back into its sheath and sauntered toward us, eyes as wide as mine. "What are you doin' out here? Where are the pirates that took you?"

I grabbed her by the shoulders and pulled her into a hug. A surprised squeak followed the motion as I squeezed her tightly. Joy bubbled inside my chest. Someone had survived. Maybe there were other survivors too. Maybe Finn...

"Why were you in a tree? What is going on?" Nik had no use for reunions.

I released Josette and examined her face for injury or some clue as to what she'd been through.

"Keepin' watch, of course. What else would I be doin' in a tree?" she snapped.

"Where are the others? What about the mutiny? Where's Finn?" Questions poured from my mouth faster than my brain could process them.

Nik stepped forward then, looking down at Josette as if to bully her into offering up the answers more quickly. But if anyone could resist being bullied, it was Josette.

"Slow down." She held up her hands to keep us at bay. "Who's Finn?"

"Captain Worley," Nikolaus and I yelled at the same time.

"Yeesh, quiet yourselves." She looked around, taking hold of our shoulders. "This island is swarmin' with pirates. You mean to call 'em all here, do ya?"

"Josette." My jaw clenched to the point I could barely utter her name. All the relief at finding her alive subsided with her games.

She waved her hand like our questions distracted her from her real mission. "He's fine. Looks like it takes a little more than some nasty pirates to bring a man like that down."

My insides turned to mush.

He lived. Finn was alive and free. Blackbeard hadn't caught him. I would get to hold him again.

"Take us to him." Nik's voice was only a whisper. He looked to me, and I offered a genuine smile. Could it really be possible after everything?

Josette chuckled to herself. "He'll be right surprised to see the likes of you two turn up. The crew wrote you off as dead, you know. And you could have told me your relation with the captain before all this happened. Gave us a bit of a surprise when—"

"Just take us to him." Nikolaus looked as if he might explode if we didn't start moving again soon.

My heart raced with relief or some new feeling I couldn't identify. Josette started off, and we followed so closely on her heels it grew harder not to trip on one another as we went. If she'd picked up any speed, I would have been happy to run the remaining distance. Nikolaus, too, I suspected, would be just as eager to end our long journey and see the evidence of Finn's safety once and for all.

"Was a real blood bath after you left, you know." Josette spoke casually over her shoulder as if gory battles had been an everyday occurrence in her life. "Captain got downright scary. Went a bit mad, if I had to tell it. Me, I just stood there. Didn't know what in bloody hell was goin' on, but I remembered what you said and started fightin' with the captain. They outnumbered us, you know. Couldn't tell who was good and who was bad."

"And Blackbeard?" I asked, relishing in the story. "Is he here?"

"On the island? Yeah, sounds like. Never made it to us, though. Not many of us got out of that fight, but Captain Worley sent us right to the ship to sail. Said he knew where Blackbeard would be comin' from and didn't want to wait around for him."

"And?" Nik's walk picked up to a job to keep even with her stride.

"And what? He sent us on with the ship this way with that Stevens fellow at the helm, told us to come to this end of the island and find some crew to fight along with us while he ran into the jungle. Came back a day ago all distressed, but didn't say where he'd been or what he found. We figured he musta gone after the pair of you, but nobody wanted to ask for certain. We kept to our mission: findin' crew. Strange bunch we're gettin', too, but we got 'em. Can't stay long with Blackbeard lurking about, you know. That's why he's got some of us scouting the area for his coming."

"But Finn's all right?" I wanted to hear the words again. The rest of the tale could wait.

"See for yourself." She flashed one last grin over her shoulder before pointing through an opening in the trees.

TWENTY-THREE

ALL AT ONCE, THE SOUNDS OF LIFE OVERWHELMED ME AS WE approached the village Nikolaus had assured me we'd find. But the sight near the water kept my full attention. Hovering like a ghost off the shore was the outline of a ship I'd once feared. This time, however, I rejoiced when I saw the *Hellbound*, my home for the past year. It was fully intact, and, according to Josette, so was its captain.

A long sigh escaped my lips, and I wiped the rainwater from my face, letting my hands linger there for a moment. I'd given little thought to how I'd feel when—or *if*—I saw him again.

My stomach turned. Did he know I'd let myself into the ruffians' inner circle to protect him? It'd backfired in the most horrible way. I put his beloved brother's life at risk and announced our secret relationship. I'd blown his entire identity in one afternoon. He could be furious with me.

I deserved it.

With Nik's help, I led the enemy directly to his treasure. Would I even be welcome back into this crew? Even after all that, I didn't even save Nikolaus's life. *He'd* saved *mine*.

Josette groaned beside me.

"What's wrong?" I asked.

"It's this new crew. You'll see soon enough." She led us onward, pressing a finger to her lips and walking in such close proximity to the water's edge the waves lapped up over our ankles.

"Um, excuse me?" Someone called from a distance down the way.

Josette froze, her nose scrunching as she pulled her sopping wet braids from underneath her hat and rung them out pointlessly in her hands. She shifted to look farther up the shore, where an older man sat in a small hut behind a makeshift desk.

"Miss Josephine? You need to see me before you go back to the ship, especially if you intend to bring guests. You know the policy," he shouted.

Nikolaus and I exchanged glances. Josette's shoulders slumped, and she trudged through the thick sand to the little shanty. We followed her until we reached the coverage of the leafed-top shelter. Rain still spit through the cracks in the design, but not enough that it bothered the strange little man sitting below it.

I studied this newcomer from behind Josette. He wore crooked eyeglasses and a hat that stretched far out over his shoulders—one of the biggest shipman's hats I'd ever seen. His mouth twitched as he stared at us in a way that made his silver mustache dance below his nose.

"It's *Josette*, Roberts. Not that difficult of a name," she growled.

"Well, Miss Josette, when we have a crew of this size, it's not easy to get all the names correct. I'm still new here, remember?" Roberts chewed his tongue in a way that made his mustache come to life even more. I could hardly stop staring at it.

"Here's a good way to help you remember: I'm the only bloody woman in the crew!" She mouthed each word carefully, her hands cemented on the small, wooden tabletop, pinning his quill in place. "Well, at least I *was*. Add another one to the list, will you? This is Cecily. She's not dead like we thought."

Roberts reached forward and lifted each of Josette's fingers one after the other until he retrieved his feather quill from her. She watched him, mouth falling open without attempting to help the motion at all. She shook her head and muttered curses as Roberts shuffled through the two small pages on his desktop and dipped the pointed end into an ink dish.

"I'll break your bloody quill if you ever touch me again," Josette hissed.

"It's not very ladylike of you to swear, Joselle." He pulled a handkerchief from his pocket and blew his nose, his mustache bobbing back and forth against the cloth.

"Oh, I'm goin' to kill him." Josette moved to stand behind me, the curses flying freely.

Nik growled behind us. "Can we just get to the ship?"

"Good luck getting past this oaf." Josette's eyes crossed, and she swore when Roberts stood like he meant to leap across the table and pummel Nik if he so much as took one more step toward the *Hellbound*.

I hurriedly regained the note-taking man's attention. "I can write my own name. It's fine."

Roberts pulled the quill away before my hand could brush a feather.

"You most certainly will not. This is a first in wing, miss. Nobody touches it but me." He adjusted his glasses, his rear end shifting on the stool. "Now, what business do you have here? I don't see a Cecilia on this list, and the captain has indicated that our crew is complete. We're no longer taking on men. Or *women*." He narrowed his eyes behind his spectacles, leaning to the side to catch Josette's eye.

"It's *Cecily*," I said. How old was this man and why on earth did Finn take him in? Were things on the *Hellbound* so desperate? "This is Nikolaus. We're already part of the crew. List or no list."

Josette rolled her eyes and nodded. It appeared as if she wanted to answer me, but Roberts took the question first. "I told the captain, the first step in managing a ship properly is in the care and organization of its crew." He delicately placed his quill on the desktop. "Without proper documentation, we're nothing more than animals on a boat. Now, if you're not on this list, my dear, you need to run along." He tried to shoo us off in the jungle's direction.

Josette slammed her hands against the table once more, missing the precious quill by a fingertip. She opened her mouth, but someone coming down the beach caught her attention and kept her silent.

The three of us peered out into the downpour as a tall, thin figure moved hurriedly in our direction. His cap had toppled off, leaving his tight onyx curls to cling to his head in a twisted, sleek design. He slowed at the sight of us and whistled shrilly over his shoulder, then continued his approach.

"Roberts giving you a tough time again, Josette?" Stevens said as he came to rest at the corner of the stand.

"I hate him," she muttered.

He laughed and clapped the old man on the shoulder. "You're doing a fine job, Herman. Don't let this insubordinate tell you otherwise."

Stevens turned to Nik and me then, as if he hadn't noticed our presence until that moment.

"Welcome back, Miss Hastings, Nikolaus. It is *so* good to see you." He plucked the quill from Roberts' hand and scribbled our names across the bottom of the sheet. Roberts didn't even protest— not verbally, anyway. It wasn't worth the risk to argue with a man in charge.

Had Finn made him second in command? A hustled clanging in the distance kept me from thinking on it for too long. I followed the sound.

And there he was.

Finn walked purposefully down the beach, dressed head to toe in black. Rainwater rushed off the rim of his hat, his head focused on the ground, weapons banging against his legs with each step.

Nikolaus spotted him then. He wedged himself between Josette and Stevens and ran with all his might toward his brother, as if none of our previous secrets ever existed. It was just a boy, reuniting with his brother—his only true family left.

Finn lifted his head in time to see him coming, the sigh that escaped him obvious even from my distant standpoint. They collided, embracing each other, hushed words spoken that only the two of them could understand. A lump swelled in my throat at the sight. I wanted to run, too, but mountains of uncertainty still whirled through my mind.

I looked to Stevens, his posture relaxed against the wall of the hut, one leg crossed over the other. He beamed as he observed the captain's reunion.

My gaze fell away, giving the brothers their privacy, while my inner turmoil raged onward. How I longed to run after Nik, to feel Finn's arms around me and take in the evidence of his safety. But he might not want that. If he didn't want me...

I sensed Josette and Stevens stepping away and looked up to meet the deep sapphire eyes I knew so well. There was no trace of a smile on his face, his joyous reunion with Nikolaus like a distant memory.

The stoic presence of the captain before me set my nerves on edge.

There was only one thing I could say. "I am so sorr—"

Finn sprang forward and took the sides of my face in his hands. His lips met against mine, sealing the gasp inside me. My eyes fell closed as I clutched the wet fabric of his overcoat in my hands, wanting to keep him there forever.

He pulled away to examine my face. "You're mad! Bloody mad!"

"I—"

His next kiss knocked the wind out of me with the force of his mouth on mine. And then, "What in all God's earth were you thinking?"

"I just wanted to—"

Again, he stopped me short with his lips. I hardly minded.

He pulled back, his forehead resting against mine, his hands weaving into my soaked curls. "Never again, yeah?"

"Never." This time, I took hold of *his* face and brought him against me once more, our arms wrapping around each other in the embrace I thought I wouldn't experience again.

TWENTY-FOUR

With my name securely in its place alongside the other crewmembers—despite Roberts' reluctance—we headed toward the rest of our shipmates. The rain still pelted my skin, but I stopped caring. For the first time in days, our family was whole again.

Upon returning to the others dutifully stacking barrels of supplies for the longboats, the men stilled, attention focused on their captain. Finn resumed his powerful pose, while Nikolaus and I stood together at his side, ready to take the newest set of orders from our captain.

"Crew of the *Hellbound*, lend me your attention," he called above the rain. "We are hunted men. Though our crew has grown in number, we are still small. This island can no longer be a place of respite to us. The storms have arrived and soon will make it impossible to sail. So, we race against the winds today. Batten down the hatches. Make preparations. We leave at my command."

The group took in their captain's every word. I studied them through the downpour. Though I could hardly make out their individual characteristics, their obvious respect for Finn showed through the gloom. They each held a sense of determination on their faces. Where had he found men to sail with him in such horrendous conditions and on such short notice?

Finn continued, "Most of you know your duties. If anyone needs assignment, see Matthew Stevens, quartermaster of the *Hellbound*." He reached a hand up to touch Stevens' shoulder. "Or I'm sure Herman Roberts can be of assistance." He lazily gestured toward the waving man that stood near the gangplank. I couldn't help but notice how Finn's eyebrow quirked when he said the name. "You'll notice the two new faces beside me, and while they may be strangers to the lot of you, they aren't to me. This is my brother, Nikolaus Worley."

Nik stiffened and clasped his hands behind his back as he looked over the men. His blond hair darkened in the rainwater, and his pale blue eyes widened in shock at the forward introduction.

Finn had told the truth. Nik's identity on the *Hellbound* wasn't a secret anymore.

"You'll do well to give him your utmost respect, as he's no doubt the finest sailor on board." Finn nodded to his brother, revealing the deep love he had for him. "And this is Cecily Hastings. And..." He took a step around the others to stand closer to me. Our eyes met as if he needed my permission to continue, though all he did next was take my hand and turn back toward the crew. "Well, to be honest, I'm in love with her. And if any of you lay a finger on her, I'll stick you where you stand. If she doesn't do it first."

Of all the things he could have said. My hand slowly rose to cover my mouth when the shock of it all set in.

The crew met the declaration with hushed compliance—except for the muffled giggles that undoubtedly belonged to Josette standing behind us. And then there was the strange scratching sound that weirdly overpowered the pouring rain and took me a moment to identify—until I spotted Robert's quill pen rushing across the page.

Finn cleared his throat and returned his focus to the awaiting men. "Anyway. Back to work."

As the others darted off to secure the ship for sail, Finn gave Stevens and Josette instruction to remain on deck and take charge. The two of them had gained high command in so little time. Surely, their proof of loyalty during when the mutineers attacked had afforded them such trust.

Finn instructed Nikolaus and I to follow him to his chambers. To discuss a plan, I suspected. And I had a million questions regarding that.

It took little coaxing to get me inside the cozy room I loved so much. After a hellish journey across the sea, followed by danger upon danger when we arrived on land, I'd longed for the comfort of this room and the company that came with it. This time, we didn't need a guise to bring me here. Finn had announced our relationship. I might be free to enter this room any time I wanted.

Inside the familiar chamber, Finn had bread and water on the center table, blankets piled on the corner chair, and a warm bed awaiting use. It would have been hard to decide where to begin if I hadn't already chosen my utmost desire in the quarters.

As soon as the door clicked shut, I spun on my heels and threw my arms around Finn once more. His arm wound around my waist, and he reached with the other hand to pull Nik into us.

"I really thought you were dead," Finn whispered.

"We thought the same of you." Nikolaus laughed into Finn's shoulder.

"I came after you, assuming the worst. When I found the others' bodies, and you were nowhere in sight, I ran back here. Figured you'd go to the closest village." He tousled Nik's hair.

"Just like you told me to. Though, you must have found the shortcut." Nikolaus pushed Finn's hand away with a sheepish grin. "I couldn't remember it, so we just followed the shoreline and—"

"That explains some things." Finn gestured toward the table where food and fresh water awaited us. "You both look famished."

I sank into the chair and let my head fall against the high-backed seat, unsure if I held the strength needed to eat anything. My dry throat begged for some water, which I obliged. But if the rest of the world could disappear for only a moment, I'd want nothing more than to curl up beside Finn and sleep for a week or two.

"How did you get away?" Finn's gaze only flickered in our direction as if he hadn't fully decided he wanted to know the answer.

"The weapons inside the cave. We lied our way through the jungle to get that far, barely escaping death. Then we waited till the treasure distracted them. Cecily had knives and a pistol; I took up a sword." Nikolaus shoved another piece of bread into his mouth.

Finn kept his focus on the table in front of him. "So, you—"

"Yeah," Nik said.

"And you're—"

"I'm fine," Nikolaus said with his mouth full. He held up his hand to stop the brief interrogation.

"I never wanted that for you," Finn whispered. "Either of you."

Nik swallowed loudly. "I know, but it had to be done."

Finn nodded and looked to me next, a longing in his eyes I could interpret in a hundred different ways.

"He saved my life several times over the past few days. We wouldn't have made it without his wisdom and skill." I reached for a piece of bread to settle my empty stomach, while Nik waved away the praise.

Finn whispered soft words in Finnish toward his brother. Nik's cheeks flushed, and he shoved a chunk of dried beef into his mouth, smiling shyly as he chewed.

We all sat in silence for a moment. Somehow, we really had survived an agonizing few days and found our way back to each other. But the fact remained: we weren't even close to being out of danger. I tightened my fist around the roll in my hand. "You do

179

understand that trying to sail out of these storms is complete madness?"

"Without a doubt, it's madness." Finn pulled his tricorn hat from his head and shook out his dripping hair. "We do madness very well on board this ship if you've forgotten. Besides, I've sailed in worse. Once, I only had half my blood in me."

A half-smirk played at his lips, and I took what comfort I could gather from it. There were so many things I wanted to say to him, so many things I wanted him to say to me. Yet, as always, an impossible mission lay in front of us, letting us know our time together would be as brief as ever.

"Finnigan Worley, you are madness defined." I tried to smile back at him but couldn't. Instead, I stared mindlessly at him from across the table.

The ship swayed. Finn clasped hold of his cup to keep it from sliding off the edge of the table. He released a long breath. "That normal life away from piracy looking a little better to you now?"

Rain hammered the glass behind him. Though it was midday, the sky had turned dark as night. "Maybe a little, especially when we're being hunted."

"That does make it a little less appealing." Finn's balled fist knocked on the tabletop.

Not much of this life called to me anymore. Nothing except the two men sitting before me. "Not to mention the part where the people I love most could end up dead at any time. I'm ready to get off this cursed island."

"Agreed. Sailing is our only choice," Nik said. He'd eaten three rolls in a matter of moments and now sat back in his chair, patting his stomach. "Won't be easy."

Thunder clapped outside the window, proving his point. Finn nodded and sat forward in his chair. "That's why I need my best men out there."

Nik's shoulders sank when he reached for another roll. "I know, you—"

"Nik, I need you in the rigs with Cecily." Finn's slow exhale showed just how hard this was for him to say. "I hate to ask it. This storm is bigger than anything we've ever battled before, and this is the most dangerous task on board. But you're the best I've got."

Nik's chair crashed to the floor behind him when he stood. "Yes." He ran his sleeve across his forehead and blinked like he might be dreaming. He still clutched an uneaten roll in his fist. "Really? I'm out of the galley?"

Finn's hesitant smile spoke of so many things. He had to let go of his brother, had to trust him. With the danger we faced ahead, no place on board brought any safety. If anyone on the *Hellbound* could execute the rigging to perfection in hurricane winds, it was Nik.

"I need you there, Nik. I know you'll look out for each other." At that, Finn nodded to me, and my heart melted a little more for these brothers. Nik had more than proven his strength and abilities in the jungle, and I trusted him with my whole life.

Nik dropped the bread on the table. "I'll start now!"

And without another word, he rushed from the room before Finn changed his mind and sent him back to peeling potatoes. The door slammed shut behind him, and for the first time, it wasn't because they'd fought. This marked a new chapter in my time on board the *Hellbound*, and it filled me with so much joy.

I shifted in my seat toward my captain. "I know that wasn't easy for you to do, but I'm glad you did it."

"He really could sail this entire ship, you know? He's brilliant." Finn beamed with pride. "Both of you are." His face turned more somber, and he scooted his chair back from the table. "I really never thought I'd see you again."

The invisible tug in my chest pulled harder than ever before. I went to him, placing myself into his lap and wrapping my arms tightly around his neck. His tricorn hat toppled to the floor. My fingers found their way into his hair, and I kissed his forehead, still trying to convince myself he was real.

He buried his face in my neck, clutching my waist with one hand, the other draped across my leg. "I cannot believe you have stuck with me this long, after all I've put you through."

I cupped his chin to draw his attention and smiled. "That's only because the last pirates that took me weren't as handsome as you, so I came back."

He laughed, hearty and carefree, the way he used to when none of the horrors of this life existed. "Cecily Hastings, you are my favorite person on this earth."

"The feeling is mutual, Captain." I bent forward to kiss his nose and drank in the sight of him. Thank the Lord he'd told the rest of the crew about our relationship. I doubted I could keep myself from him ever again. "I was so afraid you'd be mad at me for what I did."

Finn reached up to tuck a lock of my unruly hair behind my ear. "You were right to want to get rid of those men. You *tried*. In the end, you succeeded. They're gone." He ran his hand down my arm and linked his fingers with mine. "I'm just so glad you're all right, I hardly even know what to do with myself."

He chuckled again, then wrapped his arms around me even tighter, knocking me off balance. I slid from his lap, and he tumbled after me. My side ached when we hit the ground, but I didn't care anymore, not when Finn's hand cupped my cheek. Not when he looked at me this way. Not when he brought his lips to mine...

Finn shot upright and snatched hold of my wrist. "What was that?"

A faint thump reverberated in the distance.

"Sounded like—"

A loud explosion rang out, splintering the wood along the wall. The grand bay window shattered with the vibrations, and earsplitting screams flowed into the room. I curled into a ball under Finn, hands covering my head as my wits slowly returned.

All at once, Finn snatched me up and dragged me across the room, but we both knew there was nowhere to hide from cannon fire.

TWENTY-FIVE

Nothing could have prepared me for what awaited us on the other side of the door. As the ship rocked, the men ran about in shock and horror. The bow of the ship bore a gaping hole, smoke pouring out of the wound as flames licked up the sides.

"Abandon ship!" Finn screamed across the deck and rang the bell with such force he nearly ripped it from its hinge. Echoes of his command followed the splashes that dotted the angry sea with each body plunging over the side.

Nikolaus jumped from the ladder and crawled across the deck toward us. As Finn shouted his commands, I wrapped my arms around Nik like a protective mother hen. Finn ushered us to the railing, all of us examining the cloudy sky for the next attack, but the weather made it impossible to see.

I heard Josette from somewhere down the way, enough to know she was alive. Stevens hurried past us, only pausing to nod at his captain before backing up the order to jump into the sea. He shouted a prayer of protection as he went, and I so hoped it worked.

We'd barely made it to the railing when another explosion

rattled the ship, and we fell to the floor in unison. Finn's arm stretched over my body, and he tugged me closer, my back burned with the pressure of his hand against the lingering bruises. The ship shifted onto its side from the force, a growing crackle at its center drawing my attention. Ropes snapped from their places as the mighty mast tore free of its hold and tumbled into the raging waters. The nest sent water exploding into the sky when it fell. My home, my job on board the *Hellbound,* vanished into the ocean.

"Jump!" Finn shouted.

I did as he said. A scream escaped my lips when we plummeted over the edge and hit the ocean's surface. The waters had grown increasingly colder in the storm and sucked the air from my lungs when it engulfed my body, making it harder to return for air as it knocked me under again and again. Still, I kicked and fought until I broke through and searched frantically across the waves for the others.

Fires raged on board the ship, crackling louder than the thunder. Nik grabbed my wrist and yanked me toward the shore. His body brushed against me, and we swam together against the stormy waves. Our lives depended on making it to the beach, yet I couldn't keep from turning back to watch as our home crumbled.

The mighty *Hellbound* surrendered to the sea.

Wind and wave fought our every movement. My mind numbed, the only thing I knew was to get to shore. Some of our crew swam past; some screamed. Finn and Nik had vanished from my sight when the ocean leapt up between us and tore us apart.

I swam harder. I swam until I had nothing left to give.

At some point, my body sank into the wet sand, though the waves still reached out to pull me back with the tide. I crawled farther onto the shore and collapsed. Finn and Nik fell beside me, like they'd come from the sky instead of the ocean. Coughs and moans escaped the rest of the crew who survived the explosions—not as many as I'd hoped.

Ash and smoke spit across at the sky. Remnants of our home lingered on the waterline, pieces floating off into the unknown, while others broke apart and sank below the waterline.

Finn righted himself enough to sit in the sand as if he'd turned to stone. His arms rested on his bent knees, his stare fixated on the empty horizon. Hair hung loosely around his ears. And his eyes were as gray and melancholy as the sky. He said nothing, made no attempt to wipe the water from his face or brush the hair from his eyes.

I took hold of his arm, but he didn't respond to my touch.

Nikolaus knelt a distance away. His shirt had already torn during our trek through the jungle, but the unplanned swim and raging waters made him even more unkempt.

Josette rushed around the beach to assist any of the struggling crew, even swimming out to pull the remaining straggler in. I didn't know the man she helped, but he seemed in desperate need of her strong ability to swim. Stevens assisted, too, uttering unceasing prayers as he moved. A little farther down, Roberts rang out his overcoat, his cherished quill peeking out from in between the buttons of his shirt.

I found my strength again and hurried to the water's edge to offer Josette my hand and pull her from the water. She gave my fingers a squeeze, while I wrapped an arm around her waist to bring her further inland where we crumpled to the sand together.

"What do we do now?" she asked through ragged breaths.

I wished I had an answer. "I really don't know."

She gestured toward Finn. "The captain?"

"He hasn't said anything..."

He hadn't even blinked since he came out of the water.

"Who was it?" Josette closed her fingers around a pile of wet sand beside her legs. "I watched a man take his last breath after that cannon fired. I want to know who's responsible."

We scanned the horizon, but nothing showed the source of the cannon fire over the crashing waves and dark, rainy skies. It was as if a ghost ship had come upon us, then vanished. "Finn will probably have the answer for us when his wits return."

Josette nodded. I touched my hand to her shoulder and stood. I needed to return to Finn and help him regain his strength, but how? He just lost his home, his command. It all just vanished in a matter of moments with no warning.

A lump caught in my throat.

As I approached him, he rose from the sand, but his expression remained the same, his tattered appearance untouched.

"Finn." I spoke softly, my fingers brushing against his forearm. Again, he didn't budge at my contact. I followed his gaze, and the lump in my throat choked me. How could I be strong for him now? We were only together again in the beautiful captain's quarters for a moment of peace, and now...

An eerie horror crossed Finn's face as he shifted slowly from the wreckage of the *Hellbound* to a point on the horizon not so far from it. His mouth quirked, and he released a haunting laugh as he shook his head.

"*Itse paholainen*," he breathed.

I took hold of his arm and turned to see what held his attention. Emerging from the thick, foggy storm was the ghost ship I'd imagined, its tangible form causing the hairs on the back of my neck to rise.

The full-rigged vessel had no less than forty cannons. The dark sails that clung to the rigs appeared as dark as the stained wood that made up the rest of it. The *Hellbound* would have fit inside the beast's hull. If this wretched thing hadn't already sunk it. A black flag displayed from the highest mast, whipping angrily in the wind. Though I couldn't see the decoration there, I knew.

"Heaven help us," I whispered.

"Amen." Finn's mouth tightened around the word. The shock had faded away, and something else took its place. I could feel his arms tensing under my grasp in a way that reminded me of a boiling pot on the brink of spilling over. I took a small step backward in anticipation of just that.

"Everybody into the jungle," Finn commanded through his clenched jaw. "Stay together. Those with weapons, draw them. Ready yourselves for anything."

The men quickly obeyed, gathering what little they'd salvaged as we abandoned the *Hellbound* to its watery grave and began running toward the cover of trees. The sight of the ominous ship on the horizon was enough to motivate anyone to flee. A ship that large would host a crew that significantly outnumbered us, most of which had probably sailed longer than a day. Even the slight relief that came with finding all three of my daggers still fastened to my belt didn't instill enough bravery to fight such a foe.

The rain softened, distant thunder still beating its wartime drum as the storms approached. Already scarce sunshine grew fainter by the minute with the promise of a dark evening and an even blacker tomorrow.

Josette caught up to me, a sword in one hand and a pistol in the other. "Gun powder's ruined. We've got no firepower."

"We can only hope our blades are enough or that we can escape this whole thing entirely." If they came with cannons, what else might they have in their arsenal?

"Looks like Stevens took a head start on escaping." Josette's voice took on a biting tone when she glanced over her shoulder.

I followed her gaze. Toward the end of our group, I caught sight of him, darting off in the opposite direction. No one else seemed to notice his alternate route, even as he searched over his shoulder to ensure it stayed that way.

As Finn's quartermaster, Stevens should have been at his captain's side. He was our *friend*.

My fists clenched around my knife. "He's abandoned us?"

"Coward." Josette spat on the ground beside her.

My jaw clenched so hard I thought my teeth may shatter. How could he pretend to be so loyal, become the captain's second in command, and then disappear and leave us to our fate? The thought made me want to run after him and drag him back to the front lines by his hair.

A gunshot cracked across the sky, silencing both my disdain and the rolling thunder above us.

Our movement came to an abrupt stop, the twenty-some odd men glancing at one another as if to find out where the bullet found a home.

The sad truth came out when a man at the front of our group sank to his knees, his hands gathering the blood that pooled at his torso. My mouth fell open, but no sound came out as I watched another of our crew collapse into inexistence. It seemed only a matter of time before we all met the same unavoidable fate.

Our men drew their weapons, myself included, though I knew my shaking hands could never deliver an accurate throw. Steady, we waited just beyond the reach of the jungle's edge, a place we no longer wanted to explore, knowing without a doubt that the gunshot had come from inside it—our only chance at safety.

And then laughter filled the air.

As I covered my ears from the piercing howl, I almost crashed to the ground. That laughter. That savage mirth that dripped with hatred and destruction—I knew it better than any other sound. I'd dreamt of it for years.

But this wasn't a dream, and I couldn't wake up this time.

He was here. The man that burned my former hometown of Barry, the one who shot Mrs. Collins dead at my feet, who cracked my head and left me for Death.

A crew of large men stepped from the tree cover in perfect synchronization, each with pistol raised and ready. There were so many of them they had no problem forming a quick circle around the lot of us, our few swords and knives powerless to their readied guns.

And at the very center of their line was Blackbeard.

Years and oceans had separated us, yet he still came to finish the job.

TWENTY-SIX

Lightning crackled across the sky and made my vision blur. Fear kept my feet planted in the jungle floor. My head wobbled on my shoulders, but I shifted enough to regard my fellow crewmates. One caught my eye more than the others, as he always did.

Finn stood tall, his body lacking the violent shaking that overtook me. His head cocked to one side, eyes still narrowed as they had been before when I expected him to explode in rage. This time, one eyebrow peaked, adding an inquisitive air to his manner. It just made Blackbeard expel another amused chuckle that further soured my stomach.

"Ah, Worley," Blackbeard hissed through his beaded beard that smoked at the ends like he'd walked straight from the pits of hell.

"You sunk my ship, Teach." Finn crossed his arms over his chest and let his weight shift to his other leg. My eyes grew wide at the casual way he addressed his enemy.

"And you stole my treasure." Blackbeard's raspy voice suggested he dined on meals of fire and stone.

Finn shrugged. "You left it there. I could only assume you didn't want it anymore."

Blackbeard held our lives in his calloused hands, yet Finn spoke as if they'd met to have drinks in the pub.

"Where is it?" Blackbeard's smile faded away.

"Hmm?" Finn tilted to imply he hadn't heard the question.

It took every bit of strength in me not to scream at him to stop taunting the devil to his face.

"The gold, Finnigan." Blackbeard stepped forward until he met Finn face to face. "Tell me where it is."

"Surely your men would have relayed such information. So kind of you to grant us the pleasure of their company, by the way," Finn replied.

Did Blackbeard know his men had died? Did he still expect them to come through the trees at any moment with proof they'd found his wealth?

Blackbeard released a deep, hoarse chuckle as he took a step back. Whatever humor he found in Finn's words, I only found a greater source of nausea.

One nod from him, and his men moved in closer, every one of them raising a pistol aimed directly on us. Josette's arm pressed to mine, and I very nearly took her hand to have something to hold on to in this. Roberts came up beside me, his hand on his chest where the feathered quill peaked out of his coat. Nik stepped slightly ahead to be closer to his brother. It should have been Stevens, as second in command. His cowardice still cut deep, even as we faced death head on.

"My crew already outnumbers yours. Can you afford to increase that gap?" Blackbeard ran his finger along the barrel of the largest pistol strapped to his baldric.

The rain slowed, though I could almost sense the heavy storm clouds creeping in on us. Finn swallowed hard, his tense stance unwavering as he stood face to face with the most terrifying man I'd ever beheld. His gaze didn't waver. He gave nothing to insinuate weakness.

"Does Hornigold know you're here?" Finn rested his clenched fist over the hilt of the sword sheathed to his belt.

The name startled me. The last thing we needed was another villainous wretch joining this war. Did he have a connection to Blackbeard?

Blackbeard's shoulders rose, and he inched closer to Finn. "He's no ally of yours, mate. None too happy with your lack of allegiance."

Finn chuckled. "You didn't answer my question. Does he know you're here?"

"'Course he does. He'll be here presently himself."

"Good. So, he knows about the treasure then." Finn shook his head to force his wet hair off his brow. My heart couldn't take his lax treatment of the situation. If the guns didn't kill me, Finn's taunting might.

Blackbeard roared louder than before, and I sensed the shudder of the men behind me, the same one that ran through my soul. "I must admit, it had been my hope to retrieve it before he arrives." His gaze drifted lazily toward Nikolaus, and his ugly teeth appeared through the part in his thick, twisted beard. "He looks just like you, you know."

With a speed I'd never seen before, Blackbeard pulled a pistol from his chest and held it outstretched, the barrel pointed directly at Nik. That got Finn's attention—and mine. But Blackbeard didn't hold pause, and with a flick of his hand, he cocked the hammer and pulled the trigger.

My feet sunk miles into the sand, rendering me immobile as my knees gave out. The hard beach rose up to meet me when some force knocked into me. From the ground, I watched in horror, unable to move. Finn had Nik by the arm, the two of them somehow still on their feet with their bodies supporting the other.

Something brushed my leg, some*one* laying in the sand beside me.

It wasn't Nikolaus that had taken the bullet. I spared no time in getting to him.

Roberts?

I lifted his head into my lap and brushed away the drenched, gray hair from his brow. He coughed and clutched hold of his shoulder. Blood seeped through his overcoat and onto my legs. His beloved quill tumbled from his coat pocket.

"The boy," he whispered.

Finn still held Nik tightly in his grasp, while Nik stared at the man who had pushed him out of harm's way.

"He's fine," I whispered. "Because of you."

Blackbeard's laughter rose again, but I ignored him to hold on to our dying comrade whose life dripped out of him in a scarlet river.

Dear Roberts. He'd seemed such an odd man when we first met at his makeshift hut only hours before. Today, he'd saved Nik's life. And now we would be ever-indebted to him without the chance to repay the deed.

My hands turned crimson with the blood I tried in vain to stop from pouring out of him. Tears dripped down my cheeks. By night-fall, this could be every one of us, bleeding out onto the jungle floor.

Time stopped, but only for a moment. Then I noticed the laughter again. That wretched chuckle that echoed in the circle around us rose when Blackbeard's army joined him in celebrating a life lost.

And I couldn't take it anymore.

Without warning or will, all my fears changed into something so much stronger. I was ready to fight. For my life. For Finn's and Nik's and Josette's. For Roberts' agony in the sand and the *Hell-bound* in its grave and all the others brave enough to stand beside us in the face of certain death.

The thunder rumbled behind us. Had the ground literally

shaken, or did my imagination get the better of me through the red smeared across my vision?

I cupped Roberts' head with my hands and gently moved him from my lap. His final exhale rendered him motionless. The rain washed the tears from my face. Roberts' blood dripped from my hands.

When I stood, the sand coated my skin in the places where my trousers had torn. My hair matted against the back of my head, barely tied at the base of my neck. I repositioned in front of Finn, taking hold of his wrist and leaving a painted mark.

Blackbeard's laughter faded as he looked me over, his tall, broad stature towering over me. I only stood up to the middle of his wide, gun-heavy chest. The singed ends of his beard had finished smoking, but the scent of the burned hair wafted on the stormy breeze. I wished I had the means to ignite him all over again in my own special way.

"And who might you be, milady?" He bowed mockingly, an arm drifting up above him, still holding the pistol he'd meant to use to take Nikolaus away from us.

"Oh, stand up, you yellow-bellied, jelly-legged, scum-sucking, rat maggot, and look me in the eye," I spat.

His crew silenced, inching forward with hands over their weapons, waiting for the command to strike me dead. Blackbeard, however, only stiffened and smiled as he replaced the pistol in his baldric armory with a rattling clunk.

"I'm sure I could wager a guess who you might be." He scratched his chin and hummed to himself, an eerie display I hated to think too deeply on.

"My name is Cecily Hastings. And if it's treasure you want, take it. I'd be happy to point you in the right direction." Beside me, Finn balled his fists at his sides. It only urged me onward. "You'll fit nicely in that tomb with the rest of your pudding-headed corpse crew."

"You're awfully bold, girl." Blackbeard waved an arm to

encourage his anxious men to stand down. It was clear from their baffled expressions that none of them had ever been permitted to speak to him in such a manner. Even the man standing on Blackbeard's right held his breath in anticipation of how his captain would handle my outburst. He had a rather noticeable limp of his own, most likely given to him by his commander.

"She's a pirate. It comes naturally." Finn's fingers pinched the back of my wet shirt and tugged gently but forcefully. He meant to draw me back to safety behind him.

Instead, I stepped farther in front of him. Finn couldn't put this fire out so easily. "Perhaps we could spark a deal, you and me. You'll end up with the treasure. Your men return to your ship, mine go free."

"Yours?" Finn tugged harder on my shirt, but I planted my feet firmly in the sand.

I was so close to Blackbeard, his nauseating aroma pooled in my nostrils. "I'll lead you there myself."

"What? No!" Finn reached for my wrist this time, but I pulled it from his grasp.

"Are you jealous, Finnigan? Your girl has more power on your ship than you do," Blackbeard cackled.

"You sank *my* ship!" Finn reminded him with a half-scream that revealed the hidden madness underneath his calm exterior and broke off another piece of my already shattered heart.

"Very well." He held out his hands in condescending surrender.

Before I opened my mouth again, Blackbeard caught me by the arm. He spun me around until my back slammed into the jagged accessories across his chest, and the knife he'd retrieved from his belt pressed into my collarbone.

Finn lurched forward, stopping only when I gasped as the knife drew a few drops of blood—Blackbeard's threat to make it worse if Finn came any closer. I stiffened and swallowed back the whimper, giving Finn a look that urged him to stay put. The wiry curls of my captor's facial hair may as well have been spiders pouring down my cheek and neck.

"Oh, I would like very much for you to lead me to the treasure, love." Blackbeard muttered into my hair. "But my crew will join us. As will *yours*."

His men moved in, stripping each of them of any remaining weaponry and holding them without mercy. They even took Finn's captain's coat. Black ash smudged his cheeks, making him appear more of a young peasant than an established captain.

Nik, too, had gone limp in the tight hold. I couldn't find Josette with my limited perspective, but I could still see Roberts in the sand. I looked to the heavens then and awaited the moment I might join him there.

TWENTY-SEVEN

THE JUNGLE SWALLOWED US WHOLE, SUFFOCATING ALL WHO dared enter the oppressive humidity. Rain spat from the sky a little harder this time and drummed across the leafy trees overhead. Sweat dotted my skin, and my mouth turned to cotton, all while my blood boiled inside my veins.

"Your men, huh?" Finn kicked the fallen leaves at his feet, making his captor work harder to keep him in his grasp.

"Don't start with that now." I stepped onto a log and lingered for an awkward moment to throw off the balance of the man at my back. If we couldn't fight back, we could at least make things more difficult for them.

"I was just wondering how you expected your plan to play out exactly. You and the deadliest pirate at sea, strolling through the jungle alone until you found some treasure? Then what, Cess?" Finn continued.

"You know, Finnigan, I was once led to believe that *you* were the deadliest pirate at sea." I scowled in his direction and yanked my arm to readjust the pirate's hold against my sore elbow.

"Close second, maybe." He returned my irritated expression.

I ducked to miss a heavy wet branch, causing me to bow closer to Finn as we moved along. "Besides, that plan worked well enough the first time I tried it."

"Because of me." Nikolaus wiggled around just enough that we could see him roll his eyes before the nasty pirate straightened him out again. He'd struck me as oddly calm since nearly being killed hours before on the beach. Even now, being held captive and walking to what I assumed to be our imminent death, he held his head high. He didn't always make sense to me, especially in moments of danger. Or maybe after what he and I had been through together at the hands of the other mutineers, nothing bothered him any longer.

"Where next?" Blackbeard's voice boomed above my thoughts.

Finn forced a smile. "It's a straight shot. Not hard to find. Just keep marching along."

There he went again, taking a dig at the man that held the power to end him.

Blackbeard plucked a small dagger from the inside of his overcoat and ran it between his fingers, "You know, Worley, you're a lucky man."

"You and I must have a very different definition of the term *lucky*." Finn shook his head so his wet hair detached from his cheek again.

Blackbeard chuckled. Then, in one quick move, he cracked Finn across the mouth with the butt of his blade.

I toppled back into my handler, a shriek caught on my lips. Finn stayed on his feet, somehow, and spat out the blood that pooled around his split lip.

"You're an idiot, but you're a fortunate idiot." Blackbeard wiped the droplets from the knife's handle onto his jacket. How many men had he bloodied with it in his lifetime? "It sure would have been nice to take your lady fair off your hands to lead me to the treasure while you watched from the beach. Until I gave the order for your death, of course."

"Naturally," Finn grumbled.

I couldn't even pretend to hold back my shut-your-mouth cough. Every time they laid a finger on him, it only twisted the knife deeper into my heart.

"Unfortunately, Hornigold wants to have a conversation with you. I'm sure you know why. And I'm sure you know the end result will be about the same."

"As *I'm* sure he'll have a good many things to say once he finds out about the treasure."

"Oh, he isn't going to find out about the treasure." Blackbeard ran his filthy fingers down his beaded hair as he forced out the words. Whatever power this treasure had, it made Blackbeard nervous. And whatever Finn knew about it, he kept it up his sleeve to use as leverage.

"Then let us hope that my good fortune is contagious, yeah?" Finn lost the cocky grin, his face hardening.

"So long as my *insurance* for your silence doesn't meet an untimely end before I need her, I'm not terribly worried..." The gold flecks in Blackbeard's teeth caught the light of a nearby torch when he raised an eyebrow in my direction. His jacket swooshed when he turned away to head up the march toward the rock formation that would reunite him once again with his wealth.

Finn lowered his head, jaw tight.

Certain Blackbeard was out of earshot, I stretched within my captor's grasp to regard my bloody-faced captain. "What in all of blazin' hell is going on here?"

The pirate at my back jerked his body, and I tripped over a stray log. Only his strength kept me from toppling to the jungle floor. "Would you shut your trap?"

I righted myself but kept my chin to my chest. "I believe Teach's only orders were for silence amongst his crew, but he's not *my* captain."

The pirate growled under his breath, his anger manifesting through his grip on my arm. I wouldn't give him the satisfaction of my pain. I knew he couldn't argue with me. Blackbeard was a smart man. He meant for his crew to be his ears amongst us. They couldn't speak. But Finn and I could argue as much as we desired, so long as we stayed alive until they wanted us dead.

"I'm fine. Thanks for your concern." Finn wiped his bloody mouth on his shirt collar.

"I'll make you bleed so much worse if you don't tell me what this has to do with Hornigold," I murmured. "Or if you don't stop taunting the enemy to his face like a ruddy fool! Why are you like this? For God's sake, Finnigan!"

"Good heavens, Cecily. You're less and less of a lady every day," he replied.

"Stars, you people are maddening," a female voice muttered from behind us. I took what comfort I could in having Josette so close to me.

Finn cleared his throat to speak and issued a quick look of disgust at the man that held him. Surely, the pirates surrounding us leaned in to hear what Finn had to say, ready to earn their captain's praise when they reported it. "I have a small confession to make."

"There are no small confessions with you." I pulled my body closer to Finn, and my captor allowed it—just as I'd suspected. "Just say it."

"It started a long time ago when we joined the Republic of Pirates, when I first took the *Hellbound*." It clearly hurt him to say the ship's name out loud after such a loss. "We stumbled upon other crews in the Caribbean. There were hundreds, maybe thousands of pirates here. Like this scum." Finn nodded toward the man holding him. He responded with an elbow to Finn's shoulder blade. Finn winced, but shook it off and continued, "That's when I met Benjamin Hornigold. He'd heard about me, informed me of the Republic, and invited us in...if we paid our share."

"Paid your share?" I didn't like where this was going.

Finn sighed. "They're pirates, Cess. They rob and plunder and kill." He turned again to the man at his back. "Don't you?"

The man shoved Finn forward, which should *not* have made Finn laugh. But it did. As if he hadn't already bordered on insanity, his ship sinking had sent him over the edge completley.

"Anyway, you know how things work on the *Hellbound*. Worked, I guess." Finn's smile disappeared as quickly as it had arrived. "We couldn't contribute from a plunder we didn't have. When we found this treasure, we used that. I guess it started to look familiar after a while." He nodded toward the front of our group to Blackbeard. "That's when we had to disappear, tried to stay hidden."

I let his words sink in as I walked. His stare burned into the side of my face, waiting for a response.

Handmade torches dotted the pitch-black jungle. We had to be well into the night. My aching body craved rest, but my mind rushed with too many worries and thoughts to slow down now. If Finn was right about his route being faster than the one Nikolaus and I had taken after our escape, we would reach our deadly desti- nation by sunrise.

"Why did we come back *here*? If you knew Blackbeard was looking for you, and you knew Hornigold wanted payment, then why would you bring us all to the pirates' main territory?" I asked.

Finn kept quiet, almost as quiet as I'd posed my question.

His answer wouldn't have mattered. I would have gone with him regardless of his absurd answer. "Why wouldn't you tell me?"

"I thought I could fix it before you had to be involved." Deep remorse filled his sigh, his head shaking. "I thought if we could get back here, I could turn over the whole thing to Hornigold and buy my way out before you ever knew. Like it never happened. I could have gotten us out of piracy completely, given you real freedom."

At that, it was my turn to be silent. When I joined him at sea, agreed to be a part of his crew and his life, I thought I'd finally found my freedom. But he was as much a slave to his masters as I had been to mine. Maybe true freedom was a myth, merely a whim- sical thought to fall asleep to at night.

"I'm sorry." His soft whisper rang in my ears as if he'd shouted it. "I never should have brought you with me. You were better off where you were than out here in my mess."

The suggestion broke something deep inside me, memories flashing across my mind in a whirlwind. I felt the sting of a lashing across my back, the inhumane names Mr. Collins called me, and the deep rumbling in my stomach after days with no food. My skin prickled with the memory of those chilly nights curled up on the floor without a bed to warm myself and the mud that caked my skin from a day's labor on the farm.

Now, I felt the ache in my wrists from the ropes tied there, my shoulders echoing the strain. Surely by now, my arms would show the purpling of bruises from the tight grasp, and my legs would be adorned with the multitude of cuts from skewed branches and the sharp thorns of the jungle floor. Though I hadn't had a decent meal or night's rest in days, my body had grown stronger than it had ever been before.

Even if we marched to our death, if Blackbeard meant to take the treasure and end us, I really was hardly worse off than I'd been in Collins's hands. Finn hadn't chosen piracy for me. I'd chosen it for myself.

I'd chosen *him*.

The rain grew heavier overhead, and a sweeping wind whipped at my side. An excited commotion rose from the front of the group and trickled back to us. The guards assigned to keep us moved to obey some unspoken command. With a simultaneous sweep of their legs, they knocked all of us off balance until we dropped painfully to our knees, guns readied in their hands.

The torches grew brighter when encompassed by the dark rocks that broke from the earth. We had reached the rock formation that signaled the end of our journey.

Blackbeard had found the treasure's keep—the vault that would surely become the final resting place for the crew of the *Hellbound*.

TWENTY-EIGHT

THE HEAT FROM THE ISLAND WINDS COULDN'T MATCH THE sharp chills crawling up my spine as Blackbeard returned to find us forcibly knelt before him. With each step, the weapons on his person clanked with a terrifying reminder of his deadly capabilities.

For a moment, the courage I'd gathered when confronting him on the beach dwindled, but I kept my chin up, willing it to remain as high as my aching body could hold it. He'd taken so much from me, from all of us. All we had left were our lives, and I wouldn't give mine up without a fight.

"You've learned this island well, Worley." Blackbeard stood tall, enjoying the chance to dominate the enemy bowing before him on the damp, muddy floor. "Now, I should probably clarify a few things."

Finn maintained his silence without giving Blackbeard the satisfaction of eye contact. Though, I stared hard enough at the villainous monster for the both of us.

"I want my treasure," Blackbeard said.

"You've been fairly clear on that point." Finn's eyes flickered to

Nik, who sat back on his legs, stone-faced and unmoved by the conversation.

"I am a man who knows what he wants. I believe we share this trait." Blackbeard smiled and twisted his finger around a strand of beads. "And I've promised Hornigold that I would spare your life if I found you first, which I made certain that I did. But I made no such promises about the rest of your men...or *women.*"

He reached down and took hold of my tied hair, yanking hard enough that it brought me to my feet with a pained scream. Finn shouted and lunged, but his captors teamed up to hold him back and keep him quiet. My head and neck throbbed as he dragged me a few steps away, where he kicked Nikolaus hard in the back and nodded for his men to lift the boy to his feet. I could hear the heavy gasps as Nikolaus fought to catch his breath from the pounding.

Blackbeard grinned, and his men chimed in with a roaring chuckle. "Shall we keep going? I trust you wouldn't lead us astray so close to our destination, but one can never be too certain."

I couldn't fight back the tears that accompanied the pain of trying to stand with the constant tugs in my hair. Rocks scraped my knees with each tumble through the maze of jagged boulders, and panic crept over me each time I lost sight of the others. Nik and I were leverage in the deal, disposable collateral. Fear painted Finn's face in a way I'd never seen, despite the peril we'd experienced together over the past year.

There was no plan that could get us out of this, and we both knew it.

The black night faded into a gray morning as the rock walls regained their color and cast shadows of their own over us. The men fought to keep their torches lit through the downpour, but the lightning overhead illuminated everything well enough.

And then we reached the mouth of the cave, even more terrifying than I remembered it. A new smell caught on the breeze, and several of the pirates gagged when it reached their noses: the stench of death, rotting corpses deep down in the cavern's belly, left there by Nikolaus and me less than two days before.

Blackbeard looked down at me, still clutched in his hand. His face twisted in disgust, then quickly changed into his usual evil grin. "You're welcome to take the lead, dear lady."

Thinking of walking the cold, dank decline of the cavern's throat into a golden grave made me forget about the pain. My nausea increased with every second that passed. It would only get worse as the day warmed. And who knew, with the rains pouring down as they did, perhaps the entire room lay under water. I tried to look for Finn, but Blackbeard's guidance wouldn't allow it. He pushed the back of my head until I fell to the ground in front of him, certain that chunks of my hair remained in his hand.

I crawled a few paces until I could right myself on my feet. Though I longed for a deep breath to get my bearings, it wasn't worth the risk of breathing in the scent of decomposition. With my head bowed, I took a step into the cave, then another and another, but halted when I heard something coming from below. It was hard to make out what only touched my ears as an echo, but it couldn't have been the heavier trickling of water ringing a different tune as it poured in. This sound was much more distinct.

Voices. I was sure of it.

I backed up. Blackbeard's hand dug into my shoulder to keep me from retreating any further.

"Move," he growled.

"But..." I shivered at the thought of what spoke in the darkness. Ghosts? On top of everything else? Cantrill and Dull had died. No doubt about that. Had Norris come to and called out for rescue?

Blackbeard raised an arm to quiet his crew. He heard it, too, now. The noise grew louder, clearer. Whoever, or *what*ever, lingered inside was on their way out. A shrill whistle from behind us caused everyone to turn from the entrance and retreat to find the source. In a moment, the men had drawn every weapon on their person.

I ducked down, trying to keep my body close to the wall of the cave, while Finn slipped between two of the men to get to my side, his hands still bound behind his back. Josette fell against the rocks beside me, too, her dark eyes revealing the terror she couldn't hide. We watched as the rest of our crew separated themselves from Blackbeard's bunch to duck for cover behind the mountainous rocks. All except for Nikolaus.

I wanted to yell, to signal for him to join us at the wall so we might remain together, but he stood firm, looking about in wonder. His deep breaths made his chest rise and fall rather noticeably.

"Lower your weapons," someone shouted from above us, causing all of Blackbeard's men to aim toward the sky, some even firing at an invisible enemy.

"I said put down your weapons, you morons," the voice yelled again.

This time, Blackbeard himself straightened and gave the command for the men to stand down. He spun a slow circle, his expression perplexed in every way. When his gaze fell on Finn, a menacing scowl appeared.

"Edward, your men are trigger-happy," the mysterious booming voice called out.

A broad-shouldered man appeared atop a large boulder, one leg propped higher than the other to give him a rather casual appearance. He had to be a man of prominent position, another captain perhaps, judging by his fancy coat and feathered hat. His long, sandy hair tied at the base of his tricorn hat. His short beard hugged his cheeks, but didn't come together at his chin the way most men's did. A wide smile painted his face, a noticeable contrast against the dark sky and even darker company.

"Benjamin, my apologies. I hadn't expected to find you in the jungle's midst." Blackbeard tried in vain to mask his anger with surprise.

This had to be Hornigold. The recognition on Finn's face

proved my guess correct, though his equal surprise at the man's appearance left many unanswered questions.

"I knew I could count on you and your men to deliver." Hornigold moved from rock to rock until he touched the ground and straightened his delicate overcoat. He then reached out to take Blackbeard's hand. Had I met him under any other context, I might have assumed him a gentleman.

"Indeed," Blackbeard said with a flourish. Did he even know what he'd delivered on?

"Some of my men are still examining the contents of the fortune, but it is an impressive find if I've ever seen one." Hornigold patted Blackbeard on the shoulder as he looked behind him to Finn, who had stiffened at my side.

Hornigold chuckled and shook his head as he approached. "Worley, you've certainly looked better."

I braced myself for whatever comeback Finn would offer at such a statement, but he remained quiet, which was even more alarming.

"Quite the treasure you've compiled here. And to think you kept it all to yourself with no contribution to the Republic." Hornigold clicked his tongue as if he scolded a wayward child and not a notorious pirate captain.

If Hornigold believed the treasure to be Finn's, then he didn't yet know it had belonged to Blackbeard beforehand. How much *did* he know, exactly? I could see from behind him that Blackbeard was equally intent on listening to the conversation and deducing the extent of Hornigold's knowledge.

Finn forced a smile. "You are mistaken, sir. It was my intent to give the entire sum to the Republic. That's my business here in the Caribbean."

"How very generous." Hornigold looked at him flatly before letting his attention drift over to me and then back to Finn. "It wasn't simply your charitable nature, though, was it? After all, you haven't contributed your share in a year. And with all this treasure at your disposal?"

"You try finding a loyal crew to transport a treasure of this size and let me know how quickly you can manage it." Finn nodded toward his own meager group as if we proved the statement true.

Hornigold smiled. "I have such a crew, and we will happily accept your donation. Though, I must say, I'm disappointed. You had such potential, Finnigan. I'd hoped you'd one day be like Edward here."

Blackbeard's fists clenched so tightly they squeaked around his hilt.

"There's no one quite like Edward." Finn sneered in his rival's direction.

Hornigold breathed a quick laugh, then set his attention on me once more, and I fought the urge to slink even closer to Finn and hide myself away. Blackbeard had frightened me with the sheer terror of his presence, but Hornigold exuded a sense of power that made me feel as small as a field mouse.

"You're a lucky man, Finnigan." Hornigold walked a few paces past Blackbeard.

"So I've heard," Finn replied with an irritated nod.

"You've proved yourself a powerful and wise captain." He stopped walking when he reached Nikolaus and placed a heavy hand on the boy's shoulder. "But if it weren't for your brother here, this whole encounter might have gone very differently." Hornigold gestured to his closest men. "Release him."

Nik's chest puffed, and he shook out his freed hands and nodded his appreciation toward his superior.

"Nikolaus, you've done well." Hornigold slapped Nik on the shoulder, almost knocking him off balance.

The entire jungle seemed to light ablaze around us. My head grew faint. What had Nik done?

"Thank you, sir." Nikolaus regained his composure, keeping his gaze averted from mine and Finn's, though we desperately tried to attain it.

"Nik?" Finn stumbled toward his brother, but a wall of opposition met him.

"Yes, he's been quite the informant. Told us all about your affair with this servant girl and all the *distractions* that came with her presence. It is lovely to meet you, my dear, after hearing so much about you. Cecily, is it?" Hornigold flashed a clean smile in my direction, and the breath caught in my throat. "Made a little deal with Nikolaus, I did, or perhaps I should say, *he* made a deal with *me*. He'd sent word of this treasure and of your intentions to leave the Republic. Well, as you know, it's not our way to simply release those we've accepted into such company."

At that, Nikolaus looked up and met Finn's hard stare. Neither of the men moved, though I felt the harsh stab of betrayal from my place beside him. No one among us could have expected the youngest member of our group to be responsible for this encounter. Even Blackbeard himself hadn't seen this one coming, judging from the way he glared at the younger boy, his hand fidgeting with a pistol on his chest.

"And what deal did you strike?" Finn asked, the question directed to Nikolaus more than to Hornigold.

But it was Hornigold who answered. "The full amount of treasure for your life, obviously, as I'm sure you're aware your late payment to the Republic would have cost you both." Hornigold crossed his arms over his broad chest, his focus shifting between Finn and Nikolaus. "He gave me the exact location of your fortune, though he didn't mention leading Edward here as well. That's rather convenient, I must say. Nikolaus, you really will make a wonderful addition to my crew."

"To *your* crew?" Finn's outburst made me jump.

All this time, Nik had already made a bargain with the enemy. No wonder he never seemed flustered in the jungle when our lives hung in the balance. He already knew the outcome, had already gone to the one who held all the power here.

Hornigold only nodded with a thoughtful hum. "Well, yes, that was part of the bargain. Your ship and your best men become mine, or property of the Republic, as it is. You've accumulated quite the debt, unfortunately."

Blackbeard chuckled to himself, prompting Hornigold to turn and inquire with a quizzical brow.

"His ship's at the bottom of the ocean. We had a small miscommunication, you could say," Blackbeard's gruff voice muttered.

Finn's face flushed red. In one day, we lost our home, the crew broke apart, and Nikolaus had betrayed us to the enemy. The winds picked up, and a crack of thunder tore through the sky, prompting both Hornigold and Blackbeard to look toward the heavens.

"Unfortunate. That was a fine ship, but the gold will buy us finer," Hornigold said. "We must make haste if we intend to beat this storm. Untie them all. We need all the hands to transport the goods."

I no longer noticed the stench wafting out of the cave or cared about the rain battering my skin as it fell from above. The world as I knew it had fallen apart.

TWENTY-NINE

WE'D BARELY DRAGGED THE TREASURE A FEW MILES BEFORE we reached the sea and saw his warship anchored in the bay. It was at least a thirty-gun sloop, sails stretched into the low-hanging clouds. The waves caught at the sides of the vessel, but the beast stayed afloat. The journey from the beach to the ship would not be a smooth one.

"Men, load the boats." Hornigold instructed his mates, some that had accompanied him on the hike and others that had awaited our arrival on shore. "Edward, have your men watch Worley's crew and take a walk with me."

Blackbeard nodded and gave instruction, all the while making frequent glances toward Finn. Finn, however, kept his eyes on his brother. Nikolaus stood at a distance from the rest of us, helping Hornigold's men to load the boats. He put in significant effort to keep his back to us.

"What's goin' to happen now?" Josette crept to my side.

There was no easy answer. She joined the crew and hadn't even gotten the chance to sail with us, as was the case with most of the men standing in a huddle together, awaiting their fate. "I don't know."

"The cabin boy gave us up?" She leaned in closer, her watchful eye examining the surroundings. "And he's the captain's own brother?"

I swallowed hard. She hadn't known any of us long, but I could see the shared hurt in her expression. Her rough fingers wrapped around my wrist and squeezed.

She nodded toward Finn as he paced back and forth under the close watch of six guards. "You should try to talk to him."

"And tell him what?" I'd never held a shortage of words for Finn, but when the world came crashing down around us, there seemed nothing left to say.

She shrugged. "You'll think of something."

I reached out to catch her arm, but she'd already left me to join the rest of our men. Hopefully, she could rally their spirits better than she had mine. At least she'd gotten me out of my daze, and I found myself moving toward Finn.

One of the pirate guards slammed a palm into my shoulder, knocking me backward. "What do you want?"

"Get your hands off me." I slapped his arm away and regained my composure. "I just want to talk."

He raised his fist to strike again, but something caught his forearm mid-swing. I opened my eyes to see Finn standing between us to shove the man away.

"Don't touch her." Finn took my hand to pull me into the ring of armed guards. "No one said anything against talking."

I could see the assaulted pirate wanted to have a few more words, maybe even violent actions, but the disruption had also captured both Hornigold's and Blackbeard's attention. Hornigold nodded, and the pirates surrounding us stood down, muttering their disapproval with colorful words and warnings. Our first assailant patted his hand on the pistol at his hip to remind us of our powerless state.

"Filthy pirates," Finn muttered, his attention returning to Nik.

"Did you know?" I stood close enough at his side that my chin brushed against his shoulder when I spoke. It didn't matter if the others heard, but I still felt exposed at the center of their circle.

He just shook his head.

"Has he said any—"

"No. Hasn't even let me get close enough to ask a single, bloody question." Finn sucked in a deep breath and lowered his head. "I should have listened to him. I should have given him more responsibility on the ship sooner. Treated him as an equal—I don't know." He let his face fall into his hands before sliding them over his hair.

There seemed to be no reassurance I could give, and it ate at my insides. My head grew heavy on my shoulders, exhaustion clouding my every thought. I weaved my fingers into his.

"I'm sorry." I stared at the wet sand, now marked with craters from heavy rain and weighted footprints. "About the ship, about Nikolaus, about this past month and not trusting you. I didn't know about the Republic, but I think I get it. The treasure, too. It's…" I touched the palm of my hand to my forehead as if to force the thoughts into place. "You just wanted your freedom the same way I wanted mine. You deserve to be free."

His fingers tightened around mine, our expressions sharing the same sadness and defeat. We weren't as different as I once thought us.

This felt like goodbye. It most likely was. "Finn?"

He leaned into me, his rough finger brushing away the tear on my cheek.

I had to tell him. If death took us today, I couldn't let him leave this earth without knowing. "I have never regretted any of this life with you. Even *now*. I've loved you every second of it."

His eyes closed, and he lowered his forehead to touch mine. "*Minun ankurri*, I—"

"Captain Worley," Hornigold called out.

My blood turned cold when Finn winced against me.

The pirates on guard separated from us without needing more than a wave of the hand to command them. Hornigold continued, "We've come to a decision."

Finn's fingers clutched mine with even greater force now, and he positioned himself slightly in front of me like a shield between the two pirate forces and me. From the corner of my eye, I spotted Nikolaus stand at attention to observe the interaction. His neck strained as he leaned as close as he could without moving his feet.

"Edward and I disagree on your sentence, but seeming as you have already lost your ship and we have possession of your entire treasure, I believe I have come up with the perfect solution that will make everyone happy while still honoring the agreement I've made previously with young Nikolaus. After all, I'm a man of my word," Hornigold proclaimed, as if this somehow made him an honorable man.

Honor didn't exist in the demon realm.

At Hornigold's side, Blackbeard fidgeted with the handle of his sword, a scowl peeking out from his bushy beard when he glared at Finn. His anger hadn't subsided any. And why would it? He'd lost his treasure in its entirety to Hornigold and the Republic. Though Finn hadn't divulged the information that the treasure had originally belonged to Blackbeard—and neither had Nikolaus, it seemed. There was no win in it for him, but there was no win in any of it for us either. Such was the masochistic life of a pirate.

"As you know, Nikolaus has already agreed to join my crew. I will happily take him on as my apprentice now that Edward here has been rather successful on his own." Hornigold patted Blackbeard on the shoulder, a friendly act that made Blackbeard flinch. "Nikolaus can learn from a *real* captain and have a true life at sea."

I couldn't tell who squeezed whose hand first, but both Finn's and my grasp locked tighter. The words hurt him; they hurt me. I didn't have to know Hornigold or Blackbeard to know that Finn had every bit the skill these men had at sea, and more, and that no matter what happened next, Nik was about to be ripped away from us forever.

"Alas, as I've recently acquired the *Ranger*, and the crew to man it, I find no need to take on more bodies than necessary." He took hold of the edges of his coat, rolling onto the tips of his toes. The prideful display seemed particularly sickening.

Finn lifted his chin and set his jaw. "What's it to be then?"

Hornigold stepped closer to our men, his stature seeming to grow with his mighty stance. Silence overtook the lot of us. Blackbeard's arms folded over the loaded baldric on his chest. He took immense joy in this moment, despite his losses.

"Finnigan Worley, you are an enemy of the Republic. As such, your fate should have already been determined. Because I am a man of my word, no harm will come to you from my hand," Hornigold stated.

Finn's lips pursed firmly.

I felt a scream rising from the depths of my stomach. I couldn't take this anymore.

Blackbeard didn't wait for the command to speak, all his former rage melting away with the ability to finally say the words. "As a compromise, you will come with me."

"No," I whispered. The rain fell heavier than ever before. If it knocked me to the ground, I might never rise again.

Blackbeard couldn't have him. If Finn stepped foot on his ship, Blackbeard would surely kill him, or worse, and there would be no one there to interfere on his behalf. He didn't deserve that fate, not after everything he'd done for me and so many others. He'd given me hope and a new life. And I loved him for that and so much more.

"That wasn't part of our deal." Nikolaus stormed past the other pirates, tromping through the sand to face Hornigold straight on. "You said you'd leave him unharmed. Him *and* the rest of the crew. That's what we discussed. That's what you agreed to."

"Nik..." Finn's voice was quiet, defeated, but Nikolaus wouldn't turn toward the sound of his name.

"Dear boy, I have remained true to my promise that *I* would leave him unharmed." Hornigold smiled, lifting his hands as if the burdens we faced were nothing to him. Because they weren't. "The rules of the Republic are finite, and I've already broken them at your request. I can do no more. Your meager crew is still free to go. I have no use for them."

"You can't leave him with that blackguard." Nikolaus's jaw clenched.

Blackbeard took one angry step toward Nik before Hornigold's hand stopped him in his place.

"He's no longer your problem. You sail with me now." Hornigold gestured for his crew to come and claim the boy. "We can still make Nassau before the worst of the storm if we make haste."

The world darkened around me, and my knees wavered as burly hands encompassed my body, tugging me out of Finn's grasp. It wasn't real. A scream broke through the sky that sounded infinitely far away, but I knew it was mine. Finn's sad eyes pleaded for me to be strong and silently said so many things I refused to accept.

I let my weight drop, putting my feet to the sand and twisting until my elbow collided against my captor's stomach. As he bent over, I drew my arm up to hear a violent crack as my forearm snapped the bones in his nose. He dropped to his knees, and I rushed back to Finn's side. Both Blackbeard and Hornigold drew their weapons upon approach.

"Take me!" I shouted and hurled my body in front of Finn's. "Take me instead of him."

I stared into the dark, dead eyes of Blackbeard, unwavering as he came closer and closer. Finn's hands pawed at my waist as he tried to switch our places. Neither of us were armed and stood no chance in a fight against the two leaders. But I'd rather die than take another breath, knowing I didn't do everything I could to save him.

Blackbeard laughed. "I don't want *you*."

I knew that. Deep down, I knew he only cared for revenge, but I had to try. I *had* to.

"Cecily, you need to go. Get away," Finn whispered against my hair. His fingers dug sharply into my sides, as if he couldn't decide whether to force me away or keep me close. "It'll be all right. Just run. Get far from here—"

"No." I raised one hand to Blackbeard and put the other on top of Finn's. I held the attention of all three crews now. Hornigold had eased off his hilt to scratch at his muttonchops. "Leave him and take me instead. I'm the reason he stopped contributing to your Republic. I'm the one that killed your men. Your revenge should be with me, not *him*."

"She doesn't know what she's saying," Finn's voice grew more urgent now. "Cecily, just go. *Please*."

My entire body trembled as I fought to keep him behind me. My heart couldn't take his pleading much longer, and I wanted to be put out of my misery no matter what end it came by.

Blackbeard's eyes narrowed as he watched us like two play characters sent to entertain him. Finally, he clapped his hands together. "I would like to propose a change in our plans, Benjamin."

This caught Hornigold's attention, and he returned to his comrade's side. "We set our sentence, Edward. What change could you make now?"

Finn continued to plead into my hair in a way that made my tears fall faster without the slightest hope to control them. Blackbeard's men had arrived at his side, awaiting the command, whatever it may be.

"Leave Worley to the island, and allow me to take his crew to the Colonies with me," Blackbeard said. "All of them."

The *whole* crew? My legs wobbled under me.

"Cecily," Nik hissed and beat his hand to his forehead. "Why don't you ever just shut your mouth?"

"Not *them*." I couldn't raise my voice loud enough to get our captors' attention. The crew didn't deserve to suffer damnation at my side. I only meant to save my captain from an unbearable fate.

I could do nothing more than sink against Finn's chest. He still swore in continuous, hysterical streams as his hands found their way to my face. His head shook against mine, his words a mixture of Finnish and English. "Cecily, why are you doing this?"

"I just wanted you to be free," I whispered.

Hornigold crossed his arms over his chest and lifted his chin to examine the scene unfolding before him. "If you wish."

Blackbeard cleared his throat. "Might I also take the boy as my apprentice instead of yours?"

"No!" Finn shouted above the thunder.

Hornigold raised his brow, which caused his men to take hold of Finn's shoulders, pulling him from my grasp.

"This is almost the opposite of what we discussed," Hornigold said. "But I still leave with the treasure, and the *Hellbound* and its command no longer haunt the seas. If you'd prefer to handle its crew, it's your choice. Though, Worley is hardly receiving a sentence worthy of his crime, and you seemed adamant he be punished to the full extent of the Republic's law."

"You're absolutely right." As Blackbeard stepped closer to Finn, his men approached us from behind to hold him in place. "Might I recommend sending word to the Republic of his betrayal and placing justice in *their* hands?"

A brutish pirate slapped his hand across my mouth to withhold my scream. I writhed in his grasp, though my strength had weakened as we suffered one blow after the other.

Hornigold nodded toward his companion, considering the proposal. "I'll pass the word along to the others. Now, we must be on with it, or this storm will kill us all."

As the reigning captain hurried to the longboats, Blackbeard took command. "Load the ships! Tie this sorry excuse of a captain to a tree. We'll see if the lightning takes him before the Republic gets their chance."

The men wasted no time obeying orders, and I pressed my lips to Finn's until the monsters tore us apart. They dragged him from me, while he kicked and thrashed against them. Still, they bound his hands and feet and pulled him through the heavy wet sand to a nearby tree and tied him to the base. From his position, he had no choice but to watch his crew being taken away on the shoreline.

"Let's sail," Blackbeard spat.

Nik had moved to my side, his face reflecting the same exhausted horror I felt. Blackbeard approached with heavy breaths that mimicked the blowing winds of the oncoming hurricane. He jammed the weighty barrels of his guns into our backs simultaneously.

His beaded beard slithered across my exposed shoulder. "This is a much better punishment for that scum of a man. I appreciate the suggestion." He sneered and dug the butt of his gun harder into my spine. "Now walk."

Despite the cold pistol wedged in my ribs, I chanced one last look toward Finn. He'd gone silent, sunken at the foot of the tree.

He was at the mercy of the Republic now, and I belonged to Blackbeard. With a painful breath of the warm island air, I turned to walk the shoreline with my face to the weeping sky and my life in the hands of the enemy.

THIRTY

The ride to Blackbeard's ship on the choppy waves whipped our bodies around the longboat. Still, I strained to catch sight of Finn's place on shore, though he'd disappeared in the stormy haze long ago.

When the longboat collided with the ship, the pirates worked with pained effort to attach the pulleys and bring us aboard. Nikolaus's shoulder slammed into mine, and I scooted away as far as the ropes allowed. For the first time since we'd met, it hurt too much to be near him.

He'd made a deal with the enemy. And I'd made it so much worse.

The men moved us so quickly from the boat to the deck, my feet barely brushed over the floor until they forced us down at Blackbeard's feet.

"Throw them in the cells, and then we sail," he commanded. His men gathered us up again, until their captain reached into our group and grabbed Nikolaus by the front of his shirt. "Not this one. He stays with me."

The pirates ushered us on again toward the stairwell, giving us no time to react to losing one of our own. Perhaps most of our crew had grown accustomed to us being divided and lost. But how could I ever get used to seeing Finn and Nik taken from me over and over again? They were the only family I ever knew. Despite our love for one another, the three of us lived an unending lie and exhausted our efforts to keep our family from harm. We'd lost all hope—and each other now. To save Finn from Blackbeard's clutches, I placed Nik, and everybody else, directly in his path.

In the hull, the pirates wordlessly opened the cell doors and pushed half the crew inside the first and half in the second. They kept hold of me, only to shove me into a third cell by myself. If they kept us together, the men might turn on me. Blackbeard didn't want that. No, he'd keep that privilege for himself.

The grime on the cell floor coated our feet and made it difficult to stand. The darkness came over us like a curtain when all light vanished with the pirate's exit. I backed up until my leg bumped into something, sending it crashing to the floor. Not crashing. *Rattling*. Like bones.

I gasped and took hold of the cell bars. How long did Blackbeard keep his prisoners in these cells? I closed my eyes despite the blackness and focused on breathing through the rotten stench around us.

"How much time do we got before he kills the lot of us?" someone asked.

"Worley's wench led us all to the grave!" Another shrieked near hysteria.

Someone rammed himself into the cell bars that separated us, shouting in another language. It set my nerves on edge.

"This storm will take us down before the captain gets his chance. We're all going to drown!" The man beat his fists against the floorboards. "Where is *she*?"

I deserved to die at their hands after what I did. There was nothing left to live for, anyway. Blackbeard had taken it all from me.

"Oh, would you all shut your ruddy gobblers? You act as if we've already died ten times over." Josette scoffed from the opposite cell. "Bloody Norah! You think they didn't already plan to kill us all before Hastings opened her big trap?"

Her attempt at standing up for me might not have been the most flattering, but it seemed to quell the men around me for a moment. I took a chance and called out to her. "Josette?"

She hummed to the affirmative and then, "You should know I am most definitely planning to murder your cabin boy if Blackbeast hasn't done it already." Something cracked against the bars when she finished. "Can't say I've ever touched a human bone before."

Did this woman know fear? No wonder she'd survived this long with a doomed crew.

Something ground against the wood of the ship, and we swayed more violently inside our hold.

They'd lifted anchor.

Finn could only watch us sail away from his place on shore and wait for those who hunted him.

Loud footsteps sounded on the narrow stairs, accompanied by the eerie jingle of steel meeting steel. A lantern illuminated the dark space, but I kept my eyes from drifting to the corners to meet my decomposing cellmates face on. Instead, I focused on my captor through the bars as he stopped at the base of the stairs, resting one foot on the last step to steady himself against the waves.

He briefly inspected the prisoners in all three cells and smiled when he found me. I hated him more with every passing second.

"It would seem your former captain kept me from my treasure after all, but I believe I've found a solution to make up some of the difference. You see, the Colonies have placed a high price on pirates' heads, and I now find myself in the company of quite a few pirates to present them." He paused, while the men murmured around him.

The madman meant to take our lives, whether here or on our arrival. What did it matter now?

Blackbeard held up a finger as if another thought had occurred to him. "That is, if any of you survive the journey. If you do not drown down here when the waters rush in, starve, as I won't be feeding you, or die at the hands of my men in their boredom, I will, indeed, take enormous pride in delivering you to the governor."

All around me, the men's breathing hitched louder than the sounds of the waves crashing against the hull. Caught up in this cage, we really had no escape. The last time I was held captive in a pirate's cell, I'd been fed, given dry clothes, and had a cabin boy to ensure I didn't drown when the waters raged in on me. Here? We were all as good as dead.

"I am a man of mercy, however." Blackbeard paced between our cells, letting his metal lantern clang against each of the bars like he meant to set us ablaze if none of his other death plans worked. "If you join my crew on the *Vengeance*, you will receive clemency." He paused for a moment. "What say you?"

I pressed my weight into the back wall and crossed my arms over my chest. I would rather hang from ten gallows than submit to such a man.

"Aye!" The man in the cell beside me rushed to the front. Then another man echoed and joined him. All around the hull, the crew of the *Hellbound* changed allegiance. They would sell their souls to the devil for a fool's chance.

Their new captain lifted the light to reveal his sinister grin. He jingled the keys in his hand and unlocked the cell opposite mine. The men shuffled out, and Blackbeard pointed them toward the stairwell. With the force of new life in their bodies, off they went to get their assignments on board the *Vengeance*.

After releasing the men to my left, he turned to me and clicked his tongue. "Not as brave as your fellow men?"

"Not as daft, more like." I had nothing to lose by speaking to him this way. He could make no threat to hurt me more than he already had. "You still mean to turn them over in the Colonies, don't you?"

Blackbeard shrugged. "I still need my coin, lovey."

"Of course." My chest tightened, and I unfolded my arms to grab hold of the cell bars as the ship bucked in the waves.

"And I shall get a pretty penny for you. The closest accomplice to the Blood Pirate's crimes? Oh, yes. They'll be delighted to have you," he said. "The gold I get for your head will pay for the reward on Worley's."

I spat on the ground in front of me. If I'd had any sort of range, I might have tried to hit *him*. He laughed aloud and left without another word. Just before the light vanished from the hull with him, I caught sight of one other figure remaining in the cell. I could hardly wait for Blackbeard to vanish before the excitement got the better of me.

"Josette, you angel on earth." I sighed as my hand fell over my heart.

"No need to get dramatic." She chortled and smacked the cell wall again—probably with the same bone she played with before.

My fingers coiled around the grimy bars, and I imagined her face before me in the darkness. "You stayed. Why didn't you go with the others?"

She hummed an odd tune. "Well, I suspected he'd betray the takers, and I was right 'bout that. I considered for a moment, just to get my hands on that wretch of a cabin boy. But I'd also rather die than take orders from that pig-scum captain. Knew you wouldn't take 'is bait. Figured facing the gallows isn't the worst I could do with my life, and least it'd be more tolerable with a friend. It's just you and me now, milady."

As I imagined her bowing dramatically the way she would, my heart warmed—even though the comment bordered on insanity. Still, she'd called me *friend*. Even on this ship of horrors, I wasn't alone.

Blackbeard didn't scare me anymore. He didn't scare either of us.

"Josette?"

"Aye?" she answered from across the hull.

"What do you say we leave the gallows for another day and burn this ship to its shell instead?" I clutched harder on my cell bars and waited.

Something skittered across the floor in the other chamber. Then her voice came louder, almost closer than before. "I'd say that's precisely what I'd hoped to hear."

THIRTY-ONE

IT TOOK ALL OF MY STRENGTH TO HOLD MY BODY IN PLACE against the front of my cell as I schemed with Josette into the night. My eyes grew heavier, and Josette stopped answering me. At some point, I gave in to the exhaustion as well and drifted off to sleep.

A clang at the iron door shook me from my slumber, but it was the hand yanking at my shirt collar that fully woke me. The pirate spun me around and pulled me across the grimy floor. I shrieked, waking Josette. She scampered across her cell and tried to reach for my foot, but my captor kept me out of her grasp. I couldn't speak a word to her, the pain in my back too horrendous as the pirate continued to drag me up each step.

When I went for his hand behind my head, he jerked his arm until I hit the side of the stairs. He kept silent. Had Blackbeard sent him for me, or did he come for me on his own terms?

The moment he pulled me out the door, rain spattered against my face, soaking my entire body in mere seconds. We crossed the deck as men worked and yelled commands to each other. Some of those workers I assumed to be my old crewmates.

My pirate captor hauled me up yet another staircase, and I

groaned louder in protest. This stairwell led to the helm. Though I couldn't see the captain, I could sense him.

The pirate used all the force in him to throw me to the ground, causing me to roll into the wooden helm's base. I pushed myself up with my hands and backed away as much as possible.

"What do you want? I'm not joining your crew," I spat.

Blackbeard kept his eyes on the gray horizon. "You're a pathetic excuse for a pirate. I have no intention of *allowing* you to work on this magnificent ship."

"*Magnificent* is a generous word for a floating rubbish hold." My words had hardly escaped my mouth when Blackbeard's thick hand wrapped around my neck. His charcoal eyes blazed.

"Do I need to remind you that your ship rests at the bottom of the ocean? I'm sure its captain won't be far behind." He thrust me backward into the chest of the pirate that previously held me. My knees buckled, but I quickly regained my strength. The anger raging inside me made my eyes burn, but I couldn't let them see my forming tears as weakness.

I kept my focus on maintaining my stance on the unsteady deck and tried to do a sweep of the ship for any sign of Nikolaus. "Why did you bring me up here? I was perfectly content to rot in my cell, away from you."

"Because I'm bored, and I have my enemy's wench in my grasp. I might as well enjoy the moment while you still have breath in your lungs, eh?" Blackbeard waved his hand, and the pirate behind me grabbed me harder and yanked my arms behind my back. "We've decided the *Vengeance* needs a bit of decoration. And you shall make an adequate figurehead."

A figurehead? My mind couldn't process fast enough to fight off the man wrapping frayed ropes around my wrists. Blackbeard laughed at my struggle, loud enough to draw the attention of the crew on deck. The pirate dragged me down the stairs again, pain ripping through my shoulders at the odd way my arms bent. Some men stared as we passed, others averted their eyes—my old crewmates.

The rain hit harder as we moved across the ship. Would they really string me up at the bow? He might as well sentence me to keelhauling. My arms would rip from my body at this treatment.

At the front mast, my captor stopped and pressed me to the wooden hold. The air rushed out of my lungs, the bone in my wrists cracking together. The pirate flung a rope around my middle as if this wasn't the first time he'd done such a thing. I kept quiet. Mere moments before, I'd schemed with Josette on how to take down this vessel. Now, here I was, a ragged ornament.

Over the thunder and the pattering rain, I heard the captain cackling at the helm. Though they hadn't hurled me off the front of the ship, the rain beating at my face would take its toll as the day progressed. Did he mean to keep me here for the duration of the journey? A trip to the Colonies could take many months in this weather.

What hope did any of us have left? Unless Josette could single-handedly carry out a plan on her own, I might as well succumb to the storm. I still hadn't seen Nikolaus to know what Blackbeard had done with him, or what Nikolaus had become for Blackbeard. His betrayal rang too fresh in my mind. The image of Finn crying out from his hold on the beach stayed at the forefront of my mind, as it may be forever. How long until those hunting him claimed their prize?

My head fell back on the splintered post, and I cried out with the all the anguish that had built up inside me.

Why didn't Blackbeard and his men just kill us in the jungle? To play with us like this proved cruel in a way I'd never experienced. Even the Collins's farm seemed an oasis compared to Blackbeard's lunacy. Then again, he was a man of show. Whatever he could do to earn the greatest reputation amongst his fellow men, he wouldn't dare hesitate.

I lost count of the times the ship's bell tolled the hour. The crew carried on around me, only offering an occasional jeer to remind me of my existence. I couldn't see any of them, my body tied too tightly to the post. My only view included the choppy waves meeting the gray clouds that went on endlessly into the horizon. The thunder drummed overhead. It wouldn't take long until I went entirely mad here.

How had I ever thought piracy a good idea?

We'd escaped the Royal Navy, and somehow I assumed this to be the worst we could face. In such a wretched profession, opposition would always come for us. If not Blackbeard, then someone else. An infinite sea of them.

If only I could go back in time. I would have pulled Finn and Nik from the ship in Ireland and ran them off into the countryside with the rest of the prisoners Finn had rescued. We could have lived a long and *safe* life together in the hills, forget this entire existence altogether. We could have *lived*...

THE FEW LANTERNS THAT WITHSTOOD THE RAIN REMAINED the only light on deck. The bell chimed another hour, which brought with it a change in shifts.

Every part of my body ached under the tight ropes. I tried to sleep, but my neck strained from the burden of my head falling from side to side. My legs could hardly hold up my weight, though the restraints left me no other choice but to stand.

The bucking ship made my empty stomach queasier by the hour. I had nothing in me to vomit up. At least the storm hadn't gotten worse. I would have been able to tell if it had. Perhaps we'd gotten ahead of it. But if Finn had taught me one thing about this time of year, it was that there was never just one storm. Another would soon follow.

Footsteps padded across the wooden deck behind me, quieter than the way most men walked about the ship. The night crew on board the *Vengeance* must have been excessively considerate to their fellow demons, who did not grant the same courtesy during the day. Then again, Blackbeard would have also retired to bed by now.

The sound of tip-toeing boots stopped just to my left, and I dared turn my head what little I could. My breath caught. He looked so much like his brother. It ground my heart to sand inside me. Even acknowledging Nikolaus alive and well before me didn't soothe the pain. It only further mangled my gut.

"I brought you some bread," Nik said in a quiet voice that mimicked the waves crashing alongside the ship.

I shifted away from him to save myself the pain of studying the angles on his face. "I don't want it."

"You haven't eaten in two days." He further closed the gap between us.

My lips barely parted as I growled back at him. "I don't care."

"Cecily, I won't let you die."

"Death is the end result when you make a deal with the devil, Nik." I strained my head to look at him now, though it hurt in so many ways.

His hand slammed against the wooden mast beside my head, and he showed immense restraint in keeping his voice steady and low. "I did it to protect my brother. To protect *you*. I knew Blackbeard would kill you both if he got to you before Hornigold knew about the treasure."

"Which went splendidly, didn't it?" I spit out the rain water that flooded my mouth when I spoke. "Blackbeard still got what he wanted."

"Yeah, well, thanks to your attempt at a *sacrifice*, we're all at his mercy now," he muttered through clenched teeth. "He wants Finn's head, you know. The price he'll pay could earn a poor man a galleon of his own." He kicked hard at the wooden beam holding me and bit down hard on his bottom lip.

All the horrors replayed in my mind, and I couldn't stop them from surfacing. "Our men turned themselves over to Blackbeard as part of the crew, and he still means to turn them over in the Colonies on arrival. The one remaining crewmember loyal to our captain is locked away in the hull, kept in utter darkness, and starving—"

"She's being fed. She's got water," Nikolaus snapped.

What delusions had Blackbeard fed him? He'd given us no previsions. "Just go away."

He moved closer still. My skin prickled, every part of me calling out to lean in toward the familiar, the only family I had in this world.

No, I had Finn, too.

My heart choked me from the inside.

"Do you really think I wanted it this way? You really think I planned to lose our home? To turn Finn over to his worst enemy and risk his death? We lost everything, Cecily. *Everything!* I never wanted any of that. Piracy is a game, and I tried to play it to save my brother because he couldn't do it for himself." He swore, his balled fists pressed to his forehead.

Now I had nothing to say. Obviously, Nik hadn't wanted that. He and Finn had been through so much together. Their freedom had long drowned in crippling lies and the risk that they might one day lose it all.

Piracy really was a game. We'd gotten lucky too many times. Cheated our way through it until now. We had no moves left. We'd lost.

"Your plans go about as well as mine do." I tried to laugh, but it came out as a forced puff of air.

"Don't think that didn't occur to me." His half-hearted smile proved all he could manage in return.

What else was left for us in this moment? I couldn't even embrace him. Couldn't forgive him when he'd done nothing wrong but try to protect us. We'd both failed our captain and each other. I had no words of comfort. I had nothing.

"I promise my next plan will be better," he whispered.

"Wha—"

Nik shoved a piece of bread into my mouth to keep the rest of my words inside.

"Don't die. Keep your eyes on the weather." He nodded, and as quietly as he'd appeared, he vanished.

THIRTY-TWO

THE NEXT DAY PASSED IN UTTER AGONY. I DOUBTED I HAD ANY skin left on my arms where the wet ropes rubbed. Shouldn't I have lost feeling by now? Could I somehow escape my mind enough to ignore the pain altogether?

My only distraction came from watching the weather as Nikolaus had instructed me. Though, what in all the gray, churning ocean was I supposed to look for? The winds picked up. I could hear as much in the whipping sails, a sound my mind knew all too well.

I drifted in and out of sleep for what could only be mere minutes at a time. My head ached worse than anything I'd felt before.

The bell tolled its evening chime.

Something cracked against my holding beam, and I crashed to the floor. My tired arms couldn't catch me before my head smacked the wooden planks. I squinted against the blazing sunset to find my bearings, searching for the one responsible for cutting me loose.

"That was more fun than I thought it'd be. I only wish Worley could have enjoyed the view as much as I did." Blackbeard used his foot to knock me off balance once more. "Bring her."

Thick hands wrapped around my waist. The pirate minion dragged me across the deck, my legs too weak to hold up my weight; not that fighting against the man's grasp would have helped, anyway.

We followed in Blackbeard's wake, the ship swaying under us in a way that mimicked my roiling stomach. Blackbeard threw open the door to his quarters, and the pirate brought me inside, dropping me to the floor between them. Something mushy thumped my leg with a splat.

I blinked back the lingering rainwater to see a rotting orange lying beside me.

"Eat. I'd hate to have you die in such an unsatisfying way as starvation," Blackbeard said.

My heart seemed to resume its angry beat, pumping blood through my dead limbs. My fingers coiled around the fruit, testing their ability to grasp. Satisfied, I hurled it at my captor.

The orange thwacked the side of Blackbeard's boot, leaving a trail of juice trickling behind it. He guffawed as he looked from me to my weapon of choice. Hatred raged in my eyes, and I made sure he saw it.

"So, you've still got some fight in you after all that? Worley might be proud of you if he were still alive." Blackbeard nudged the fruit away from his boot and smiled wickedly.

I tried to stand, to lunge at him with every breath in me, but I couldn't budge. The pirate behind me placed a gruff hand on my shoulder when I rose even an inch. They meant to keep me beneath them in every way.

A knock sounded at the door, and someone entered. He walked past me and stood before Blackbeard with legitimate authority.

"Nikolaus, my boy, my *apprentice*," Blackbeard greeted, ensuring he enunciated that last word for my benefit.

I hardly recognized Nik. He stood so tall, had changed from his torn trousers and loose-fitting shirt into a jacket, tricorn hat, and boots that reached his knees.

Blackbeard leaned against a massive gold-plated desk, his hand gesturing to Nik. "Do you see this man? He knows how to be a pirate. How to take care of himself when need be. He doesn't let his *feelings* lead him to a death sentence. Now he's arranged for a fresh start on my grand ship as my navigator, while you waste away before our eyes."

Nik stood taller and cleared his throat. "Captain, the *Ranger* has passed out of view. It seems Hornigold still means to stop in Nassau." When Nik spoke, his voice deepened, but not with age—with *rage*. He'd used this very tone with his brother when he didn't get his way, when he felt himself deserving of more responsibility on the *Hellbound*. Usually, he just shouted at Finn. He couldn't shout at Blackbeard.

"I fail to see a problem." Blackbeard raised a thick eyebrow as he stared at his younger counterpart. "That's always been his intention."

"You still mean to continue on?" Nik asked.

The pirate behind me twitched, though I dared not look at him. Nobody questioned the captain. Nik had crossed the line.

Blackbeard stood to demonstrate his height over the younger boy. "My orders do not change."

"But do you think it wise to go north?" Nik didn't flinch. The pirate behind me took a few steps back. I suspected the many injuries among the crew—the limps, the wrapped arms, the missing fingers—all reminded them who held the power here.

"What gives you rank to question me?" Blackbeard twisted his greasy fingers around his stringy beard.

Nik didn't falter. "A larger storm brews east that will surely take us off course if not run us aground. If we go inland—"

"I have sailed these seas longer than you have been alive. We keep to the course," Blackbeard growled.

The pirate behind me took action then, moving forward to take hold of Nikolaus. Blackbeard held up a single finger to stop him.

"Leave him, Barnes. He's testing his place here on the *Vengeance*. For once, he holds superior rank to the girl. For once, he's no longer in his brother's shadow, being overlooked time and time again in favor of *this*." Blackbeard's lip curled when his gaze found me.

"Don't listen to him, Nik," I mumbled from the floor, my throat raw and scratchy from battling the elements at the front of the ship. I crawled to my knees and tried to stand. Barnes grabbed at me again, but I smacked his hand away and reached for Nik.

"Get back, Cecily," Nik snarled.

I refused. "You know these are lies, Nikolaus. Finn never meant—"

"Back!" In a flash, Nik turned and clutched my shoulders, shoving me backward until I crashed into Barnes' firm hold.

What about watching the weather? What about the plan? Did he mean nothing by that but to give me false hope?

"You disappoint me." Blackbeard said from across the room. "I had hoped for a better show than that."

I wriggled in Barnes' hold. "You'll get no such thing—"

Nik raised his hand so quickly that, for a moment, I thought he might strike my face. His hand stopped a hair from my lips and kept me quiet. He turned back to his commander. "Captain, I meant no offense. I trust your judgment. If you mean to sail into this storm, might I suggest calling all hands on deck for the night?"

I gagged at the words spilling out of his mouth like poison.

"Perhaps you can leave that decision to your superior, Worley. This storm shows no sign of being any worse than the last," Blackbeard said.

My eyes rolled in my head. The imbecile meant to risk his ship and crew for the sole reason of squashing Nik's advice. "I may want to throw Nikolaus overboard right now, but if he says the storms will worsen, take note." I squirmed again to readjust Barnes's tight grasp on my chafing arms, but he quickly threw his filthy hand over my mouth to keep me from speaking out against his captain.

Blackbeard smiled wickedly and held up his hands in surrender. "It would seem I'm outnumbered. But since I'm in the company of such magnificent sailors, I should use the talent I have. Worley, why don't you switch to rigs? You'll have the best view of the storms from that perspective so you can keep me updated. Do let me know if lightning strikes."

Nik nodded, revealing no disappointment at the new command. In fact, Finn had given Nik the same task before the *Hellbound* sank. Nik really was good at rigging, storm or no storm. Blackbeard's pitiful attempt at a punishment wouldn't bother a Worley. Though, I hated to think of Nik battling the wind without being at his side to help.

Blackbeard turned to me then. "As for you, you can join your mouthy friend and swim with the rats when the water rises while I contemplate some more fun we might have together."

Barnes accepted the command and dragged me from the room. I tried to catch Nik's eye, but the codfish wouldn't look at me. Had Blackbeard just sentenced us both to our deaths, or was this just another way to entertain himself along the way to his actual plan for our demise?

With each step into the ship's belly, my mind raced back to the day I chose to lock myself in the ship's cell. That was the day I learned what Finn had really done with the captives he held aboard the *Hellbound*. I would have drowned that night if he hadn't come for me. He wouldn't come for me this time. Just as I couldn't come for him.

The darkness began to swallow me. My foot brushed the top step that led to the hull. Behind me, Barnes's yelped and jerked forward, releasing my arms. I grasped for the railing but stumbled down the first few steps from the force of our momentum. My shoulder slammed into the last step, but I righted myself quickly, expecting Barnes to come tumbling after.

The clanking of keys hit the floor beside me, and Barnes swore loudly overhead. I began fumbling around on the floor, searching for the keys before he could reclaim them.

A lantern lit beside me, and I cowered at the shadowy image atop the stairs. I blinked a few times just to be sure I saw what I did. It was Nik. In the crook of his arm, he held Barnes captive, a blade pressed to his neck in warning.

I turned toward the lantern light at my right to see Josette's smiling face behind the bars.

"You still want to burn this place down?" she asked.

My mouth could hardly form the words. "Very much."

"Well, if you'd grab those keys, it'd be very helpful," Nik said from the top of the stairs.

I searched around until I found my target. Josette immediately reached through her cell and snatched the keys from my grasp. She hit every bar with her lantern on the way to unlock her cell. "Took you long enough, Cabin Boy."

"I can still leave you here, you know." Nik groaned as he escorted the now-captive enemy pirate down the narrow steps.

I shook my head and took in the sight. "What is going on here?"

Josette lifted the light high, opened her cell door wide, and shrugged. "You left me, so I made other plans."

Nik moved forward and shoved Barnes into the cell with impressive force. As quickly as she could, Josette slammed the door behind him. Without the immediate danger of a knife against his neck, Barnes yelled and beat against the bars to draw attention to the hull.

Josette said something else about their scheming, but I couldn't make out a single word with the ruckus.

Nik rammed his body into the cell and lifted his knife so it gleamed in the lantern's light. "I didn't plan to gut you, but I am not opposed to changing my mind."

"I'll do it." Josette reached to take the blade, but Nik pulled it back toward him. Thank heavens. The woman was a readied

238

cannon. She might slaughter the entire ship if we would only light her fuse. Barnes seemed to suspect as much, too. He quieted and took a step back.

Josette's toothy grin grew. "Already bit this bloke twice."

"Not just *him* from what they're saying on deck." Nik sheathed his blade and turned toward the stairwell. "But you need to save that fight for this storm."

"So, we're really doing this? We're really going to take on Black-beard?" I asked.

Nik lifted his fist out in front of me. "I told you I wouldn't let you die here."

I pressed my balled fist against his, and Josette followed suit.

Thunder clapped outside the ship, and Nik pulled his hand from ours. "Enough chatter. We need to move."

THIRTY-THREE

Barnes screamed every profanity I'd ever heard, and some I hadn't. He called for help. He cursed our names. But outside the walls of the ship, a storm raged that whipped the sails and beat against the wood. No one could hear his warning.

We were coming for them.

Nik led us into a dark corner behind a row of hammocks. He flung open a chest and began throwing clothes at us. "Put these on and hide your faces as much as you can. We're going to run this ship aground."

"Wreck the ship?" I dropped the stinky trousers I held in my hands.

"There's no way the three of us are taking down this vessel with our battle skills alone." Nik raised an eyebrow in my direction and handed Josette a kerchief and hat.

He meant it as an insult, surely, but I couldn't take offense at the truth. I'd been hardly any help in the treasure cave. When Finn and I had waged a similar mutiny a year ago, I only succeeded in bumping men overboard and tripping the captain so he fell out a window.

"Right. If you let me at the sails, I can catch this wind," I said.

"That is exactly what I'd hoped for. I'm already supposed to be up there, and Blackbeard is bound to realize I haven't arrived to my post. He's hardly let me out of his sight since we arrived, and he won't want to miss my struggle in the storm. I'll switch my clothes, and you take mine." Nik then handed us each a small blade to attach to our belts, then stretched to see above the hammocks and ensure no one else had come around. Blackbeard really must have called everyone on deck to tackle the storm, despite his arrogance.

Nik grabbed a set of trousers and a ratted shirt, then sunk behind a few barrels to change, throwing his clothes overtop for me to wear.

"You still need a distraction while you two fly?" Josette asked as she fought with a belt to keep her pants around her middle.

Nik stood and answered with a salute in her direction. When had they started getting along? I thought they hated each other.

"I can disable the rudder," Josette added.

Nik frowned in the dim lamplight. "I told you that was a bad idea. It won't work."

"Look here, Cabin Boy, I spent some rather boring days staring at the back of your *Hellbound* floating off shore and wondering how much effort it'd take to do it, and now I want to see how close I was to bein' right." Josette pulled her overcoat closed with a huff.

"You're going to be killed." Nik spoke the seriousness words rather casually.

I could only stand there and button my shirt as if eavesdropping among strangers.

"You're a dear to worry, but I haven't died yet. I'm giving it a go." She punched him in the shoulder enough to knock him back a step.

Nik tried in vain to suppress a smile. "You're hopeless."

"What exactly happened while I was tied to the mainmast?" I motioned between the two of them, then began tucking my hair underneath my hat.

Josette released a hoarse laugh. "Cabin Boy brought me food, and I decided to let 'im live. Simple as that."

"Do you not know my name?" Nik interrupted.

"Course I do. Keep your trap shut." Josette turned to me. "We devised a simple enough plan over stolen bread. We're avenging Captain Worley and rescuing his archery by whatever means. That's pretty much all it was."

I hardly knew if she spoke English anymore. "His *archery*?"

Nik's hand wiped down his face in slow motion. "*Ankurri*. His *ankurri*. The distraction, wench. Take your chaos to the deck."

Josette rolled her eyes and rushed off to cause some distraction they'd seemingly pre-planned and yet somehow disagreed on. Nik followed slowly, and I trailed behind until we reached the bottom of the steps that led to the main deck. I grabbed hold of Nik's arm to keep him from running off just yet.

"Nik, what's *ankurri* mean? You were talking about me just then, yeah?" I stared deep into his blue eyes, so much like his brother's. Finn never told me what the word meant, but he spoke it often in our quiet times together. I could almost hear his voice saying it inside my head. It hurt more than all my other memories of him.

"We don't have time, Cecily. We have to go *now*." He motioned for me to follow, but I clung to his arm.

"*Please*. He always called me that." I couldn't stop the tear that pricked at the corner of my eye and quieted my voice.

Nik's shoulders sank, and his arm sagged out of my grasp. "It means anchor. *Minun ankurri* means 'my anchor'. My brother is absurd like that, as you're well aware. Now, can we please go wreck this ship and try not to get killed?"

With that, Nik ran off.

I listened for a long moment, hoping with every ounce of me I didn't hear a gunshot or screeching captain that implied Nik had been caught. I needed to follow him, but my feet stuck to the floor with the resound of Nikolaus's words.

His anchor? Finn had called me his anchor all this time? My mind raced over each instance I remembered him speaking it to me. He always held certain tenderness in his voice when he'd said it. I assumed it to be a Finnish term of endearment, but I wouldn't have guessed it meant *that*.

I wiped my eyes with the palm of my hand and listened to the sails clapping overhead. Finn had been my anchor, too. He kept me strong when I thought I might drift away. Our last few weeks together, I hadn't shown him enough how much I needed him.

But I could show him now. I could take down his enemy in his stead.

I swallowed hard and sucked in a deep breath of the salty sea air drifting down the steps, and off I ran to climb the rigs with Nikolaus.

The moment I stepped foot on deck, I heard someone yell and stopped short.

"A longboat's been cut loose!" the voice bellowed.

They hadn't caught me. That must have been part of Josette's distraction. And perfectly timed, no less. I leapt onto the ropes and climbed high, my fingers slipping in the rain. My boot heel was the only thing keeping my foot from shooting through to the other side of the webbing.

Near the top, I clung tighter and dared look for the captain. I found him at the ship's helm, issuing what must have been a series of commands to another man. He hadn't seen me either.

Next, I squinted through the rain to find Nik. A few other men scurried around, one furiously fought a rogue rope, and another worked to mend a ripped sail.

The *Vengeance* swayed, and I held tighter. Any moment, my hat would blow from my head, freeing my hair and giving away my identity if Blackbeard only looked up. I needed to keep moving. At least our entire objective revolved around wrecking the ship. That'd prove infinitely easier than trying to sail it. Though, how exactly did we mean to survive such a crash? Did they neglect to mention we would go down, too, in our mission for revenge?

Wiggling my way out onto the first sail, I kept hold of it with all my might as the wind shook the beam below me. My instincts made me check again for Nikolaus, though I knew I needed to trust him to do his part and keep safe.

I found him near the bucket. He had overpowered another rigger and tied him to the mast, but not before the man shouted over the howling winds.

My gaze darted to Blackbeard, who withdrew his hat to see up into the rigs. We had to hurry. I took out my knife and began cutting away at the ropes. The wind cracked louder against the sails as they loosened.

I'd nearly snapped the second when the ship lurched violently. My head banged against the wood, but I wrapped my arms around the beam before I fell. Below me, the men shouted and scurried about. Did we hit reef? Or, even more impressive, had Josette actually disabled the rudder?

Blackbeard swore loudly at the helm.

A gunshot followed.

I dared search the area for his aim and found Nikolaus frantically crawling away from the bucket. Another shot erupted and tore through the sail just over Nik's head. He tried to move, but the sail snapped, knocking him off balance. He hugged the beam, feet dangling. Blackbeard would have an easy target now.

I had to get him off there. Another gust of wind caught the sail, and the idea came to me.

"Nik, hang on." I inched my way across the slick rig as quickly as I could and took hold of the ropes that manipulated his sail. If I could just catch the wind in the right direction...

I pulled with all my might to tighten the cloth as the whistling wind caught and twisted the mast just enough. Shouting my plan to warn Nik wasn't an option, though maybe I should have. The force of the turning mast threw him from his hold and sent him plummeting over the side of the ship.

My eyes went wide. Though my plan had worked, it appeared much more violent against my own man than I'd expected.

The towering drop shouldn't kill him...as long as he didn't hit something on the way down. I stretched to look overboard, but couldn't see into the black water.

On deck, Blackbeard yelled again. He'd spotted me, realized what I'd done. He stormed from the helm, clinging to the railing as he tried to remain steady on the bucking ship.

I scrambled across the beam toward the edge of the rigs. I had to make the jump, too, if I could just get close enough.

Another gunshot sounded, and I froze, waiting to feel the pain of a bullet hole in my belly. No such pain came. Instead, I heard a ruckus of clanging below, and the type of monstrous growl that only the foulest of beasts cried.

I followed the clanging to where I'd seen Blackbeard on the stairwell. He'd drawn his sword and engaged another man in combat. Had his own men, or maybe even our former crew, chosen this moment to mutiny alongside us?

But his foe moved in that graceful way I hadn't seen from many other pirates. Only two others, if I thought about it. I clutched harder to my beam, afraid I may topple prematurely if I leaned any closer to the battle going on below me.

Blackbeard's opponent shifted, and I caught sight of a blond lock of hair spilling out of his bandana. A half-smirk playing on his lips as his blade clanged against the captain's.

My head spun. It couldn't be him.

It wasn't possible

A ghost, perhaps? Did I hallucinate from a gunshot wound? Had the storm made me entirely mad?

The mast shook with a loud crack.

"Take cover!" someone shouted below me.

It cracked again, shaking me loose.

"It's gonna fall!" another screamed.

Piece by piece, the mast split under the wind's pressure.

Someone called my name, and I searched the chaos to find the source. A man with a dark head of curls waved his arms wildly at the mast's base. I lost all strength in my body.

Stevens? He'd run off in the jungle when Blackbeard appeared. He couldn't be *here*...

The apparition motioned toward the water, and I blinked hard against the rain. The mast lurched once more with the reverberation of a cannon blast. If I jumped now, I risked the entire beam falling into the water on top of me. I had to ride it down and hope for the best.

My stomach dropped when I noted the distance between my position and the ocean's surface. I tucked my knees and tried to get my footing on the edge. The black waters rose rapidly like it meant to grab hold of me midair.

I kicked off the beam with all my might and let the water have me.

THIRTY-FOUR

THE SHARP CORAL CRADLED MY BODY ON THE OCEAN FLOOR. I frantically tugged at the rope wrapped around my ankle, the heavy mast keeping me weighted under water. Sand and shell whirled around me from the wreckage. The rope loosened enough for me to slip my foot through and kick toward the surface. My lungs burned from lack of air.

I burst above the choppy water and gulped for breath, only to choke on a wave that knocked me back under. The ocean whirled in every direction. Blackbeard's ship loomed in the distance. Had it run aground yet? Could Blackbeard see me in the water?

Pushing against the waves, I tried to put some distance between myself and the enemy ship. If I meant to go farther out to sea, I needed something to hold on to. I swam toward a piece of debris, perhaps some remnant of the ship's bucket, and tried to gather my bearings. Lightning reflected off the caps on the water, and thunder competed with the roar of the sea.

The waters parted just enough to reveal a figure appearing at my side. I hurried to readjust on my boards to strike out against the attack or even weaponize my raft. But my opponent grabbed hold of my arm and stilled my board.

I nearly sank to the depths all over again when I saw his face. "You're here."

Finn's hand reached behind my head and burrowed into my wet hair. His lips found mine. Tears mixed with the rain as I tasted the salty sea, felt his warmth, and melted in the rhythm of his heart beating so hard under my palm.

He lived.

Finn broke our kiss first and touched his forehead to mine. "I plan to kiss you from now until eternity, but first, we need to get out of here."

It wasn't until he pulled back farther that I realized we weren't alone. Stevens swayed in the waters behind Finn. He had a deep cut on his forehead, but it didn't keep him from smiling.

"Fancy another swim in the shark-infested waters, Miss Hastings?" he asked.

He came back for us. I hadn't lost him either.

"Come on," Finn commanded.

We all clutched hold of my board to ensure the waves didn't separate us and kicked together. I could hardly keep from looking at Finn every few seconds, as if he might disappear with each wave that crashed over us. Even greater than the threat of Blackbeard's reappearance, I feared Finn's presence being a result of an unconscious dream after falling from a wrecked ship. Though, most of my life since meeting him had been like a dream, really, and a nightmare at times.

A sharp crack echoed across the sky, followed by another.

"Guns? Again?" I shrieked. "Where's Nik?"

"We have to keep going! Put as much distance between us and that ship as we can." Finn motioned farther out to sea.

My body ached, my fingers cramping from their tight hold on the board. "We're going to drown!"

"Not if my plan goes accordingly," Finn replied.

A wave broke over our heads, and Stevens laughed as he spit out the water. "Relatively few of those plans have gone accordingly thus far. But the Lord is definitely at work."

A loud crunch reverberated across the sea. We turned in unison to see the *Vengeance* tip to the side, splintering as it collided with the rocks.

Finn's mouth fell agape, and he glanced toward the heavens. "I should say He is!"

The sight kept me silent, the storm seeming so small compared to the massive ship collapsing before us.

"We need to go in that direction." Finn pointed into the distance. I strained to see, but could only make out a dark formation. Did he mean for us to swim directly into the rocks that wrecked the *Vengeance*? That was suicide. The waves would launch us right into them.

"Wrong way," Stevens shouted above our furious splashing. "They're here!"

Panic coursed through my body as I searched the wreckage, expecting to see Blackbeard rowing toward us with his army of men.

Finn's hand wrapped around my waist and pointed me in the opposite direction. A longboat did approach us.

With Nik and Josette inside.

"You almost made it all the way to those rocks, eh, Captain? I very much thought you'd be dead by now," Josette called out.

"I appreciate your confidence," Finn yelled back.

Nik's oar clattered inside the boat, and he leapt headfirst into the water. He surfaced directly beside us, reaching out to take hold of his brother and pull him into a tight embrace. His voice broke against his brother's neck when he tried to say something in their native language.

Finn kept one hand on the board to hold them afloat, wrapping his other arm tightly around Nik. "I know. I shouldn't have assumed anything. I'm sorry, Nik. I'm so sorry."

Nik pulled back to look his brother in the face, his eyes red from a mix of tears and seawater. "I can't believe you're here."

"I can't really either." Finn drew Nik into him again and kissed the top of his head.

Stevens and I swam to the longboat and fought our way aboard. Nik followed behind us, and I reached into the water to give Finn a helping hand. He swung his legs over, but didn't let go of me when he made it in safely. Instead, he tugged me closer and pressed his lips to my ear. "They kept me from answering you on shore. But I swam all this way to tell you: I've loved every second with you, as well," he said.

He shook his head, seemingly still in a state of disbelief, and released me to snatch up an oar.

I could only watch him, all the pieces of my heart slowly coming back together as I reminded myself repeatedly he was really here. He was alive. My Finn came back to me.

"We need to get away from the wreckage. I don't know if Blackbeard survived, but I don't want to wait around to find out. And these storms will only get worse. Nik, will you take the other oar? I need your help," he called over his shoulder for us to hear.

Nik scrambled to obey, taking his place beside his brother to command our tiny vessel.

I searched the bottom of the boat but found no other oars.

"There's just the two." Josette clung to the edge of the boat at my side. "The others fell out when I knocked it off the side of the ship."

Lightning lit the sky behind her, which struck me as entirely too appropriate for the situation. "Josette, you are a force. I can't believe you disabled the rudder."

"Nah, I didn't do that. Nasty thing wouldn't budge. I jammed it a bit, but would have liked to take it down," she said.

"Well, it's down now. Nice work." I settled lower into the boat and hooked my leg against the wooden benches. The waves tossed us all around, trying to throw us to the sea all over again. "How'd you come by this boat if you cut it loose from the *Vengeance*? These waves should have ripped it clean away!"

She nodded toward Finn in front of us.

Stevens chuckled on the other side from his hunkered down position. "As I said, Miss Hastings, the Lord is at work. I cut the captain loose, and we stowed away on Hornigold's ship just before they set sail. I've memorized every inch of that vessel, and hiding is much easier when the whole crew is distracted by a storm." He pointed to the sky and laughed even louder. "We jumped when we got close enough to these islands, hoping to catch the *Vengeance* before the ships got too far apart. And then we see an abandoned longboat..."

None of them could have planned for such an exchange.

"You came back for Finn?" I still could hardly believe any of them survived after what we'd just been through, but Stevens' appearance truly had me baffled.

He pressed his fist against his chest. "He's my captain. I apologize for disappearing in your hour of need, but I knew Teach would recognize me. I'd been in his presence many times while sailing with Hornigold. If he noticed me, I stood no chance of helping. I kept watch from a distance, trying to determine when best to reappear. When they bound the captain on the beach, I waited only long enough for everyone to set out in the longboats."

If it wouldn't topple the boat, I'd have leapt to the other side and thrown my arms around him. He, too, had been scheming in our absence. And for once, all of our plans worked together to bring us out of trouble, rather than send us deeper into it.

Finn and Nik maneuvered the boat farther around the rocks until land was in sight. The closer we got, the clearer the view became. A long pier stretched out into the water with ships of varying size waiting out the storm in the port.

As we approached the shoreline, a wave caught the back of our boat and tipped us into the water. We swam from there, checking furiously in all directions to assure we'd all made it out together.

Finn waved toward the pier. We ran on tired legs, knowing an attack may follow behind us. Finn's hand reached for mine, our fingers intertwining and giving me the strength to run the last stretch.

We slowed underneath the cover of the pier, the rain only trickling beneath the breaks in the wood overhead. It was the best break from the rains we'd had in hours.

Josette collapsed in the sand, rolling onto her back and draping her arm over her face. "I hate pirates. I can't believe I became one."

"It's a mistake we've all made." Finn's attempt at a laugh turned into a cough as he still fought to catch his breath. "What do you say we give it all up?"

"Piracy?" Nik had sunk to his knees and brushed his long wet hair out of his face, revealing his pink, rain-battered features.

"Yeah, I can't do this anymore, Nik. I can't keep putting you in danger. I know this is a life I chose for us, foolishly thinking I could manage it, but I can't. When I watched him drag you away from me on that beach..." Finn lowered his head and tapped his fist to his brow. "I won't do it again."

Josette sat up. "Well, what do you suggest? The Caribbean is crawling with pirates. It's a rotten, horrible place, and I still want out."

To think how I'd fallen in love with the islands. How I'd longed to make this place my permanent home. Josette was right, though. The beauty had faded. The storms came and washed it all away.

"But where would we go? We've lived on the *Hellbound* for three years. We have no place to call home," Nik said.

Stevens watched our group silently, his hand clutching the rosary around his neck. The image flooded me with a peace I hadn't felt in months. His serene expression took me back to the relief I'd seen from Finn's captives the moment he released them in Ireland. We had become like those fugitives, seeking refuge from a life of captivity and hardship.

I cleared my throat. "I may know of some friends in the Irish countryside willing to help us."

Finn took a few steps until he stood in front of me. "Of course. And I've always been rather fond of Ireland myself." He took my hand, turning my wrist and bringing my palm to his lips. The stubble from his newly formed beard tickled my fingers. "Would you run away with me one last time?"

I nodded and placed my hand against his jaw. "Finnigan Worley, I would run away with you *every* time."

"Stop." Nik groaned behind us.

Josette, too, gagged and spit dramatically into the sand.

Stevens stepped forward, holding up his hands through laughter. "All right. We're done with piracy, but we don't have a means to get off these islands. And if Teach survived, he's almost certainly plotting his revenge."

"Plus, there's these damned hurricanes," Josette deadpanned.

"Meh, it's heading northwest." Finn waved his arms in a pointed direction. "If we can get past this one, we'd be clear the rest of the way to Donegal."

Donegal? The name made me smile, especially the way Finn spoke it with a hint of a Finnish accent. The town now held all our hopes of a fresh start and a new life together. That was something worth fighting for...even if it meant we had to hold on to our pirate nature a little longer.

"What if we take one of the ships in the harbor?" I asked.

Finn leaned against the beam beside me, tilting his head to follow my line of sight. "You want to commandeer another ship? This already goes against everything we discussed just now."

"Only this one last time. There's a caravel that would suit us rather nicely." I grinned.

"I'm afraid I've been a terrible influence on you." Finn shook his head and searched the distance to inspect the ship I had my eye on.

Stevens winced. "I would rather not resort to theft from an honest angler."

Nik stood and fumbled with something in his pocket. "How about theft from a pirate?" He opened his fist to reveal a thin brick of gold. "I took this from Blackbeard's quarters in case I needed to bribe anyone on his ship to make our escape. He meant to use it toward the price he had on Finn, but since I found him first..."

Finn looked around at our small crew, pride swelling within him. "Well, then."

We held no secrets this time. We knew where our loyalties belonged. We now shared one goal, unbound from the shackles that held us hostage for so long. We were free.

"All hands on deck?" Finn asked.

"Aye," we said as one.

THE END

ACKNOWLEDGMENTS

Lord, this has been a bumpy ride, but you saw me through it. Thank you.

Matt, Ross, and Lizzie- Thanks for keeping me grounded when I wanted to scream during revisions. I'm so blessed to have you three in my life.

My family and friends- Your support and enthusiasm for this crew makes me want to keep aiming for the horizon. I love you all to Barbados and back (and then some).

Chasia, Kate, Michelle, Maria, Alex- What would I do without you? You read some pretty terrible drafts of this book—when it was mostly just some friends riding around in a boat—and you helped me shape it into a real story. I want to keep you forever.

ABOUT THE AUTHOR

Stephanie is an author specializing in pirates and women's fiction. She works as a freelance editor, cleans when she's stressed, and hates cooking but loves to eat. Away from her desk, she's a wife, mother of two human children, servant to eight cats, and wrangler of one bulldog.

Subscribe to Stephanie Eding's newsletter for all the latest updates from her or visit her website!

Made in the USA
Columbia, SC
14 September 2020